The warmth of his fingers
stirred senses she had tried to forget. . . .

She could have rebuked him for his forwardness, and pulled away quite easily, but she didn't. He looked deep into her wide green eyes. "Become my wife. You will lack for nothing, and your son will be amply provided for. I will also instruct my lawyer to make every possible investigation regarding the false will. If Falk Arnold's villainy can be exposed, it will be."

She managed to overcome the spell he'd suddenly cast over her. "But why? What possible reason could you have for helping me so much? Society would regard such a match as scandalous. The Arnolds have branded me a kept woman who has a son out of wedlock. Even supposing some people believe I was married, can you imagine with what shocked disapproval they would regard so hasty a second union?"

"Chitter-chatter is of no concern to me." Rowan paused. "But before making your final decision, be warned that it will not be a marriage in name only. If you enter my life, you enter my bed as well."

Marigold's Marriages

by

Sandra Heath

A SIGNET BOOK

SIGNET
Published by the Penguin Group
Penguin Putnam Inc., 375 Hudson Street,
New York, New York 10014, U.S.A.
Penguin Books Ltd, 27 Wrights Lane,
London W8 5TZ, England
Penguin Books Australia Ltd, Ringwood,
Victoria, Australia
Penguin Books Canada Ltd, 10 Alcorn Avenue,
Toronto, Ontario, Canada M4V 3B2
Penguin Books (N.Z.) Ltd, 182-190 Wairau Road,
Auckland 10, New Zealand

Penguin Books Ltd, Registered Offices:
Harmondsworth, Middlesex, England

First published by Signet, an imprint of Dutton NAL,
a member of Penguin Putnam Inc.

First Printing, May, 1999
10 9 8 7 6 5 4 3 2 1

Chapter One

The summer of 1806 was to end uproariously, with among many other things, a talking wren, a demon duck, and ancient druidic magic gone very wrong indeed, but it began on a somber note that gave no hint of the amazing events ahead. At the reading of her late husband's will, Marigold would never have guessed that within weeks she would not only be deliriously happy for the first time in years, but her enemies would all be changed into chickens and sold at Salisbury market!

None of these astonishing things seemed in the offing as everyone gathered in the great hall of Castell Arnold to hear Merlin Arnold's will. They were all waiting for Merlin's brother, Falk, and at last he arrived, but as he took his seat it was clear he relished the coming minutes. There was an air of gloating anticipation on his face, as if he knew that all his devious ambitions were soon to be realized. Everything about him warned his elder brother's widow that things did not bode well for her. Or for her son.

Conscious of the intense dislike Falk had always had for her, Marigold smoothed her black bombazine skirts, then clasped her gloved hands pensively in her lap. Of late he had become more arrogant than ever, conducting himself like a medieval baron who enjoyed absolute power over everyone and everything in his domain. There were whispers that he was to marry this summer, although no one seemed to know the identity of the unfortunate bride. One thing was certain, the poor creature had her sister-in-law's complete sympathy!

Marigold drew a steadying breath. Today was too important to indulge in trivial thoughts about Falk's forthcoming nuptials. He wanted this castle and everything that went with it, and although she and her son stood in his way, Falk was the sort of man to stop at nothing to get what he wanted. His recent astonishing victories in the law courts had so gone to his already swollen head, that he'd begun to think success was his by right.

Falk was the most litigious man she had ever encountered. Ever since she'd known him, he had pursued doubtful claims through the courts, but until the beginning of this year he had never won. Then two important, seemingly impossible cases had inexplicably gone his way, followed by several smaller victories, so that a considerable amount of money had now fallen into his grasp. Since then he had confidently embarked on more, mostly ancient and very tangled disputes over land and titles. He didn't doubt he would win every one, for when it came to legal matters, Falk Arnold of Castell Arnold on the Isle of Anglesey seemed to have become invincible.

Marigold couldn't help a secret smile, for since she'd been banished across the straits to a dower house in Caernarfon for nearly twelve years, she wasn't supposed to know what went on here. The Arnolds wanted to ignore her existence, but she had managed to keep a finger on their pulse. She'd had to, for her son's sake. With an uncle as rapacious and cunning as Falk, thirteen-year-old Perry needed all the help and support his mother could give.

From behind her veil, she watched as Falk sat down heavily next to his black-clad mother and maiden aunts. He wore black too, and as usual, everything was too tight for his considerable bulk. It was as another Beau Brummel that he liked to imagine himself, but it was of the unstylish, overweight Prince of Wales that people thought when they saw him. He had split his breeches on sitting down to dinner recently, and Marigold wished it would happen again now. It would certainly enliven proceedings that were the end in dullness.

At forty, Falk was two years his late brother's junior, and his image in many ways, except that Merlin had been thin. Both were vain, with enviably thick golden hair and strange amber eyes. And both were disagreeable, unfeeling, and overbearing. She wished she could hold her late husband in higher esteem, but there was no denying the truth. Her love for him was long since as dead as he himself now was, in fact all she felt at his demise was relief.

She clasped and unclasped her hands, for although she'd seen little of Merlin since their son's birth, it was still hard to believe he'd gone forever. He'd died two weeks ago, when returning from one of his infrequent visits to her. As usual his purpose had been to nitpick with every item on her household accounts, and again as usual, they had parted acrimoniously. According to the groom accompanying him, they'd just alighted from the ferry at the island, when a robin had suddenly burst noisily from a rowan tree. Merlin's startled horse had thrown him, and he'd died that night.

She looked out of the tall east-facing windows. Cloud shadows raced across the rolling park toward the narrow Menai Straits, which separated Anglesey from the northwest tip of Wales. The shore was deserted now, but in the mists of prehistory, the island had been a druid stronghold. In their hundreds they'd waited on the sand to confront the invading forces of Julius Caesar, gathered half a mile away on the mainland. The druids had been overwhelmed, and their sacred groves of oak and mistletoe destroyed.

Her gaze moved to the distant peaks of Snowdonia, still whitecapped even though it was the end of May. Today was the fourteenth anniversary of her arrival here at Castell Arnold, and she remembered first seeing those beautiful mountains. Her thoughts wandered back over the years. From the wiser age of thirty she could see Merlin's faults so clearly, but at sixteen she had been a naive Lancashire lass who was readily impressed by his London airs and facile charm. When she'd met him at the Preston subscription ball—to which he and his society friends had come merely to amuse themselves with the local rustics—she had been flattered and taken in completely. How could the stepdaughter of a mere country doctor fail to be? Her strict stepfather forbade her to see "that strutting London popinjay," but in her passionate innocence she thought she was in love, and so she ran away with her seducer. Her stepfather had promptly disowned her.

With hindsight she marveled that Merlin had actually married her, for it was surely against all the odds. The rest of the Arnold clan were appalled, especially Falk, who loathed her from the moment he learned her name. Privately she thought that for some reason Falk was actually afraid of her; for there'd been something almost panic-stricken about the way he'd kept on at Merlin to send her to the dower house. She had to admit that the name Marigold wouldn't have been her choice, but she didn't think it warranted such a vitriolic reaction. She'd been given her name because her parents were particularly fond of Shakespeare's *A Winter's Tale.* "Here's flowers for you; Hot lavender, mint, savory, marjoram; The marigold, that goes to bed with the sun. And with him rises weeping." Her mother had told her she'd nearly been called Lavender Marigold, but her father, who had died before his only child was born, had always liked marigolds. And so Marigold Lavender it was.

Such a touching story carried no weight with Falk, who turned on Merlin for refusing to send her away. Merlin had loved her in the beginning, and as the elder brother, he was heir to everything, but Falk, supported by the rest of the family, gradually gnawed away at his influence. When old Mr. Arnold passed away within six months of the marriage, Merlin should have become the absolute master of Castell Arnold, instead it was Falk whose commands were always obeyed, Falk whose permission was always sought, and Falk whose preferences always came first. Falk was everything, Merlin virtually nothing.

Realizing what his wife had cost him, Merlin began to treat her cruelly. Too late she realized her mistake in marrying him, but in the time-honored phrase, she had made her bed and now had to lie in it, for she was expecting his child. And so she had consented to go to the dower house, accepting the situation because she was intent upon guarding her child's inheritance against Falk's ambition. On the whole she had been well provided for, even when Perry went away to school, and then on to Eton, where he now was, but over the years she had endured Falk's vicious sniping, put up with the constant criticisms of his old buzzard of a mother, and submitted to the spite of his spinster aunts. Above all she'd suffered the vindictiveness of his sister, Alauda, a raven-haired beauty who in spite of her exquisite exterior and stylish Latin name—meaning skylark—was in fact a vulture fit only for Hades itself!

Marigold pursed her lips. Everyone at Castell Arnold possessed a name relating to birds in one way or another. Even Perry, whose peregrine falcon was sometimes seen over Anglesey. Why the Arnolds seemed so obsessed with birds, she did not know. She wished they would all up and fly away! Excepting Perry, of course. Her eyes slid toward Alauda, who was now the Countess of Fernborough, and was one of the acknowledged belles of London society. Lovely to a fault, with tumbling dark curls, dewy lips, and shining brown eyes, she possessed the sort of curvaceous figure that looked seductive even in mourning. More than anyone, Alauda had striven to make Marigold's life a misery. Even after leaving Castell Arnold, Alauda had written numerous spiteful letters to Merlin and Falk, inventing sins Marigold was supposed to have committed. Without fail, the letters were believed, and retribution fell upon the dower house in the form of temporarily withheld allowance.

Alauda was a woman of loose morals, and the once adoring Earl of Fernborough had soon become so tired of his beautiful wife's constant indiscretions that he was now her equal in the adultery stakes. Her latest love was Lord Avenbury, who was apparently the personification of all that was fashionably Gothic and mysterious. Marigold knew nothing of Lord Avenbury, except that he was reckoned the most romantically handsome man in England, as well as one of the most accomplished lovers, and most notorious duelists. Falk spoke of him as "doomed" Lord Avenbury, and when Alauda laughed at this, Marigold had put the remark down to the fact that his lordship would soon go the way of all Milady Fernborough's lovers.

Momentarily catching Alauda's gaze from behind both their veils, Marigold quickly looked away. She turned her thoughts to things more pleasant: her adored son, Peregrine, who would now inherit his father's great estate and fortune. Perry was in his third term at Eton, and was as golden-haired but much more handsome than his father and uncle. He'd declined to attend his father's funeral, nor would he come here today for the will reading, for he felt nothing for the man who had ignored him virtually all his young life, and had treated his mother so badly. Marigold could not blame him, nor did she attempt to persuade him to change his mind, for in her opinion he was justified. The Arnolds, on the other hand, were outraged.

Suddenly a shiver passed over her, and she glanced instinctively toward Falk, only to find his amber eyes, cold as a hawk's, already upon her. The chill glitter in his gaze reminded her of the unease she'd felt as he first entered the hall. Something was wrong. But what? A hush descended over everyone as Merlin's lawyer, a hook-nosed, shifty-faced fellow by the name of Crowe, took his seat in the middle of the long polished oak table. The entire Arnold family, Marigold included, faced him, with the multitude of servants ranged behind them, all wearing black, like a clustered flock of rooks. The lawyer broke the seal on the will, cleared his throat, and then read out in his harsh, guttural voice. "This is the last will and testament of the late Mr. Merlin Arnold, made on the fourth night of May, in this year of 1806. I, Merlin Peregrine Arnold, being of sound mind, do hereby . . ."

As the lawyer's grating tones echoed around the vast hall, where a huge painting of the Anglesey druids in one of their groves had pride of place on the vast chimney breast, Marigold's lips parted with shock. Less than a month ago? A *new* will? Why hadn't she been told? Her eyes moved warily toward Falk, who was still smiling faintly. Suddenly she realized that he already knew what the will would contain. More than that, he *liked* what he knew! Her heart sank like a stone.

Chapter Two

The opening paragraphs of Merlin's last testament were dull, as such things always were, but just when it seemed the main points would never be reached, suddenly came the momentous words. ". . . I have to confess to a monstrous deceit, perpetrated over many years, to wit that I was never legally married to the woman known to you all as my wife."

Falk's cunning smile didn't waver as Marigold stiffened with shock. There was a gasp from the servants, but old Mrs. Arnold did not react, except for her clawlike hands tightening upon her silver-handled walking stick. The old witch knew, Marigold thought. So did Alauda, who raised her veil to briefly reveal her astonishingly lovely face, and a smug smile that was an echo of her brother's. The spinster aunts fluttered, but it was only a token show. Everyone had known, except the servants, and the hapless widow.

Mr. Crowe held a hand up for silence, and as the stir died away again, he continued. "In order to secure Miss Marigold Lavender Marchmont's seduction, on the second day of May, 1792, I deceived her by hiring an actor to play the part of clergyman at the parish church of Kirkham in the County of Lancashire. After resorting to such a course, I was surprised to find myself in love with her, by which time it was too late to admit my sin without risking losing her. To this day she remains Miss Marchmont. I meant to take the secret to my grave, but my feelings have changed irreparably because Miss Marchmont has become increasingly ill-disposed toward me. So also has her son, who clearly can no longer be regarded as legitimate. In view of this, I do not feel I owe them anything further. What they have been provided with thus far is therefore *all* they will receive. My entire estate goes to my younger brother, Falk, who is my legal heir."

No shocked gasps from the servants now, merely a stunned silence as all eyes turned toward Marigold. She was shaken to the very core, and could not move. The hush was so complete that she heard something tapping at the window. It was a robin, his red breast feathers puffed, and his head cocked to one side as he looked intently at her. He shook his wings, revealing several unusual white feathers, then he trilled a little, still looking at her. Had he spoken she could not have understood his message more clearly. "Go on," he was saying, "Go on, and tell them what you think of this so-called will!"

Suddenly she found herself getting up from her chair. She tossed her veil back to reveal her pale face and the glint of her red-gold hair, and her bombazine skirts rustled in the hush as she approached the table. "Mr. Crowe, is this truly the last will and testament of the late Mr. Arnold?" she asked, her voice carrying with unexpected clarity.

"It is indeed, Mrs. Arnold. I, er, mean, Miss Marchmont." The smirk in his voice matched the one in his shifty eyes.

"I do not believe you. If there was coldness between the late Mr. Arnold and me, it began within months of our marriage, and was certainly not a recent thing. Why then would he wait all this time before casting me off? I'll tell you why, sirrah, it is because he and I *were* legally married. This will is a fake!"

There was immediate uproar. Falk leapt to his feet, his spinster aunts had the vapors, and old Mrs. Arnold collapsed, but not so completely she could not gasp for a large restorative glass of sherry. The servants babbled together, sounding for all the world like a flight of wild geese. Alauda rose in a graceful swirl of black brocade, and advanced accusingly toward Marigold. "How *dare* you suggest that Merlin's will is false! My brother is dead, and this family is in the deepest mourning! Have you no shame?" she cried above the noise.

Silence fell, and as Marigold turned to face her; she was still conscious of the robin's bright gaze. She had the uncanny feeling he was egging her on, and suddenly she felt almost exhilarated. The years of humiliation she'd suffered at the hands of this woman and her unpleasant family suddenly became too much. It was time to deal the creature in kind! *"Shame?"* she repeated challengingly. "Come now, Lady Fernborough, people in glass houses should not throw stones. I was always a faithful wife, whereas you . . . Oh, dear." Marigold tutted reprovingly, and as the robin fluttered joyously against the window, she swept recklessly on. "Shame is *your* forte, not mine, Alauda. Who is your lover at the moment, my lady? One of the guards' regiments? Oh, no, that was last week. Let me see. Ah, yes, it's Lord Avenbury now, isn't it? Or has he already discarded you for pastures new? From all accounts his conquests outnumber even yours!"

Alauda's lips whitened at the edges. "Hold your tongue!" she breathed.

"Gladly, but only if you will oblige me by doing the same," Marigold retorted, all thought of caution now dispatched with the four winds.

Falk intervened. "That is enough. Alauda, please be seated again. As for you, Miss Marchmont, under the circumstances I think it appropriate for you to leave Castell Arnold before the passing of another night. And do not think the dower house remains at your disposal, for of course, it does not."

Marigold's green eyes were withering. "This family's concerted efforts to have my marriage set aside fell on stony ground fourteen years ago, and have continued to do so ever since. Until now, of course, when Merlin is conveniently dead and unable to prove or disprove anything!"

Falk's expression became venomous. "What are you implying, madam?"

"Do I need to spell it out? You have always wanted Castell Arnold, now you have set out to get it illegally."

Old Mrs. Arnold rose unsteadily, and pushed back her veil to reveal her long pointed nose and small eyes. Her first name was Merle, the French for blackbird, and seldom had it seemed more appropriate to Marigold than now. Indeed, at this moment they *all* resembled the birds after which they were named. Mrs. Arnold pointed a quivering lace-mittened finger at Marigold. "Oh, monstrous ingrate! You have been feeding off this family's bounty for years, and now have the *gall* to—to—"

"The gall to speak out?" Marigold interrupted, her chin raised defiantly.

Falk seized her arm. "Enough of this unseemliness, madam. The will is genuine, and you and your son no longer have a place in this family." He pointed toward the staircase. "The dower house has been cleared of your property, and the room you have temporarily occupied here is being attended to right now, so I suggest you oversee matters before the carriage arrives at the door."

"How very premature to issue such orders before the seal on the will was broken. But then, I suppose if you already knew what the

document contained . . ." As she allowed her voice to trail sugges-
tively away, she again heard the robin's encouraging chirrup. She
couldn't help recalling how Merlin had met with his death. A
robin. The same one? No, that was preposterous. . . .

"Just prepare to depart forthwith, madam! This family no longer
welcomes you," Falk replied, toying with the old gold ring he always wore. It was formed like an eagle, with outstretched wings
and eyes of coral.

"This family *never* welcomed me, sirrah, but Perry is Merlin's
legitimate child, and therefore heir to all this!" She swept an arm
to encompass the hall, but in her heart of hearts she no longer knew
anything for certain. What if an actor had indeed been hired to play
the clergyman?

Falk saw the uncertainty pass briefly through her eyes, and he
smiled anew. "No, Miss Marchmont, your son is my brother's *illegitimate* child," he declared, trying to usher her toward the door.

She resisted, shaking her arm free and whirling to face him
again. "I will fight you through the courts!" she cried.

To her astonishment, the entire family broke into laughter. Even
Mr. Crowe was moved to smile. "My dear lady," the lawyer said,
"even presuming you had the funds for such a legal battle, you
would still lose. Mr. Arnold is unassailable."

"Unassailable? How so?" she demanded.

"It is quite impossible for you to win, Miss Marchmont," Mr.
Crowe insisted, declining to explain more.

Falk addressed her again. "Enough, madam. I wish you to be
gone from this house before another night passes. Is that clear,
madam?"

"Why do you always measure time in nights, not days?" She
couldn't help asking, for it was something that had always puzzled
her about the Arnolds. A week to them was seven nights long, not
seven days. Even Merlin's will referred to the fourth *night* of April.

Falk didn't answer the question, but turned to snap his finger at
two footmen, who came immediately. "Miss Marchmont is leaving," he said.

"I despise you, Falk Arnold," she whispered, and a pin could
have been heard to drop as she went on in a clear tone that could
be heard by everyone. "You have always coveted my son's
birthright, and the only way you can lay your grasping hands upon
it is by falsifying your own brother's will! Is that how you

achieved your other legal successes? Have you cheated and lied your way through the courts?"

He turned to the footmen. "Remove this person," he said tersely.

The robin pecked at the glass, then burst into a defiant little song. Again he inspired her, and her next action was gloriously impulsive. There was an elaborate silver inkstand in front of Mr. Crowe, one of its bottles containing red ink, the other black. Before the footmen could take hold of her, she seized the red ink, and tossed the contents at Falk. There were startled cries as scarlet spots spattered all over him. "Throw her out!" he shrieked, searching for a handkerchief with which to mop the stains.

But Marigold had already gathered her skirts to walk proudly toward the great staircase. She glanced at the window, and saw the robin fly away. As she ascended to the floor above, her head was held high, and no one could tell how utterly devastated she was. She reached her room to find two maids hastily packing her things. They faced her uneasily. "It was Mr. Falk's orders, madam," said one.

With great difficulty, Marigold contained herself. It wasn't their fault, so it would ill become her to blame them. So she said nothing as she went out onto the balcony. Her brief moment of doubt concerning the legality of her marriage was already a thing of the past. The odious Crowe had forged a new will to suit Falk, and she knew she stood little chance of proving it. The hopelessness of her situation made her feel numb. What would become of her now? And of Perry? She was without income, and disowned both by her own family, and by the Arnolds. How was she going to provide for herself and her son?

Several minutes passed, and she could hear the maids whispering together, but suddenly they fell silent. Turning, she saw them gazing nervously at the door as Falk's angry steps approached. The moment he entered, they gasped at his red-spotted appearance, then scurried out. He'd tried to wipe the ink, but had only succeeded in smearing it, and his continuing fury was such that he trembled visibly. She knew he'd dearly like to strike her, and she steeled herself. His amber eyes were like stones as he crossed the room to block her escape on the balcony. "I've waited a long time to be rid of you, madam, and believe me, in spite of your childish outburst, I am enjoying every moment."

Never had he seemed more large and frightening, and as she pressed back against the balustrade, she was uneasily conscious of the drop to the gardens below. But to her relief he came no closer. "I could never understand what my brother saw in you, and I certainly can't imagine why he had to go the length of making you his wife."

She gave a sharp intake of breath. "So you *admit* he married me?"

"We are alone, my dear, so why should I pretend? Yes of course the will is false, but as you so shrewdly observed, I would go to any length to have your son's birthright. It is now mine, and there is nothing you can do about it. Crowe is my creature through and through, and all trace of the marriage ceremony has been expunged. But there *is* an actor in my pay, and he is very eager to earn a fat purse for swearing before witnesses that he 'officiated' at a fake ceremony between you and my late brother. Attempt to take me to court, and you will very shortly be out of countenance, for I cannot lose when it comes to the law."

"We will see about that," she replied in a trembling voice.

He laughed. "I have protection, my dear."

"Protection?"

"That is what I said."

Suddenly the robin fluttered down beside her on the balustrade. In its bill it held a marigold flower and a rowan leaf. Falk froze, and stepped involuntarily backward as she instinctively held out her finger to the little bird. For the briefest of moments she again thought he was afraid of her, but almost immediately his face became a mask. Then he lunged forward to grab her by the arms, and the robin dropped the flower and leaf as it flew into the room in alarm. Falk shook her roughly. "Who are you?" he demanded.

The fall to the gardens threatened, and she was afraid. "I—I don't understand. You *know* who I am!"

"Don't meddle in my affairs, madam, for you have no idea of my power," he said softly, his face so close she could feel his breath.

"Power?"

Releasing her, he slowly crushed the flower and leaf with his heel. "Just remember nothing can defeat me, my dear. This is the last time you and I will ever speak, madam, a fact for which I am eternally thankful."

"The feeling is mutual, sir," she replied.

"Be gone from here within the hour." He turned to leave, but the robin flew down from the top of the bed canopy, where it had taken refuge. It skimmed so close over his head that he was forced to duck, but then the bird swooped over him again and again, until he was obliged to raise an arm to fend it off. It seemed to Marigold that there was a definite purpose in the robin's attack, and at last she saw what it was. Making a particularly daring dive, the bird seized Falk's splendid golden hair with its tiny claws. For a moment Marigold couldn't believe her eyes, for the thatch of curls lifted slightly, and she glimpsed gleaming bald pate beneath. Falk Arnold wore a wig!

With an apoplectic oath, he swiped at the robin, which darted out of reach before returning to another angle of attack, this time seeming concerned with Falk's coat pocket. A handkerchief protruded, and the robin seized it with its bill, then tugged with all its might. The handkerchief came out in a rush, bringing with it a red billiard ball that fell heavily to the floor. The ball would have rolled beneath a chest of drawers, had not Falk put out a foot on it. Its purpose evidently fulfilled, the robin flew out past Marigold, then away across the park, chirruping triumphantly as it went.

Marigold was bemused by the truth about Falk's hair, but even more by the bird's incredible antics. As she gazed down at the handkerchief and billiard ball, Falk bent to retrieve both. There was a loud ripping sound as the back seam on his long-suffering breeches gave up what had been a very long struggle. In spite of everything, Marigold could have laughed. Oh, how good it was to see his humiliation. But somehow she kept a straight face as he stuffed the ball and handkerchief into his pocket again, then carefully backed out from the room.

Chapter Three

A fortnight later, the June sun was setting as the London to Bristol stagecoach rattled into the yard of the Spread Eagle Inn, which stood in the shadow of Windsor Castle. Horses stamped, bells rang, and ostlers shouted as a single passenger stepped down to the straw-strewn cobbles. It was Marigold, and she was to stay here overnight, before visiting Perry, who had still to be told the awful truth about their savagely reduced circumstances.

She wore a lilac silk pelisse and matching gown, and her rich red-gold hair was swept up beneath a gray jockey bonnet from which trailed a long cream gauze scarf. For the sake of Perry's rightful claim to his inheritance, she was still wearing her wedding ring and calling herself Mrs. Merlin Arnold, but she had discarded black because of the peculiar Arnold tradition of wearing mourning for only a month.

The last two weeks had been very wearying. She'd left Castell Arnold within an hour of her confrontation with Falk, and traveled to Lancashire to see her mother and stepfather, in the vain hope of finding refuge there. Her mother would gladly have taken her in again, but her stepfather was still obdurate. In his eyes a sin committed at sixteen remained unforgivable at thirty, and that was the end of it. From Lancashire she'd come south to London, to inquire about positions as governess or lady's companion, for there was little else that a respectable woman could do. Needless to say, there were more impoverished ladies than positions, and there was nothing immediately available. For a week she'd struggled to find something, but already what little money she had was running out, and there would be fees to pay when she removed Perry from Eton. So this morning she'd woken up knowing she could no longer postpone the evil moment of telling her son he must leave the school he loved, and that instead of being master of Castell Arnold, he had nothing. What Fate had in store for them after that, she hardly dared think. Tonight, however, she'd put on a brave face, and keep up appearances by staying at a good inn.

She stepped aside as fresh horses were brought for the stagecoach. The first lamps were being lit around the galleried yard, and there were lights inside too, giving everything a warm and welcoming glow. The innkeeper's name was written above the taproom door; HENRY G. FINCH, LICENSED TO SELL LIQUORS, BEERS, WINES, AND SPIRITS. A bird within a bird, she thought, looking at the inn sign of an eagle with outspread wings. The design was an unpleasant reminder of Falk's ring, and therefore of Falk himself, and all the feathered inmates at Castell Arnold. She would have preferred the inn to be called the Rose and Crown, the Royal Oak, or even the Pig and Whistle! But then she chuckled quietly as a fat pigeon perched on top of the sign to roost for the night, and promptly deposited a runny white memento which trickled down over the painted eagle. How very appropriate, she thought, thinking of Falk again.

Taking a deep breath, she gathered her skirts to walk around the stagecoach toward the taproom, but suddenly a scarlet curricle swept smartly in beneath the archway from the street, and the nearest of its two dapple gray horses almost knocked her down. The gentleman at the ribbons hauled his unnerved team to a halt, and leapt furiously to his feet. "Have you no sense, madam? You might have been killed!"

"Forgive me, sir, I fear I wasn't thinking." She looked up at him. There was something compelling in his quick hazel eyes. He was several years older than she was, and his sky blue coat and white breeches showed off his tall, broad-shouldered shape. A top hat was tilted back on his unruly black hair, and his tanned face was ruggedly handsome, although marred now by his anger.

"In future, pray save your preoccupation for safer surroundings!" he snapped.

Annoyance stirred belatedly through her. It wasn't entirely her fault, *he'd* been driving too fast. "And perhaps in future, sir, *you* should drive with more care in such a confined area," she replied, with a flash of her old spirit.

For a long moment he met her gaze. That he found her retort annoying she did not doubt, but he said nothing more as he gave her the coolest of nods, then sat down to move the curricle on past the stagecoach. But at least he drove sensibly now, she thought with some satisfaction.

Later, after resting longer than planned in the third-floor room, which was all she could afford, she went down to dinner. She didn't want to enter the dining room unescorted at such an advanced hour, having found over the past week that a woman alone was a magnet to a certain species of disagreeable male. But tonight she had no choice. She had to eat, and the landlord, Mr. Finch, a burly ex- pugilist known as "Bull" Finch to his friends, had flatly refused to send a meal up to a guest who was clearly of little consequence. Bracing herself, she paused to adjust her gray-and-gold cashmere shawl, then she caught up her lilac skirt to go inside. To her relief it proved almost deserted. Shadows blackened the furthest corners, and it was partitioned into settle-backed boxes that were only lit when candles were specifically requested. Without looking at any of the occupied tables, she hastened to the far side of the room, and slipped into one of the empty boxes, then sat with her back to the rest of the room, hoping not to be noticed because of the tall settle.

The newly employed waiter, a nervous, large-nosed young man by the name of Bunting, came to take her order of beefsteak pie, potatoes, and peas. Yet another bird, she thought as she asked for a candle and some wine. She was brought both, although the latter might more accurately have been described as vinegar. However, to make a fuss would be to attract attention, so she put up with it. As she awaited her meal, she glanced around the room. It was long and low, with dark oak beams and uneven walls. The usual sporting prints hung in prominent places, especially those of prizefighters, and gleaming copper pots and pans were fixed around the stone fireplace. Pots of white geraniums stood on the windowsills, and outside the Windsor street was quiet. A lantern shone on a corner opposite, and a lady and gentleman strolled down from the direction of the castle. Several carriages passed by, and she heard a church bell sound the hour. Her attention returned to the room itself, and suddenly she noticed a picture that was far from being a sporting print. It was on the wall right next to her box, and depicted a robin with several distinctive white feathers in its wings. Her lips parted, and her heart seemed to lurch as for a horrid moment she was back at Castell Arnold, watching Falk Arnold's precious toupee being dislodged by a tiny bird that was David to his Goliath. . . . She looked more closely at the picture, and was puzzled to note that it wasn't protected by glass, indeed it had been subjected to considerable attack with what appeared to be ordinary dressmaking pins. There were pinpricks all over it.

Her gaze was torn from the picture by the sudden arrival in the dining room of two rather affected, noisy gentlemen. Gentlemen? Perhaps not, for like the wine, they were in fact examples of that more vinegary creature, the Bond Street lounger. Drawling, foppish to a fault, and lacking in all manners, they sprawled in a box across the aisle from her. The other diners fell uncomfortably silent, and a number of them hastily quit their boxes. Those who remained were careful to become as unremarkable as possible. The loungers thundered their fists upon the table for service, for there was no sign of Bunting. "Waiter? Candles! And be quick!"

Marigold had frozen with dismay the moment the newcomers arrived, because she recognized them. Lord Toby Shrike and Sir Reginald Crane—bird names, naturally—were cronies of both Falk and Merlin Arnold, as well as intimate acquaintances of Alauda, albeit prior to Lord Avenbury. Marigold did not doubt that by now they would know about Merlin's will, nor did she doubt that if they recognized her their taunts would be both loud and insulting. Thrown into a quandary, she quickly averted her face and moved her own candle so that it cast more shadow over her. Should she remain and risk their jeering? Or would it be wiser to quit the room and go hungry? But just as the latter course seemed the only sensible option, Bunting scurried in with her dinner.

The loungers were displeased. "Demmee, sir! Candles, this instant!" cried Sir Reginald, banging the table. His long nose resembled a crane's bill, and his trumpeting voice was not unlike that same bird's call. He wore gray-and-black stripes, and his cheeks looked suspiciously rouged. Lord Toby flicked his perfumed handkerchief over his immaculate purple brocade sleeve. He was a pale, thin-faced man with brown eyes that somehow managed to look very cold, and he was by far the most unpleasant and dangerous of the two, for if he believed himself even mildly insulted, he demanded satisfaction. To her knowledge, at least two men had died at his hand.

The moment Sir Reginald called, Bunting turned with a dismayed start, for it was the first he'd realized the loungers were there. Sir Reginald drummed his beautifully manicured nails upon the table. "Candles, demmee. We'll take *that* one in the meantime," he declared churlishly, nodding at the candle on Marigold's table without observing whose it was. Bunting dithered, torn between duty and his dread of loungers. Sir Reginald rose with an oath that would not have disgraced the worst den in the East End, and reached over to snatch the candle. As he did, he at last saw Marigold. "I'll be demmed," he breathed.

Lord Toby looked swiftly across, and his jaw dropped. "Well, if it ain't Merlin's doxy." He laughed.

Marigold tried to get up. "Please leave me alone, sirs," she begged.

Another voice broke in from an unlit corner of the tap room. "Waiter, two pairs of candle snuffers if you please," drawled an unseen gentleman, who was apparently possessed of precisely the same affected tones as the loungers.

The harassed waiter turned. "Snuffers? Yes, sir!"

Outraged that he should apparently give someone else precedence, the fops temporarily forgot Marigold. Lord Toby jumped to his feet. "You'll attend *us* first!" he ordered the unfortunate Bunting, and then suddenly pointed toward the picture of the robin. "Remember the wheel."

Bunting went quite white. "Yes, sir," he whispered.

Marigold glanced at the picture as well. Wheel? What were they talking about?

The voice from the darkened corner came again, and this time was more commanding. "Waiter, two pairs of snuffers, *if* you please!"

Forced into a hasty decision, Bunting scurried away for the snuffers, leaving the two loungers speechless with fury. They glared at the unlit corner, where the interloper's silhouette was only just discernible. Lord Toby's face was like ice. "Demmee, sir, I'm of a mind to call you out for your impudence! Can't think why you want two snuffers when you haven't even got a candle," he said ominously, flicking his handkerchief again so that heady waves of cologne drifted over Marigold.

Bunting hastened back with the two snuffers, which were like scissors with flattened ends. He handed them respectfully to the gentleman, who then slowly stood. He'd donned his top hat, tugging it low over his forehead, so his face was impossible to make out in the uncertain light as he made his way toward the loungers, who immediately barred his way.

"I demanded an apology, sir!" cried Sir Reginald rashly.

The gentleman nodded. "Yes, my sentiments exactly," he replied mincingly. He held a snuffer in either hand, and before either lounger knew what was happening, he'd clamped them tightly to the ends of their noses. "Well, I seem to have caught me two very fine birds," he declared. "Now, gentlemen, I await the apologies upon which we are agreed."

They squealed and squirmed, with tears of pain running down their rouged cheeks, but their torturer merely gave a thin smile. "Come now, sirs, I'm still waiting." Still the affected drawl.

Sir Reginald capitulated, for his beaky nose was by far the easier target of the two. He was released the moment he gabbled the necessary words, and retreated warily until he was pressed against the table. However, Lord Toby's mouth remained firmly shut, so the gentleman brandished the free pair of snuffers toward the defiant lounger's loins. "Be warned, Lord Toby, I am quite prepared to make a capon of you." At that, Lord Toby's resistance crumbled as well, and he apologized. The loungers hoped that was sufficient, but the gentleman hadn't finished with them yet. He clacked the snuffers, and drawled once more. "I think you must also apologize to this lady, for you were unforgivably rude to her." He nodded toward Marigold.

In spite of his false voice, Marigold suddenly realized he was the gentleman in the scarlet curricle. She thought he could not possibly be aware that one of the fops he was humiliating was Lord Toby Shrike. She sat urgently forward. "Sir . . ."

He held up a quick hand. "In due course, madam, first I will have these good fellows make amends for the insulting manner in which they saw fit to address you." His attention returned to the loungers. "Now then, sirs, what was it you were about to say?"

Again Sir Reginald saw sense first, and hastily expressed penitence, but it was several moments before Lord Toby did the same. Only then were the snuffers lowered. The gentleman nodded. "Well, you were not exactly gracious, but I suppose it will have to do."

Lord Toby's eyes were cold in the light from Marigold's candle. "I will have your name, sir," he breathed.

The gentleman gave a slight laugh. "My name is of no consequence to you, Lord Toby."

Lord Toby's eyes became like flint. "Your name!" he snapped.

"My name is of no consequence to you," the gentleman repeated.

"It is when I intend to call you out."

Marigold was horrified, but the gentleman showed no concern, beyond a little mild amusement. "Then call me out, but you may wish you had not."

Lord Toby's voice was taut with barely controlled emotion. "I doubt very much if I will have any regrets. Are you familiar with the Druid Oak in Windsor Great Park?"

"It's a famous enough spot, so naturally I'm familiar with it."

"I will expect you there at dawn."

"Oh, very well. Whatever you wish."

The gentleman waved a languid hand, and his tone was weary, as if Lord Toby were no more than a tiresome fly he intended to swat at his leisure. Marigold stared incredulously at him. Was he *eager* to flirt with death?

Lord Toby quivered with rage. "I trust you still find it so amusing come the morning!" he breathed in a choked voice.

The gentleman shrugged. "Oh, I'm sure I will," he murmured.

Sir Reginald clearly thought him mad. "For pity's sake, sir!"

The gentleman glanced at him. "Toddle along, sir, and take your purple friend with you. I mislike purple, it is an unbecoming color at the best of times, but when worn by such a disagreeable bird, it becomes positively stomach turning."

Lord Toby stiffened, but Sir Reginald caught his arm. "Come, let's have done with this," he said wisely.

Lord Toby resisted, still looking at the gentleman. "I will make you pay for tonight's work, whoever you are."

"We'll see," murmured the gentleman with infuriating calm.

As the two loungers left, Marigold looked at the gentleman. "I thank you for your gallantry, sir, but have to confess I think you have taken leave of your senses," she said.

He gave a low laugh, then answered in his normal voice. "The likes of Lord Toby Shrike do not fill me with alarm."

"Then perhaps they should."

He removed his top hat and indicated the seat opposite her. "May I join you?"

"If you wish, sir."

He sat down, and then glanced at her now-cold dinner. Turning, he called Bunting, who hurried over. The gentleman gave the waiter a charming smile. "This establishment really should be more select about its clientele. This lady's dinner has suffered irreparably from the delay caused by the two recently departed fellows, so I trust you will provide her with a suitable replacement?"

He pushed her glass forward as well. "And if this is Bull Finch's notion of wine, it certainly isn't mine. Bring something better."

Bunting hesitated, for the landlord's orders were very strict.

The gentleman eyed him. "Just do as I say, and if that reprobate old prizefighter has any complaint, tell him to come to me."

Bunting blinked. "Yes, sir. Er, sir . . . ?"

"Yes?"

"Are you of the wheel?"

The gentleman looked blankly at him. "The what?"

Bunting drew back in confusion. "Oh, forgive me, sir, I—I was mistaken." He gathered up the plate and glass, and scuttled away.

"And bring two fresh glasses," the gentleman called after him. "Sir."

Marigold looked at her rescuer. "What do you think 'the wheel' could be? Lord Toby spoke of it earlier, and then pointed at that picture." She indicated the poor pinpricked robin.

The gentleman glanced at it. "Yes, I too noticed the remark. I fear I have no idea. Some club or society, no doubt. I'd hazard a guess at the Royal and Ancient Wheel of Featherheads," he added dryly.

She smiled, but then became more serious. "Sir, I don't know if you are aware of Lord Toby's reputation, but—"

"The fellow is as known to me as I am to him, but it amused me to withhold my identity. However, come the dawn, he will know me well enough, and he will certainly regret tonight's escapade."

"You speak as if the duel is bound to go your way, sir. Dare you be so confident in your own abilities?"

He sighed wearily. "*Che serà serà,* whatever will be, will be. The Russells and the Duke of Bedford are not alone in their family motto, for it is mine, too. All our fates are preordained, especially mine, so there is nothing to be gained from allowing dying to be of consequence."

His jaded tone was studied, but behind it she detected a disturbing vulnerability that reached out to her. Woe betide the woman who fell in love with him, she thought suddenly. "You should not speak that way, sir, for dying is of consequence to everyone."

The candlelight shone in his hazel eyes. "Not quite everyone," he murmured.

"Why should you be different?" she enquired.

He smiled a little, and didn't reply.

She studied him. "You would not tell Lord Toby who you are, sir, but will you tell me?"

"Certainly, madam, but only after I know who you are."

"Mrs. Arnold."

The name was common enough, and he did not give it a second thought. "Lord Avenbury, your servant." He inclined his head.

Alauda's lover? Marigold's breath caught, and she stared at him.

Chapter Four

Marigold's startled reaction intrigued Lord Avenbury. "It would appear my name is of some significance to you, Mrs. Arnold."

She collected herself. "I fear it is, my lord."

His hazel eyes shone in the candlelight as he sat back and raised a quizzical eyebrow. "You *fear* it is?"

Somehow she managed to look at him. "Perhaps it would explain if I told you that Merlin Arnold was my husband?"

"Well, what a small world, to be sure," he murmured, his gaze lingering on her red-gold hair.

"Uncomfortably small," she replied. "No doubt you now wish you had left me to Lord Toby and Sir Reginald."

"And why would I be so base as to wish that?"

She saw no point in being too delicate. "Oh, come, sir, we both know that you and Lady Fernborough are more than mere acquaintances, and that she despises me above almost all other living creatures. I'm sure she will have acquainted you with the titillating details of Merlin's will?"

"I haven't seen Lady Fernborough of late."

At that moment Bunting returned with another plate of dinner, and a very different wine from the one he'd served earlier. Lord Avenbury poured some, tasted it, and then nodded. "That's more acceptable. You may convey my compliments to Finch."

Bunting looked at him as if he were mad. Bull was already jumping with rage at having to replace both the dinner and the wine, to say nothing of losing what custom Lord Toby and Sir Reginald would have provided, so it would be preferable to go fourteen rounds with Tom Belcher than deliver another message from this particular gentleman!

Lord Avenbury waved him away, poured Marigold some wine,

then sat back again to look intently at her. "You think you cannot trust me, Mrs. Arnold?"

"Would you if you were me?"

"Probably not." He sipped his wine. "Tell me about Merlin's will."

The last thing she wished to do was confide anything to Alauda's lover, but there was something about him that would not be denied, and so much against her better judgment she told him everything.

He searched her green eyes in the half light. "You are destitute?" he said.

"Yes. By spending this one night at the Spread Eagle, I'm frittering away what little I have left."

"You're telling me that Falk Arnold has actually thrown you out without a penny to your name?"

"Oh, yes. And on top of that, he frankly admitted the will was a forgery."

Lord Avenbury sat forward incredulously. "He actually *said* it was false?"

"It amused him to taunt me with it. There were no witnesses, you see, so he knows I cannot prove anything. I could tell at the reading that the entire Arnold clan, including Lady Fernborough, knew what the will contained before the lawyer Crowe even broke the seal, so the whole thing was a wicked fabrication." She paused, half expecting him to defend his mistress, but he didn't, so she continued. "It is a conspiracy to deny my son his rightful inheritance."

"So it would seem."

"I begin to wonder if Falk has been falsifying other things too," she said then, not knowing why she was revealing so much to someone who had to be from the enemy camp.

"Other things?"

"These court cases he's won so miraculously over the past few months. Even the judges have been amazed by some of the decisions."

"Ah, yes. Well, I would not know whether or not he falsifies evidence as a matter of course, but I do know I think he is mentally unbalanced."

"Unbalanced?"

"Yes. Two months ago I encountered him at White's Club. Your late husband was with him, as it happens. Anyway, Falk was in his cups, and treated me—together with a number of other members who were present—to a most embarrassing diatribe concerning some past conflict between one of his ancestors and one of mine. He seemed to lose all control, and ended by addressing me as if he were his ancestor, and I mine. He even vowed to be avenged! Anyway, Merlin said something sharp to him—which, now I come to think of it, included the word "wheel"—and Falk was immediately persuaded to leave. If he hadn't, I fear he would have been requested to do so."

"I've seen Falk in his cups, it's not a pretty sight." She looked at him. "Are you sure Merlin said something about a wheel?"

"Quite sure. It didn't mean much to me at the time, but now . . ." Lord Avenbury shrugged.

"It's all very strange."

He smiled. "So you see, Mrs. Arnold, you may trust me after all, for after that embarrassing little episode I am certainly not well disposed to the Arnold clan, excepting you, of course."

"What of Alauda?" she inquired wryly.

He pursed his lips. "Ah, well she is another matter entirely."

"I do not doubt it, sir, just as I do not doubt that none of this makes any difference to my woeful situation. Falk is guilty, but I remain disowned by everyone, and financially and socially ruined. And tomorrow I must tell Perry how greatly reduced our circumstances have become."

"Perry?"

"My son, Peregrine Arnold. He's thirteen."

He smiled. "Thirteen? Forgive me for saying, but you must have been extremely young when you . . ."

"I married Merlin when I was sixteen."

"Merlin, Peregrine . . . Why are the Arnolds so obsessed with bird names? Falk Arnold is a rara avis surrounded by people of similar feathered nomenclature."

She smothered a laugh. "I don't know, but it is a fact. Speaking of the Arnolds' passion for things avian, when I took a room here, I began to wonder if I was still at Castell Arnold, what with a landlord called Finch, and a waiter named Bunting."

"To say nothing of shrikes, cranes, and pictures of robins."

"Yes."

"Well, this hostelry is one of Falk and his cronies' favorite nests, you know."

"Is it?" She glanced around in dismay.

"I suspect you'd have stayed elsewhere if you'd realized."

"Most certainly. I wonder what they do here? It's hardly a gaming hell or cockpit, and it certainly doesn't seem like a—a . . ."

"House of ill repute?"

"Yes."

He smiled then. "No doubt the Royal and Ancient Order of Featherheads dines here once a month. Perhaps they preen a lot, then take turns to give erudite speeches on ornithology."

She smiled. "Why are you here, Lord Avenbury? If you know this to be Falk's aerie, I would have thought that after your recent experience at White's, you'd avoid it too."

"I had an appointment at the castle late this afternoon, and it took longer than anticipated, so I decided to stay here for the night. I'm not one to stay away from somewhere because of the likes of Falk Arnold." He poured some more wine, and then glanced at her almost untouched dinner. "Have you lost your appetite, Mrs. Arnold?"

"I—I'd forgotten all about it," she answered truthfully, and picked up her knife and fork. The pie was lukewarm, but still edible.

Lord Avenbury watched her eat for a moment. "You say you have to see your son tomorrow?"

"Yes. He will have to leave Eton because I have no funds for his fees. No funds for anything, come to that." She tried not to think of tomorrow, but its advancing tread was relentless.

"What do you intend to do?"

"I—I don't know." The hopelessness of her situation breached her defenses, and for the first time her voice faltered. She put her knife and fork down, and pushed her plate away.

Lord Avenbury leaned across suddenly to put his fingers briefly over hers. "Don't lose heart, Mrs. Arnold." Then he got up. "I—I fear I have matters to attend to, and must bring this meeting to a close."

She was a little embarrassed. "Er, yes, of course, sir. Once again, thank you for protecting me tonight."

"It was nothing, believe me."

She met his eyes. "Is it considered bad form to wish someone well in a duel?"

"Shrike does not intimidate me."

"Don't underestimate him, for he is a vicious, untrustworthy maggot who would stoop to any level if he thought he would benefit."

"You clearly believe in speaking your mind."

"I have no reason not to."

He looked down at her. "I realize that," he said quietly, then drew her hand to his lips. "*À bientôt,* Mrs. Arnold."

"*À bientôt,* Lord Avenbury."

She gazed after his tall figure as he left the shadowy dining room. The impression of his lips still seemed to linger on her hand, and for the first time in her life she found herself envying Alauda, Lady Fernborough.

Chapter Five

Mist threaded eerily between the trees of Windsor Great Park as the old ostler maneuvered the hired trap off the road, and drew the pony to a standstill by a tall hawthorn hedge that was still heavy with late blossom. Dew shone on the leaves, the dawn light was silvery, and the chorus of birdsong was deafening. The ostler resented being aroused from his bed at such an hour, and so made no effort at all to assist Marigold to alight. Then, after pointing rather churlishly in the direction of the Druid Oak, he huddled on his seat to wait. She gathered her shawl warmly around her shoulders, then caught up her lilac silk skirt to make her way through the long grass.

She knew she shouldn't have come here, but she just couldn't help herself; after all, the duel had come about because of her. So, after tossing and turning most of the night, she'd been wide awake when Lord Avenbury's curricle drove out of the yard, and the urge to follow him had proved too great. The mist swirled slightly, and for a moment the silhouette of an immense tree was dimly visible directly ahead, but then the gray veils closed in again, and there was nothing. Horses snorted, and the faint gleam of polished brasswork told her where Lord Avenbury—and presumably his seconds—were waiting. She couldn't hear anyone talking, but supposed it to be because of the shrillness of the awakening birds. After going as close as she dared, she pressed back out of sight among the hawthorns.

From here she could see that the Druid Oak stood at the edge of a small grove. On the way from the Spread Eagle, the ostler had been disposed to tell her the story of how it had gotten its name. It seemed that long ago a local blacksmith had accidentally interrupted druidic rites, and for his pains had been magically impaled upon a jagged branch. The branch still jutted strangely from the main trunk about fifteen feet above the

ground, and mistletoe now grew in profusion where the unfortunate blacksmith had met his grim end. She knew the old man
had been trying to frighten her, but right now, with the dawn
mist still clinging between the trees, it seemed a little too real
for comfort.

More minutes passed, the morning chorus quietened, and the
mist thinned noticeably. Now she could see Lord Avenbury quite
clearly. He was lounging on the seat of the curricle about
twenty-five yards away across the grove, with his long legs
stretched out, and his boots resting on the rail. His arms were
folded, his top hat was low over his forehead, and his head was
bowed as if he were asleep. There was no one else with him, no
seconds, no surgeon, just him.

A robin suddenly flew down from the oak, and lighted on a
hawthorn spray close to her. With each flutter of his wings she
saw the unusual white feathers possessed by the robin at Castell
Arnold, and also by the bird depicted in the painting at the inn.
Anglesey was nearly two hundred miles away, and the painting
was clearly rather old, so it couldn't possibly be the *same* robin,
and yet . . . She tried not to think it, but when the little bird
paused and cocked his head to one side to look at her, she felt
sure it was the very one that had inspired her to confront everyone at the reading of the will. She held out her finger, and sure
enough, the little scarlet-breasted bird flew onto it. She looked
at him. "Well, Robin, my friend, why did you bring the marigold
and rowan leaf to me, mm? And why do you dislike Falk so
much?" she whispered.

The robin chirruped as if he understood, but then a carriage
was heard approaching, and he flew off. Marigold kept well
back amid the hawthorn, watching Lord Avenbury, who did not
move even though he must also have heard the carriage.

The clatter of hooves and wheels grew steadily more loud,
and then suddenly the vehicle swept into the clearing, and came
to a halt within ten yards of her. Birds were startled from the
hedge and surrounding trees, some of them so close that
Marigold was scattered with droplets of dew from the shudder-
ing hawthorn blossom. The carriage door was flung open. Lord
Toby, Sir Reginald, and two gentlemen unknown to Marigold
alighted. If they turned, they could not help but see her, but they
laughed and talked together as if arriving at a fashionable dinner
party, and Sir Reginald, who clutched a bottle of cognac and

some glasses, seemed to Marigold to be somewhat in his cups. One of the men carried a beautiful inlaid box containing a set of dueling pistols, which he opened for Lord Toby to take one out to examine. Then he placed the box on the grass in order to accept a glass of Sir Reginald's cognac. They all three sipped a goodly measure, and glanced across at the curricle and its sleepy occupant, who still seemed asleep. After a moment they looked at one another, and then Lord Toby called out.

"Hey, you, sir! Have the good manners to step down!"

Slowly Lord Avenbury lowered his legs to the board, then sat up and moved his top hat back only a little, so that his face was still not fully revealed. "Are you talking to me, sir?" he replied, adopting the same mincing tones of the night before.

The mockery provoked Lord Toby. "I'll make you pay for your insults! Step down, I say!"

"I'm always willing to respond to such an elegant avian beseechment," murmured Lord Avenbury, humming to himself as he climbed slowly down from the curricle. Only then did he tip his hat back completely.

The man who'd brought the box of pistols took an involuntary step backward. "Ye gods, Shrike, you've taken on Avenbury!" he squeaked, dropping his glass.

Lord Toby went pale, but managed to display a little bravado. "It makes no difference to me whether it's Avenbury or Beelzebub himself!" Handing his glass back to Sir Reginald, he made much of inspecting the pistol he'd selected.

"But it isn't time yet," the third man warned in an undertone. Marigold could just hear him, but he was inaudible to Lord Avenbury.

"Time?" Lord Toby's eyes flew to his friend's.

"It cannot be now, or the wheel will not turn."

"This is a matter of honor!" breathed Lord Toby.

"We have no choice. The wheel must come first. Think, man! Of all the men in England, this one must be safe!"

Marigold listened bemusedly. No choice? Of all the men in England? What on earth *was* this wheel they kept referring to?

Sir Reginald, who had been swaying drunkenly, suddenly put a hand on Lord Toby's arm. "I—I say, Tobes, this is best left, don't you think?" he said in a thick voice. "The c-candle snuffers just ain't worth the candle, and George is right, the time ain't right."

Lord Avenbury grew tired of their whispering. "We have business to attend to, Shrike!" he called.

Sir Reginald hiccuped loudly, then looked at Lord Toby again. "I've s-said my piece. I'm not getting involved in this." Turning, he walked unsteadily back to the carriage, and clambered inelegantly into it. The other two men exchanged glances, then followed him. Lord Toby suddenly found himself alone, with the pistol still in his hands. Clearly rattled, he turned to his opponent. "I—I may have been a little hasty, Avenbury," he said after a moment.

Lord Avenbury's eyebrows twitched. "Come now, sir, we came here to fight a duel, and I'm ready to do precisely that."

"I—I, er . . ."

"Yes?"

"I think this whole business is unnecessary," Lord Toby said then. His face was quite pasty, and there was little trace now of the sneering bully of the night before.

"Really? How is it unnecessary?"

"I realize that—that I was completely in the wrong last night."

"Well, what a pity you did not think of saying it then, for I fear now is too late." Lord Avenbury strode across the grass to take the remaining pistol from the box on the grass.

Lord Toby panicked, and stumbled backward. As he fell, his finger closed involuntarily upon the trigger, and a single report shattered the silence. As the reverberations died away, Marigold was dismayed to hear her hired trap being driven hastily off as the ostler decided to distance himself from possible danger.

Lord Toby sprawled where he fell, gazing up in terror at Lord Avenbury, who now cocked the other pistol. It was a menacing sound.

Lord Toby's mouth was suddenly desert dry. "Sweet God above, Avenbury, I didn't mean to—to . . ."

"No?" Lord Avenbury took pleasure in leveling the pistol.

"For pity's sake, spare me!" Lord Toby groveled before him.

After a moment, Lord Avenbury raised the pistol, and fired it into the air, then tossed it into the box. "Get out of here, Shrike, and take your friend's pretty weapons with you," he said.

Hardly able to believe he was to be spared, Lord Toby gathered the box and its contents, then scrambled back to the carriage, where his wide-eyed friends had witnessed everything. They almost hauled him inside, and the door had hardly slammed behind him before the vehicle drove off as if pursued by all the hounds in hell.

Lord Avenbury turned toward the hedge. "You can come out now, Mrs. Arnold."

Chapter Six

Horrified to realize Lord Avenbury knew she was there, Marigold emerged reluctantly from hiding.

"I trust the spectacle just past wasn't too indelicate for you?"

"Er, no, my lord."

"Lord Toby can certainly thank his lucky stars for your presence, for otherwise I would certainly not have let him off so lightly."

She didn't know what to say.

There was a fallen tree nearby, and he went to lean back against it, still looking at her. "Why did you come here?"

"I don't really know." Still clutching her shawl close, she went to join him. "Where are your seconds, Lord Avenbury? And why is there no surgeon?"

"I saw no reason to bother with such niceties."

"If Lord Toby's shot had found a mark in your elegant hide, such *niceties* could have saved your life!" She was appalled by his attitude.

"My elegant hide? What a charming turn of phrase."

"I chose it because to my mind taking part in a duel without seconds or a surgeon shows an intelligence so limited that it verges on the bovine."

"Ouch," he replied, grinning. "My, what a tongue you have, madam."

"I don't think it funny, sir," she said tersely.

"So I notice."

"Nor should you, considering you might have just been killed."

"Come now, that's rather an exaggeration," he murmured.

"Is it?"

"Of course it is. Be sensible, Shrike's shot was so wide of the mark that I doubt he even managed to hit the oak tree!"

Annoyance stung through her. "Be sensible? Sir, *I* am not the one who just foolishly brushed with death." Her tone was now very tart indeed.

He was still amused. "I find your spirit most refreshing, Mrs. Arnold."

"And I find your cavalier tendencies irritating in the extreme."

"You don't hold men in much estimation, do you?" he said after a moment.

"You sex has done very little to endear itself to me," she answered, smoothing trembling hands upon the folds of her lilac skirts, for in spite of her defiant sallies, she had been deeply upset by what had so nearly happened. Instead of being able to mock her like this, he could have been lying dead on the grass.

He noticed the gesture. "You're too fainthearted, Mrs. Arnold," he said gently.

"And you're too careless of your own safety!" she replied angrily.

Suddenly he seized one of her hands, and held it tightly. "Why did you really come here?" he asked.

Surprised by his action, she tugged her hand away. "I've already told you I don't know, and right now I wish I hadn't."

"I'll warrant that last is true, since I fancy your transport has departed without you."

She lowered her eyes. She'd forgotten the wretched trap. How was she going to get back to the Spread Eagle?"

"Rest easy, for I am more than happy to convey you," Lord Avenbury said, almost as if he'd heard her thoughts. Then he paused. "Do you believe in destiny, Mrs. Arnold?"

"Destiny?" The change of subject made her look up in surprise.

"That our whole lives are written in the stars?"

"No, I believe we are responsible for our own fate," she replied, thinking that if anyone was nearly the author of his ultimate fate, he was.

He searched her face. "Is that truly what you believe?"

She wondered what lay behind his questions. "Yes, it is. Why do you ask?"

"Because you intrigue me greatly, Mrs. Arnold."

"Lady Fernborough would not appreciate such an admission," she replied, moving to get up, but his hand shot out to restrain her. "Tell me something else, Mrs. Arnold. What would you have felt if Shrike had killed me?"

"I would have thought it a stupid waste."

"Of a noble soul?" He laughed.

"Noble? How would I know whether or not you are noble? You may have championed my cause last night, and risked your life in defense of my honor here this morning, but what I have heard of you otherwise does not suggest you are someone who could be truly described as noble."

His eyes were compelling. "Do I detect the wagging of a puritan finger, Mrs. Arnold?" he asked softly.

She didn't reply.

"And what if I were to similarly judge you? To me you seem a damsel in distress, and that is indeed what you would have me believe, but the Arnold family undoubtedly hold a very different opinion. Should I believe them?"

"Oh, I do not doubt that you will ultimately take their side, Lord Avenbury," she answered, thinking of Alauda.

"Don't presume you know me, Mrs. Arnold, for I promise you do not."

She met his gaze. "I do not need to know you sir, I have only to remember that you are Lady Fernborough's lover."

"Possibly, but you are the one I am asking to be my wife," he replied quietly.

The proposal caught her so completely off guard that she stepped hastily from the tree trunk as if it had suddenly burned her. "I—I beg your pardon?" she gasped, facing him.

"Become Lady Avenbury, and all your problems will be solved."

"Sir, I think Lord Toby's shot must have found a mark of sorts after all. Either that, or you are possessed of an addled brain!" she said.

He straightened as well. Before she knew it, his left arm had suddenly shot around her waist, and his right hand was to her chin, forcing her to look up at him. "I am in earnest, Mrs. Arnold."

The warmth of his fingers stirred senses she had tried to forget, as did the masculine scent of costmary on his clothes. She could have rebuked him for his forwardness, and pulled away quite easily, but she didn't.

He looked deep into her wide green eyes. "Become my wife, and your worries will be at an end. You will lack for nothing, and your son will be amply provided for. I will also instruct my lawyer to make every possible investigation regarding the false will. If Falk Arnold's villainy can be exposed, it will be."

She managed to overcome the spell he'd suddenly cast over her. "But *why*? What possible reason could you have for helping me so much?" she cried, pulling away at last. "Is it simply that you wish to goad Lady Fernborough?"

"My reasons are my own, but believe me, I have nothing to lose."

"That is no answer, and you know it."

"Very well, perhaps it is simply that for once I wish to do something completely honorable."

She was mystified. "You see me as a salve to your conscience?"

He smiled. "Don't look for unnecessary answers, Mrs. Arnold. All you need be concerned with is whether or not you intend to look this gift horse in the mouth. Well, do you?"

"You really mean it, don't you?" It was a statement, rather than a question.

"Mrs. Arnold, I am not in the habit of proposing marriage willy-nilly, indeed this is the first time I have ever done so."

"But I don't even know your first name!"

He released her. "That is easily remedied. My name is Rowan, and I'm the thirteenth Lord Avenbury."

Marigold stared at him. Rowan? Merlin's riding accident had been caused by a robin flying from a rowan tree; and the robin had brought her a rowan leaf, and a marigold flower. . . . Suddenly her conviction about being in control of one's own destiny didn't seem quite as certain.

He looked quizzically at her. "Is something wrong?"

"Er, no, of course not."

"I'm relieved to hear it. Now, may I know *your* name?"

"It's Marigold."

He smiled. "Marigold?" he repeated.

She colored again. "I know it's a foolish name, but—"

"I didn't say it was foolish," he interrupted quickly. "On the contrary, I find it quite charming. So, we are now fully introduced. The only other things you need to know about me are that I am wealthy, and completely at liberty to offer marriage. Oh, and that I would regard it as an honor to protect you and your son."

"Society would regard such a match as scandalous. The Arnolds have branded me a kept woman who has a son out of wedlock. Even supposing some people believe I really was married to Merlin, can you imagine with what shocked disapproval they would regard so hasty a second union?"

"Chitter chatter is of no concern to me, nor should it be of concern to you. All you should consider is your son, and if you marry me, he will be amply provided for. Go your own way, and he will not." Rowan paused, then added. "But before making your final decision, be warned that it will not be a marriage in name only. If you enter my life, you enter my bed as well."

Hot embarrassment rushed into her cheeks. "You are very direct, my lord."

He smiled, putting his fingertips briefly to her hair, which shone like spun copper in the translucent morning light. "I'm of a mind to enjoy your favors, Marigold." He gave a low laugh. "Just think, we would be a flower and a tree against all those Arnold birds."

Suspicion lingered. Was it a trick? He was Alauda's lover, so surely he had some ulterior motive for making such a dazzling offer! "But would you really be against them?" she asked.

"Yes, Marigold, I would."

"But, Alauda . . ."

"Alauda has nothing to do with this."

"Are you sure?"

"I have already said so." Rowan held her eyes. "I know that for Perry's sake you wish to accept, and yet you hesitate. Why? Is it because you shrink from attentions you may find disagreeable? If so, let me assure you that my demands for your favors will cease before the end of this month."

It was such a very odd thing to say that she looked curiously at him. "What do you mean?"

"You will find out soon enough, so I will not bore you with the details."

His refusal to explain made her draw back from the edge. "I—I need time to consider . . ."

"Time is the one thing I cannot allow, Marigold. You must answer me now, or forfeit your chance. After all, I may sleep on the matter and wake up of a different mind."

"Which statement reduces this whole thing to the farce I suspected all along, sir," she replied angrily.

"If it appears farcical, I apologize, because believe me, I am serious. So what is your answer? Will you honor me with your hand? For your son's sake I advise you to think carefully before you decline."

She tried to read his eyes. What manner of man was he? Another Merlin? Or someone with whom she could at least come close to being happy? Her head warned against the former, but her heart leaned toward the latter.

"The seconds are ticking away, Marigold," he pressed softly.

The robin fluttered down to the grass only yards away from them, and sang a little song. Marigold once again threw caution to the winds. "I accept, Lord Avenbury," she answered, hardly able to believe any of this was happening. The robin flew away, but his song echoed joyously around the grove.

Rowan smiled. "A sensible reply."

"Or a completely lunatic one," she observed. She *must* have taken leave of her senses! She'd known him for a few hours, and yet had agreed to marry him! What else could she be but moonstruck? Then an obvious question belatedly struck her. "When do you wish this, er, contract to be solemnized?"

"How very formal you are."

"I don't know how else to be, sir."

"That will soon be rectified. As I said before, time is the one thing I cannot allow, so I intend the marriage to take place in a few days."

"Why won't you explain more? What will happen before the end of the month?"

Instead of answering, he suddenly drew her closer, and put his lips to hers. It was the sort of kiss to melt her soul, for it was lingering, teasing, sensuous, and filled with sweet promise. A warm ache began to seep deliciously through her; it was the ache of desire, and all her willpower was required to prevent her from slipping her arms around him and returning it in a way that was not at all demure.

He relaxed his hold, and stepped back. "There, Marigold, we have sealed our betrothal with a kiss," he said softly.

Her senses were in chaos, and she avoided his eyes in case he realized the sort of response he had aroused in her. A sudden breath of wind rustled through the Druid Oak, and her gaze was drawn toward it. She saw the golden mistletoe swaying on the jagged branch.

Chapter Seven

Later that day Rowan took Marigold to see Perry. The great round tower of Windsor Castle was very white and majestic against the clear blue June sky as the curricle swept over the bridge across the Thames, on its way to Eton College. Marigold's gauze scarf streamed in the breeze as the team of grays kicked up their hooves. She wore her lilac silk pelisse and matching gown, and gripped the rail tightly as the curricle skimmed around a corner. If she had wondered if the past twenty-four hours was only a dream, she could wonder no more, for on her finger was a diamond ring Rowan had purchased for her at a fashionable Windsor jeweler.

Right now, however, her thoughts were of Perry. Her astonishing betrothal was for his sake, yet how was she going to explain it to him when she still hardly knew what to make of it herself? She glanced down at the ring, and wished again that she knew Rowan's reasons for marrying her. His vague replies about honor and having nothing to lose didn't explain anything, she still didn't know *why* he was doing it. But she did know it was a very unequal bargain for him. When the story got out, society would think the same, and the new Lady Avenbury would be greeted with a scandalized stir. She was thirty years old, penniless, and not a great beauty, nor did she even have a great lineage to commend her. She claimed to have been widowed for only a month, yet as things stood, the law would not only call her a liar, but also brand her son illegitimate. So why, *why* did one of England's most handsome, sought-after, and wealthy lords choose to make her his bride after a few hours' acquaintance? Oh, it would engross drawing room conversation for weeks!

Her eyes slid surreptitiously toward Rowan's face as he tooled the grays along the cobbled street. His profile was matchless—strong, firm, and yet finely molded too in that oddly aristocratic way that so set his class apart. His top hat was, as usual, tipped back on his tousled dark hair, and the folds of his brown silk neck-cloth fluttered a little as the curricle raced toward the college. His hard, lithe body set off his tight-fitting sage green coat and cream breeches to perfection, and his skill with the ribbons was such that he hardly seemed to instruct the flying team.

What sort of marriage was theirs going to be? All she had to give was herself—and he had already warned that he intended to take her—but how did she feel about it? Her reaction to his kiss told her she was greatly attracted to him, but it was many years since she had last graced Merlin's bed, and even longer since she had known pleasure there. Yet pleasure there *had* once been. If the kiss by the Druid Oak was a guide, then it seemed the sensuous side of her nature had certainly not withered along with her love for Merlin. Not only that, it was set to bloom again with Rowan, Lord Avenbury, whose lips had almost robbed her of all restraint. But there was Alauda to beware of. Beware, Marigold, beware, she warned herself.

Suddenly his hazel eyes swung to meet hers. "Have you studied me enough, Marigold?"

"Forgive me, I—I didn't mean to stare."

"Oh, yes, you did. And I know what you were wondering."

"You do?" Color warmed her cheeks.

He laughed, and did not trouble to lower his voice to reply. "You're wondering if the kiss by the oak was a prelude to a veritable symphony of fleshly pleasures."

"Hush!" Marigold was hugely embarrassed, for a lady just emerging from a haberdashery heard, and was shocked.

Rowan merely laughed, and raised his voice still more. "The answer is yes, Marigold, for when we are married, I intend to make passionate and lengthy love to you!"

Two gentlemen on the pavement turned in astonishment as the scarlet curricle dashed past, and one of them raised his hat and shouted approval. Mortified, Marigold gazed fixedly ahead. "Why do you not print a broadsheet and distribute it throughout the town?"

Rowan chuckled. "Forgive me, but I simply couldn't resist." He became more serious. "Joking apart, I trust I have answered your unspoken questions?"

"Only some of them."

"Other answers will be forthcoming in due course, I promise."

"But not yet."

"No, not yet, for I'm not quite ready to tell you everything. I will though, you have my word. And when I do explain, please try to understand."

"Understand what?"

He didn't say anything more, but tooled the team even more swiftly along the cobbles. Several minutes later they reached their destination, not the college itself, but the residence of Dr. Bethel, the classics master, with whom Perry and his friend and classmate, Percy Bysshe Shelley, were lodged. It was a three-storied town house in a quiet cul-de-sac, and as the curricle came to a halt, Marigold was startled to hear screams, shouts, and the frantic quacking of an angry duck emanating from an open window on the top floor. More than that, a cloud of foul-smelling smoke billowed out over the leafy street.

She alighted anxiously. "The house is on fire!" she cried, gathering her skirts to rush inside, but Rowan vaulted swiftly down and held her back.

"It isn't a fire. From the smell of it, I'd hazard it's a scientific experiment that has temporarily bested its creator," he reassured her.

"But, Rowan, I—"

He interrupted her. "Believe me, Marigold, all will be well. The smell is only too familiar, because as a boy I once attempted precisely the same experiment. My lodgings were somewhat odiferous for a few days, but that is all. Although what in God's name a duck has to do with it, I cannot imagine."

Suddenly a man's angry voice carried plainly to the pavement outside. "*Mr.* Arnold and *Mr.* Shelley, how many times have I remonstrated with you concerning dabbling with chemicals and keeping creatures in your room?" Whoever it was then had to shout as the quacking became positively hysterical. "Mr. Shelley, will you kindly keep your bird under control!"

Gradually the clamor of quacks died to an occasional grumble, and a boy spoke. "But, Dr. Bethel, it isn't my bird!"

"Which leaves me to presume it must be yours, Mr. Arnold?"

Perry answered. "No, Dr. Bethel."

"Then may I inquire to whom it *does* belong?"

"We don't know, sir," replied the first boy. "We, er, found it in the room."

There was a heavy silence, broken only by a quack or two. Then Dr. Bethel spoke again, and very testily. "I came in here and found you two seated on the edge of a satanic circle, with blue flames, smoke everywhere, and this poor creature in the middle of the circle! Why, sirs, I wonder you bothered with such mild magic, why didn't you go straight to the pentagram and sacrificial cockerel? A devil or two would certainly enliven afternoon tea, but a demon *duck* seems something of an anticlimax!"

Rowan hid a smile, but Marigold had grown more and more dismayed. What on *earth* had been going on here?

Perry protested. "Dr. Bethel, we don't know anything about the duck, it just appeared! Anyway, it's a drake."

"Duck, drake, what does it matter? The fact remains that I do not believe you, Mr. Arnold, instead I think you and Mr. Shelley brought the unfortunate creature here for your sorcery."

The duck began to quack belligerently. "No, sir, I *swear* it!" Perry cried. "It—it must have flown in through the window, and we just didn't see it because Bysshe's chemical experiment had caught fire and produced so much smoke."

"And that is your explanation?"

"Yes, sir."

"You must think I also believe the moon to be made of cheese! I'm sorry, gentlemen, but this behavior is simply not good enough, nor is your conduct in general. Last week you contrived to use a gunpowder device in order to blow up an old tree stump at the college, and now it is ducks and devil worship!"

Marigold's hand crept worriedly to her throat. Chemicals? Gunpowder? Devil worship? Ducks?

"We weren't worshipping the devil, sir, we were trying to raise a Celtic god," protested Bysshe.

"I don't care *what* you were attempting to raise, sir, I only care that I don't wish it to materialize in *my* house!" cried the furious master. "This is the final straw, you leave me no choice but to report you to Dr. Keate!"

Marigold's lips parted. The formidable Dr. Keate was in charge of the entire Lower School at the college, and in Perry's letters was described as a "flogger."

Seeing her expression, Rowan smiled a little. "Well, if they've been doing all *that,* they deserve it," he murmured.

"Perry was always so quiet," she said bemusedly.

"Boys grow up, and I fear that dabbling in things such as this is part of that process," he replied, endeavoring to reassure her.

"Clearly you speak from experience."

"Well, I have to confess that I was indeed a boy once," he answered dryly.

"A devil-worshipping boy?"

"Naturally, along with searching for the secret of alchemist's gold, trying to communicate with spirits, and frightening my unfortunate friend witless with imaginary monsters. But I promise I no longer communicate with Beelzebub and his lieutenants, indeed I've quietened considerably in my old age. Come on, let us enter this abode of hellfire and demon ducks." Adjusting his top hat, he offered her his arm.

Slowly she slipped her hand over his immaculate sleeve, and they went up the flight of three shallow stone steps to the dark blue door. Rowan raised the gleaming brass knocker, and rapped it twice. After a moment a rather flustered maid admitted them. The shadowy hall behind her was hazy with the noxious smoke, and there came the clatter of footsteps and the sound of renewed quacking as the harrassed Dr. Bethel, clad in his black master's robe, ushered the two miscreants—one of whom carried an indignant mallard drake under his arm—down the staircase to his study on the ground floor.

That Peregrine was an Arnold there could never be any doubt, for he was tall, handsome, bronzed, and golden like his sire and uncle, but there, as Marigold had happily observed on countless occasions, the similarity ended. Perry wasn't sly and cruel, but warm and thoughtful, and he had her expressive green eyes rather than the cold amber of Merlin and Falk. He wore a short charcoal tailcoat and gray pantaloons with Hessian boots, and a sky blue waistcoat with a plainly knotted neckcloth. Marigold glowed with pride. How handsome he was, and how much more handsome would he be when he was a man grown. He was a veritable Greek god in the making. Oh, how many hearts he would break when he entered society. The train of thought broke off sharply as she realized what a difference her brief acquaintance with Rowan had made. From the depths of despair and want, suddenly she was again anticipating her son's entry into society!

Her glance moved to her son's companion in crime. Percy Bysshe Shelley—he of the mallard—was thin, freckled, and awkward, with a long face and a markedly large nose. He was dressed in a navy blue coat and fawn pantaloons, and his neckcloth had come undone due to the constant exertions of the wriggling drake. His blue eyes were wide and rather startled, and his shoulder-length brown hair hung in curled girlish profusion. Her first impression was that he seemed even less likely than Perry to be a blower up of tree stumps, a raiser of devils, or conducter of dangerous experiments.

Dr. Bethel, a small, mild-featured man with graying hair and a worn expression, had clearly been driven to the end of his tether by his two high-spirited charges. "Well, sirs, well, sirs," he was saying, "I begin to hope you will both succumb to this epidemic of chicken pox and have to be sent home to recuperate, for I believe that is the only way I will again enjoy some semblance of peace!"

Perry suddenly saw Marigold. "Mama!" he cried, and forgot Dr. Bethel as he ran to hug her. But then he realized she wasn't alone, and drew back in puzzlement, looking at Rowan. "Sir?"

Marigold hastened to effect an introduction. "Rowan, may I present my son, Peregrine Arnold? Perry, this is Lord Avenbury."

Perry looked inquiringly at Marigold the moment she addressed Rowan by his first name, but remembered his manners, and bowed his head. "I'm honored to meet you, sir."

"I'm honored to meet you too, sir," Rowan replied.

Before anything more could be said, the drake began to quack frantically. Perry's friend struggled to silence it as it flapped and struggled in his arms, and he eventually kept it quiet only by clamping his hand tightly over its bill. Two feathers drifted to the floor as the unfortunate mallard continued to wriggle, but at last it subsided, contenting itself with a series of darkly disgruntled half quacks that told everyone exactly what it thought of the human race.

As soon as he had the disheveled drake more or less under control, Percy Bysshe Shelley stepped excitedly toward Rowan. "Lord Avenbury? *The* Lord Avenbury?" he breathed, as if in the presence of a supernatural being.

Rowan was clearly dismayed, although he hastily dissembled. "Well, I know of no other Lord Avenbury."

"The cursed lord? The one whose ancestor brought the vengeance of the druids upon his line? The one who fears nothing and gazes death in the eye without a flicker of fear or remorse?" The boy spoke with almost ghoulish relish, but then had to grapple again with the determined mallard.

Perry rounded sharply on his friend. "You shouldn't ask such things, Bysshe!"

But Bysshe only pressed the question. "*Are* you that Lord Avenbury?"

Rowan glanced fleetingly at Marigold. "Yes, I suppose I am indeed that Lord Avenbury," he murmured reluctantly.

She looked at him in astonishment. *Cursed* lord? She certainly did not believe in such things, but it was clear that the subject rattled him considerably. When Falk had referred to him as doomed, she had presumed it was on account of Alauda's proven record of casting unwanted lovers aside. Maybe that wasn't Falk's meaning after all. And when she thought a little more, that very dawn she herself had seen Rowan look death in the eye without a flicker of fear or remorse!

Bysshe was too excited to halt now. "I have Stukeley's book on the curse, indeed I believe I know it line for line."

Rowan looked as if he could have strangled the boy. "That wretched little scribble has an annoying habit of surfacing now and then," he said, then cleared his throat and firmly changed the subject. "Now then, Mr. Shelley, I fancy it is time you extended a suitably contrite apology to Dr. Bethel."

Loath to abandon such an intensely interesting subject, but afraid to argue with a peer of the realm, Bysshe turned to the master. "We're truly sorry, sir," he said dutifully, looking every inch the picture of schoolboy guilt. Perry murmured the same words, then fixed his gaze firmly upon the floor.

The drake flapped as Dr. Bethel drew a regretful breath. "Forgive me, my lord, Mrs. Arnold, but as you will have gathered, there has been yet another unfortunate occurrence here today. I regret that I can no longer let such matters pass, indeed I have no alternative but to report both your son and Master Shelley to Dr. Keate."

"Oh, dear. Must you really?" Marigold envisaged her son being flogged within an inch of his life, like a mutineer upon the high seas.

The doctor glanced at the maid, who waited nearby, keeping a wary eye on the drake. "That will be all, Bessie."

"Yes, sir." Still watching the mallard, she bobbed a curtsy and hastened thankfully away.

Dr. Bethel turned then to the two boys. "Your immediate punishment can wait, but you are to return to the scene of devastation above, and clean every inch of it yourselves. Is that clear, sirs?"

"Yes, sir," they mumbled in unison.

"Be off with you then. And take that monstrous duck back where you found it!" With that the doctor turned toward the study door, but as he stretched out to the gleaming brass knob, Bysshe uttered a strangulated warning yelp.

"No, sir! Don't touch it!"

He was too late. Dr. Bethel's fingers closed upon the knob, and there was a blue flash, accompanied by a crackling sound. The unfortunate doctor shot backward across the hall, and fell to the floor against a table upon which stood a vase of overblown roses. He was showered with petals and water as the vase teetered, but thankfully did not fall.

Chapter Eight

The two boys were speechless with dismay as Rowan helped the shaken master to his feet. Marigold hurried over as well. "Have you been hurt, Dr. Bethel?" she asked anxiously, taking out a handkerchief and mopping some water from his black robe.

"Only my dignity, dear lady, only my dignity," he replied, retrieving his aplomb in that singular way learned by teachers through the centuries.

Rowan examined the doorknob, around which a telltale length of copper wire had been wrapped. The wire led to the hinge of the door, then disappeared into the study beyond, where Bysshe or Perry had no doubt arranged the implements necessary to create the new Italian electrical invention known as a voltaic battery. He looked at the boys. "Your handiwork, sirs?"

Bysshe spoke quickly. "It was me, sir, Perry had nothing to do with it." The drake made a noise like a sneeze, and shook its head so that its head feathers stood up. Fearing another onslaught of quacking, the boy gripped its bill with his hand.

Rowan raised an eyebrow. "Well, Master Shelley, it would almost seem you are hell-bent upon expulsion."

Bysshe gave him an imploring look. "It was just a prank, sir."

"A highly dangerous one."

"It was meant for Bessie, not Dr. Bethel," Bysshe protested.

Rowan was outraged. "Shame on you, sir! What on earth has the poor maid done to warrant such disagreeable attention?"

Bysshe swallowed. "It—it wasn't meant to hurt her, sir. She goes into the study at the same time every day to refill Dr. Bethel's sherry, and I meant to observe from the top of the staircase. Unfortunately, one of my other experiments caught fire, and I couldn't leave my room. I—I didn't know the current would be so strong. I just wanted to see if it was true that her hair would stand on end. It—it was another experiment."

Rowan eyed him. "What if I were to wonder right now if *your* delightful curls would stand on end in similar circumstances?"

"Mine, sir?"

"Yes. Pray take hold of the doorknob."

Bysshe's eyes widened. "Oh, but—"

"Come now, sir, where is your backbone? If it is of scientific value when a mere maid touches it, just think how much more weighty and respected the results would be if *you* were the subject." Rowan folded his arms. "I'm waiting, Master Shelley."

The drake eyed the boy, and quacked with relish, but Bysshe swallowed cravenly. "I—I'd rather not, if you don't mind, sir."

The ghost of a smile played upon Rowan's lips. "The scientific benefits cease to appeal when yours are the dainty fingers that will suffer, eh, sir?"

Bysshe hung his head, and Rowan looked at Perry. "Were you party to this?" Guilt was written large upon the face of Marigold's son as he too hung his head. Rowan drew a long breath. "I think you should both again apologize most humbly to Dr. Bethel, then go to your room to clear up the undoubted mess therein. After that you will do penance to Bessie. Whether or not you are permitted to stay on here, or indeed whether or not you have to face Dr. Keate's wrath, remains to be seen."

"Yes, sir," they replied together, and then turned to face poor Dr. Bethel, who was still covered with rose petals. Their expressions of regret were very ashamed indeed, and when they ascended the staircase once more, their heads were bowed in remorse. The drake could still be heard long after they had disappeared from view.

Rowan looked at the unfortunate master. "Sir, is there anything I can say or do which will induce you to be lenient?"

"I doubt it, sir, I doubt it very much," came the heartfelt reply.

Rowan glanced at the door again. "On arriving, I noticed that the window to this room had been left slightly open. With your leave, I will enter by that means, and dismantle the apparatus on the door."

"I would be grateful, Lord Avenbury."

Rowan turned, and went outside. A minute or so later, the copper wire was pulled from the other side, then the door opened, and Dr. Bethel and Marigold went inside. It was a jumbled room, its walls lined with bookshelves, and there was a huge desk topped with green leather standing in the center. Various armchairs were in evidence, as was a rather battered harpsichord, with piles of music sheets and well-worn keys that bore witness to its frequent use. Bysshe's voltaic battery, which consisted of the copper wire, and a small stack of alternating plates of copper, zinc, and moistened pasteboard, had been carefully dismantled, and replaced in a wooden box, then covered with a crumpled sheet of brown paper.

Rowan assisted Marigold to a chair, and whispered suddenly to her. "I think I may be able to extricate our two demonic young scientists from this. Would you like me to try?"

"If you think you can help, I would be most grateful," she replied, for she felt quite out of place in these peculiarly male circumstances.

Rowan turned to usher the still-shaken doctor to another chair. After pressing a glass of good sherry into the master's hand, he went to the harpsichord and played a finger upon several keys. "Tell me, doctor, what would you say to owning an instrument that was once owned by Handel himself?"

The doctor lowered his glass, and turned to look at him. "By Handel, you say?"

"Yes. It's a particularly elegant harpsichord, and has been maintained in the finest order. No one uses it now, which is a great shame, but I am certain you would fully appreciate its qualities."

Dr. Bethel surveyed him shrewdly. "And in return for this fine instrument . . . ?"

"You could overlook today's regrettable occurrences."

The doctor smiled. "I'm sorely tempted, sir, just as you knew I would be, but may I be so bold as to inquire why you wish to do this? As far as I am aware, you are not connected with either boy."

"I have the honor to be Perry's future stepfather," Rowan replied.

The doctor's jaw dropped. "Indeed?" He looked quickly at Marigold, belatedly recalling her all-too recent widowhood.

"Do we have an agreement, sir?" Rowan pressed skillfully.

The carrot was taken. "We do indeed, sir."

"Excellent."

A little later, Marigold walked alone with Perry in the doctor's garden. Sunlight was dappled through the leaves of a weeping willow overhanging the small stream that formed the garden's boundary, and at last Marigold reluctantly came to the point of her visit. The coming few minutes wouldn't be at all easy, especially as she feared her news concerning Rowan might stir a dormant sense of honor in her son toward his hitherto intensely disliked sire. She sat down on the grassy bank, where daisies were scattered like tiny white stars. "Perry, there is something I must tell you."

He smothered a huge yawn, then said quickly. "Forgive me, Mama, I didn't mean to be rude."

"What's wrong? Aren't you sleeping well?"

"I sleep excellently. I really don't know what's the matter with me today. Bysshe feels the same. We're peculiarly tired. I hope it's the chicken pox." He leaned back against the willow.

"You *hope* it's the chicken pox?"

"Yes, because we'll be sent home to recuperate. Everyone else who's gone down with it has begun by feeling tired."

"You and Bysshe do not seem too tired to indulge in all manner of disagreeable experiments," she pointed out, aware that she was diverging from the point of her visit.

He looked down at her a little guiltily. "We didn't mean any harm."

"Nevertheless, harm is what you caused."

"I know."

"Where is the unfortunate duck now?"

"Sir Francis?"

"Sir Francis?" Marigold looked blankly at him.

Perry tutted. "Oh, come on, Mama! Sir Francis Drake!"

She had to smile. "How very slow of me."

"Indeed. Anyway, we think it's a good name. He seemed to think so too, because when we told him that's what he was going to be called, he got quite excited, and kept nodding his head up and down. Anyway, he's gone. Bysshe took him down to the Thames. He was going to put him on the stream here, but then decided— Oh, no!" Perry straightened and ran out of the shade of the willow to look skyward in dismay as a distant quack carried on the air.

"What is it?"

He pointed as a mallard drake flew down to the stream. "It's Sir Francis, I'd know that quack anywhere!"

As they watched, the drake swam to the bank, and after clambering ashore to shake its tail and have a short preen, it waddled up through the daisies toward them. To Marigold's astonishment, it then settled down beside her, quacked once or twice in an amiable tone, rattled its bill a little, then buried its gleaming dark green head under its wing, and went to sleep.

Perry came over and gave a huge sigh as he looked down at the bird. "What am I going to do? Dr. Bethel will think we didn't get rid of it!"

"There's nothing you can do, short of shooing it away, and that seems a little unkind." Marigold put out a tentative hand, and touched the drake's glossy feathers. Sir Francis raised his head, gave her a cross look, then muttered as he pushed his bill under his wing again. She drew her hand back, and then looked up at Perry again. "You really must behave, Perry. Lord Avenbury has extricated both of you this time, but I pray you will not give further cause for concern."

"We won't, truly." Perry gave her a quick smile, then changed the subject. "Anyway, you said you have something to tell me. Does it concern Lord Avenbury?"

"Well, yes."

"I knew something was up the moment you called him by his first name," he replied knowingly.

"Before I get to that, I think you should know what happened at the reading of your father's will. Sit down too," she urged, removing her gloves and then patting the grass beside her.

Perry obeyed, and then looked in astonishment at her left hand as he noticed her new ring. "Mama, are you and Lord Avenbury . . . ?"

"To be married? Yes, Perry, we are, but please don't leap to conclusions, for once you hear about the will, I'm sure you will understand. At least, I hope you will. Will you hear me out?"

He put his hand quickly on her arm. "Mama, you know how much I love you, and how much I despised my father and all the Arnolds for the way they treated you. Of course I will hear you out, but there is just one thing."

"Yes?"

"Isn't Lord Avenbury connected with . . . ? I mean, aren't he and Aunt Alauda . . . ?" He colored and fell silent.

Marigold felt herself go a little pink too. "Well, yes, I believe they are, but that has nothing to do with this."

"Aunt Alauda won't see it that way," Perry replied shrewdly.

"No, she probably won't, but that is Lord Avenbury's concern, not mine, or yours."

"She's a true Arnold, and therefore not someone to cross. I'm an Arnold too, but not through and through like the rest of them."

"I should hope not, for you are my son too," Marigold replied with a smile.

He grinned. "Anyway, tell me everything, Mama."

Taking a deep breath, she related all that had happened that dreadful day at Castell Arnold. Perry's eyes at first widened, and then grew steadily more stormy. "I—I am declared illegitimate?" he interrupted, shock widening his eyes and draining his face of color.

Her hand still rested over his, and she squeezed his fingers in an attempt to reassure. "Yes, I fear that for the moment you are, just as I am branded a fallen woman, but your Uncle Falk admitted to me in private that the will Mr. Crowe read out was not genuine. Lord Avenbury is to instruct his own lawyer to make every possible investigation. If it is possible to prove their villainy, it will be done, I promise you that. In the meantime, my marriage to Lord Avenbury will offer us both protection. You do understand what I'm saying, don't you?"

"Yes, I—I believe so."

She went on, but when he learned how she had been forcibly ejected from Castell Arnold, it was too much. He leapt angrily to his feet. "Uncle Falk did *that* to you? I will call him out! I will make him pay for treating you so foully!" he cried, his hands clenched into furious fists. He startled Sir Francis, who awoke with a surprised quack.

Marigold put a soothing hand up to her son. She could see how he trembled with emotion, and her heart surged with pride and love. How fine a son he was to want to defend her. "It's all right, Perry. *Please* sit down again, so I can tell you how things have arrived at their present situation. Oh, be quiet, you foolish duck!" she added as Sir Francis continued to register protests at being awoken. The mallard clacked its bill, but subsided once more into the daisies, and after a moment tucked his head under his wing again. Then Perry resumed his place beside her as well, and she went on with her extraordinary tale. At last she finished. "There, now you know why I am about to become Lady Avenbury," she said.

Perry plucked at the daisies. "But you don't really know why *he* is entering into it?"

"No."

"Isn't that a little risky? I mean, you hadn't even met him before last night, and it seems to me he should be on Falk's side, not ours."

"I wondered that, but I trust him completely." She did, although when she had stepped over that particular threshold, she really didn't know.

"Do you love him?" Perry asked.

She was aware of hesitating before answering. "No, of course not. How can I possibly love him in so short a time?"

"So you're only doing it because of me?" Resolve suddenly blazed in his eyes. "I cannot let that happen! I will leave Eton and provide for us both!"

She smiled. "Oh, Perry, how fierce you are, but there is no need, for I really *want* to marry Lord Avenbury." The words slipped out so naturally that she hardly realized she'd said them. But it was the truth, she *did* want to marry Rowan. Heaven help her, she wanted it very much indeed.

Perry was confused. "In spite of Aunt Alauda?"

"Yes."

"Bysshe says—"

"Perry, I don't place great faith in Bysshe. With your dubious assistance, he attempts to raise devils," she said, interrupting quickly in case he was about to mention the Avenbury curse, which she didn't wish to discuss until she'd had a chance to speak to Rowan.

Perry flushed. "It wasn't a devil, it was Taranis," he corrected.

"Who or what is Taranis?"

"The old Celtic god of thunder. Bysshe read about him in that Stukeley book he mentioned."

"Who *is* this Stukeley person? I've never heard of him."

"He was a famous historian. He—and Aubrey before him—researched and mapped in detail all the standing stones in the Salisbury Plain area, including the ones at Avenbury. They called them British druidic temples. Did you know there were standing stones at Avenbury?"

"No, but go on. Why did you want to raise Taranis?"

Perry colored a little. "Because there's a cricket match this evening, and neither of us wants to play. We thought a good thunderstorm would do the trick. Anyway, it doesn't really matter now, because all we managed to conjure was Sir Francis."

"I hardly think you *conjured* anything," she replied firmly.

"I swear it, Mama. We were telling the truth to Dr. Bethel when we said Sir Francis just appeared from nowhere. We didn't bring him into the house ourselves, truly we didn't. We made the demonic circle, lit the blue flames, and said the correct incantations, but all we got was this stupid mallard!" The boy looked daggers at the slumbering drake.

"Oh, that can't be possible! If you didn't take him into the house, then he must have flown in through the window," she declared.

"If he did, he was very quiet about it. Ducks make a noise when they fly, but one second there was nothing, the next he was on the floor right in the middle of the circle. And he wasn't in a very good mood, I can tell you. He certainly made a noise after that, quacking at the top of his odious lungs. We were so shocked that we forgot Bysshe's other experiment, which suddenly burst into flames. Dr. Bethel came to see what was going on, and the rest you know." Perry plucked at the daisies again. "I won't be raising Celtic gods again, and that's a fact."

Marigold was hard put to hide her mirth, for it was clear he and Bysshe really believed they'd had raised a demon duck!

Perry cleared his throat uncomfortably. "Anyway, I'd prefer it if you forgot I told you, Mama. Do you promise?"

"I, er, yes, I suppose so."

He gave her a quick smile. "Bysshe isn't mad, you know, he's very clever."

"He's a menace," she replied.

"I'm just as bad, so you mustn't blame him. Actually, he's great fun to be with, and I like him very much." He looked at her. "He does have Stukeley's book. It's called *An Account of the Avenbury Curse.* Mama, you do know about the curse, don't you? Only, when Bysshe blurted it out, I thought it came as a complete shock to you."

"Perry, I'd rather not discuss—"

He interrupted, looking intently at her. "Bysshe says it's true, Mama."

"The writing of a book on a subject doesn't make it true. You know what I think of superstition, Perry."

"Yes, you dismiss it as nonsense. But I believe in magic and the supernatural."

"Oh, Perry."

"And so does Bysshe. He's *always* reading books about that sort of thing. He says that every Lord Avenbury is destined to die young because in 1534 the first lord deliberately broke up a sacred druidic rite at the stone circle that encloses the village of Avenbury. It's the largest circle in the whole of England," Perry added.

Marigold had to look away, for she could hear Rowan by the Druid Oak. *My name is Rowan, and I am the thirteenth Lord Avenbury . . . The only other things you need to know about me are that I am wealthy, and completely at liberty to offer marriage. Oh, and that I would regard it as an honor to protect you and your son.*

Perry spoke again. "It's all in Stukeley, Mama. If you ask Lord Avenbury, he'll have to admit it."

Footsteps sounded on the grass, and Bessie hurried up. "Begging your pardon, madam, Master Perry, but Lord Avenbury says it's time to leave." Perry got up quickly, and assisted his mother to her feet. Sir Francis stirred as well, shook his feathers, then waddled after Perry, who ran toward the house.

Marigold paused beneath the willow to smooth her skirts. There was a flutter of little wings overhead, and Marigold was so attuned to the sound that she knew it would be the robin. He hopped along a branch and then cocked his head to look down at her. She saw immediately that he wasn't alone, for a tiny brown wren was at his side. They perched together, so like sweethearts that Marigold almost expected the robin to put his wing around his diminutive companion. Robin Redbreast and Jenny Wren, she thought, for in times gone by the two birds had always been spoken of as a pair.

The wren sang a few sad, sweet notes, then both birds flew off again. Marigold's eyes filled with tears as she watched them disappear, for there had been something desperately sorrowful about the brief little song.

Chapter Nine

Two days later Marigold and Rowan were married by special license at the Grosvenor Chapel in Mayfair. The midday sun was shining brightly as Rowan greeted the fine town carriage conveying his bride and her son. He wore the bridegroom's traditional brass-buttoned royal blue coat, and white waistcoat and breeches, and was accompanied by two strangers, a country gentleman and his lady who happened to be passing by, and who had gladly agreed to be witnesses.

As her bridegroom kissed her on the cheek, Marigold was immediately conscious of a change in him, and for a dismayed moment she wondered if he was about to cancel everything. It was a fear that had lurked at the back of her mind ever since the visit to Eton, and was entirely due to the so-called Avenbury curse, about which she had tried on several occasions to speak to him. But he had resolutely—even angrily—refused to discuss it. The atmosphere between them had become tense because she found it as hard to leave the matter alone as he did to speak of it. Now as he handed her toward the chapel steps, she was afraid her persistence had proved too much.

She paused in the doorway, nervously arranging her skirt and then toying with her posy of marigolds. Marigolds were said to be for marriage, but right now she felt they must be the opposite! She almost turned back to the carriage before he could shun her at the altar, but then common sense took over, and she relaxed a little. He was dressed as a bridegroom, he had secured two witnesses, and he had greeted her with a kiss; none of which he was likely to have done if he no longer intended to marry her. Nor would he have settled Perry's fees, acquired a fine suite of rooms for her at the luxurious Pulteney Hotel in Piccadilly, arranged for their departure for Avenbury Park in the morning, or sent a fashionable couturier to show her a dazzling new wardrobe of the most stylish clothes imaginable.

The Pulteney was acknowledged as the finest hotel in London, and the couturier, who was the most sought-after, had supplied the prospective Lady Avenbury with a number of clothes that had been cancelled at the last minute by a notoriously fickle duchess who happened to be Marigold's size. The gown chosen for the wedding was part of this elegant wardrobe. It was made of pearl-stitched cream silk, and showed off her red-gold hair and the marigolds in her posy.

Thus the most startling wedding of the Season proceeded without society realizing. The names of the bride and groom meant nothing to the witnesses, the couturier was prized for her discretion, the clergyman had not broadcast the ceremony, and no one at the Pulteney knew of their lady guest's intimate connection with Lord Avenbury. Perry discharged his duty proudly, in spite of looking decidedly under the weather due to what did indeed seem like the onset of chicken pox. He escorted his mother down the aisle, and then solemnly gave her hand to her new husband. There was only one brief interruption, and that was caused by another appearance by the robin.

Without Jenny Wren, he flew in through the open door and perched on the polished brass eagle lectern, where he began to sing his heart out. Marigold turned with a smile, for she had come to regard the little bird almost as a friend. As she wondered again why he seemed to follow wherever she went, the clergyman saw him too, and exclaimed in horror. Robins were bad luck indoors, he cried, and temporarily abandoned the ceremony in order to rid his chapel of such a harbinger of doom. Vestments billowing, he tried to shoo the bird toward the chapel door, and it was such a comical sight that Perry choked with laughter, Marigold wanted to giggle, and even the witnesses found it something to smile at, but Rowan frowned and turned toward the altar again. Marigold's mirth was extinguished, and her insecurity swept back. What was wrong? Why had he changed so much? She felt as if he were pushing her away instead of drawing her closer.

Suddenly the robin decided to fly away of its own accord, and the flustered clergyman returned to the altar. Marigold remembered little of the remainder of the service, except the moment Rowan slipped the wedding band on her finger, and they were pronounced man and wife. This time Rowan did not seal the moment with a kiss, but turned to politely thank the witnesses. As the small wedding party emerged into the sunlight again, Marigold felt more like crying than smiling.

Rowan made an effort to be amiable for the fine French meal he, Marigold, and Perry enjoyed afterward at the Pulteney. Perry chattered happily during the drive back to Eton, telling his mother and new stepfather about the elaborate system he and Bysshe had devised for keeping Sir Francis out of Dr. Bethel's path. The mallard, it seemed, was sticking to the boys like a shadow, and no matter how many times they took him to the river, he always came back. Now they'd given up, and were resigned to his presence.

After leaving Perry at Eton, the return journey to Rowan's town residence in Berkeley Square was conducted in virtual silence. Marigold became more and more ill at ease, and by the time the carriage drew up at the house, she was again close to tears. Had she made a monumental error of judgment by marrying this unpredictable man? Tomorrow they were to leave London for Avenbury Park in Wiltshire, where they would be alone except for the servants. Could she endure it? They went inside, and her hand trembled as she placed her posy upon the table in the echoing green marble entrance hall. She glanced around. Lofty columns rose into the shadows of the upper stories, an imposing double staircase dominated one side, and unsmiling statues gazed from all directions. It was far from welcoming.

Rowan tossed his upturned top hat beside her posy, together with his gloves. "It would seem the deed is done, Marigold," he murmured, toying with the frill at his cuff as if his thoughts were elsewhere.

She had to say *something*. She steeled herself, and then faced him. "Thus far ours is a marriage in name only, so if you have regrets, sir, there is still time to undo it."

"I do not wish to undo anything. Except perhaps . . ." He broke off.

"Except perhaps what?" she asked.

He looked at her. "Nothing you need be concerned about. Tomorrow we leave for Avenbury Park, but this evening you and I are attending Vauxhall Gardens."

She was unprepared. "Oh, I—I'd rather not . . ." she began, for she had imagined they would spend the evening quietly and then set off early for Wiltshire.

He took no notice of her protest. "I have reserved a box at the gardens. We will dine, enjoy the concert, and then observe the fire-works display afterward.

"Lady Fernborough will be there," she said quietly, knowing that Alauda would have returned from Castell Arnold by now, and that when in town she seldom missed the concerts at the famous gardens. Knowing also that it was at Vauxhall that Alauda's liaison with him had begun.

"Most of the *ton* will be there, Marigold," he pointed out, glancing at the butler, who waited at a discreet distance.

"Does she know about us?" It was an unwritten rule that a wife should never mention her husband's mistress, especially in the presence of a servant, but Marigold couldn't help herself.

There was a disapproving pause before he replied. "No."

"But, surely—" Marigold blundered on.

"My marital arrangements are no concern of hers," he interrupted tersely, and waved the butler away.

"No concern of your *mistress*?" Marigold's discretion vanished over the horizon.

"Nor are my private arrangements any concern of yours, madam," he added very coolly.

Her knuckles had been rapped, and she knew it. Resentment and humiliation flushed into her cheeks as she fell into a mutinous silence. He'd just made her his wife, so how *dared* he say his private arrangements were none of her concern!

He realized he'd been a little heavy-handed, and extended an olive branch. "Forgive me, Marigold, I did not mean to be so harsh."

Oh, yes, you did, she thought, but managed to find a smile of sorts. "You will have to forgive me as well, sir, for the lady in question has always appointed herself grand bane of my life. When I left Wales, I hoped I'd left all things Arnold, now it seems I must still endure her."

"A fact that was known to you from the outset of our acquaintance," he observed reasonably.

"Knowing and accepting are sometimes poles apart."

"You need have no fear that she will encroach."

"I sincerely hope not, sir."

"If she is at Vauxhall tonight, do I have your word that any encounter will be conducted with dignity?"

"*My* behavior has never been questionable, sir, but hers certainly has."

The ghost of a smile touched his lips. "This, er, contretemps, has only arisen because we are going to Vauxhall tonight. The whole purpose of the excursion is to acquaint London with our nuptials, so that our scandalous bones can be chewed during our absence in Wiltshire. Now then, the subject of a certain lady is banned from now on, are we agreed?"

She met his gaze. "Rowan, where you are concerned, there are too many banned subjects."

He immediately drew away. "All in good time, Marigold."

"But you can't possibly *believe* in such things as curses! This is 1806, not the Dark Ages!"

"And you, I suppose, are the personification of enlightened womanhood?"

"Well, this is supposedly an enlightened age!" she retorted. "You're being very unfair, Rowan. I'm your wife now."

"I know I'm being unfair, damn it!" He ran his fingers through his hair, and then took her hand. "I didn't expect to find it so difficult to tell you, Marigold, and if I'm treating you shabbily as a consequence, I apologize. The curse isn't something my family has ever cared to broadcast, and if it weren't for that damned Stukely volume, Bysshe wouldn't know, and neither would you."

"But I have a right to know."

"Maybe so, just as I have a right to feel reluctant to talk of something that has dogged my family ever since the sixteenth century."

She could not deny the reasonableness of this. "I—I'm sorry I've harped on so. Please forgive me."

"There is nothing for me to forgive, Marigold, on the contrary, the forgiveness must come from you to me. Were the situation reversed right now, I have no doubt that I would be far less tolerant and understanding than you. I'm not shutting you out deliberately, I'm merely trying to find the right moment. And the right words," he added, before drawing her palm to his lips.

His lips were soft and warm against her skin, and she suppressed a delicious shiver of pleasure. "There is no curse, Rowan, and I will prove it," she whispered.

"And how do you imagine you will do that?"

"I don't know, but somehow I will."

Chapter Ten

There was no bridge across the Thames near Vauxhall Gardens, which lay on the south bank, so most people arrived by water. Darkness had almost fallen, and thousands of little colored lamps twinkled among the ornamental trees. There were twelve acres of avenues, cascades, pavilions, obelisks, triumphal arches, and grottoes, all laid out in the formal splendor of the middle of the previous century. Some of the avenues and grottoes were less well lit, and as a consequence were much resorted to for flirtation, assignation, and intrigue. Music drifted on the sweet summer air, and a fashionable crowd had already arrived as the boatman Rowan had hired maneuvered his craft through the crush at the stairs, and made it fast.

Marigold wore a simple décolleté silk gown that was muted orange-gold in color, and her new maid had pinned her hair into an intricate style. As she prepared to let Rowan help her ashore, she knew she looked as well as possible. If only she felt as good on the inside, but she didn't. Her stomach was knotted, and she was almost sick with nerves as Rowan stepped ashore. The diversions at Vauxhall Gardens were breathtaking, and under any other circumstances she would have enjoyed them all, but she knew the *beau monde* was about to be startled in no small way by the new Lady Avenbury. That was bad enough as far as she was concerned, but worse by far was the possibility of encountering Alauda.

She glanced at Rowan. Oh, how easy it was to see what drew Alauda to him. Like most of the other gentlemen, he wore the formal attire that was *de rigueur* at Vauxhall, a black brocade coat, lace-trimmed shirt, white silk waistcoat and breeches, and a tricorn hat, but he stood out. With his tall elegance, and darkly handsome looks, he more than warranted his reputation as one of England's most fascinating and attractive men. But was he also the final victim of an ancient druidic curse, and doomed to die young, no matter what?

He held a hand out to his bride, and before she knew it, he'd pulled her close to put his lips to hers. It was a very public kiss, with people brushing past them on the crowded steps, but she felt as if they were alone. Wanton feelings began to race through her again, desires that longed to be satisfied. Tonight she knew he would come to her, and oh, the pleasure she would know when she surrendered to him. Let the intervening hours pass quickly, but let the night go slowly. Oh, so slowly . . . He released her, severing the train of thought as a druid's golden sickle severed mistletoe. "Come, Lady Avenbury, let us face the world," he said softly.

Marigold's introduction to the *ton* of London was postponed just a little because she and Rowan chose to perambulate the gardens before joining the main throng of fashionable guests in the Grand Walk. From then on, however, the new bride was the center of attention, and found it a most disagreeable experience. Rowan presented her as the former Mrs. Arnold, and at first, since Arnold wasn't a name exclusive to Falk's family, no one made the connection. However, the usual pleasantries soon elicited the necessary information, and after a while she was aware that her identity was known more and more to those to whom she was introduced. This was because whispers were in circulation behind her back. It seemed that some of London's most fashionable salons were already acquainted with the titillating story of Merlin's will. The Arnold version of events naturally made certain that she figured to great disadvantage, in fact as little more than a kept woman with a child born the wrong side of the blanket. She endured the stir as best she could, thinking how very unfair it all was, for she had been married to Merlin, and Perry wasn't illegitimate. Glancing around at the whispering lips, raised fans, and scrutinizing eyeglasses, she could not help wondering if Rowan had really considered the many disadvantages of marrying someone who had nothing to offer except an undeserved but shocking reputation.

She was relieved when the time came to retreat to the row of supper boxes, which stood across the Grand Walk, directly opposite the orchestra pavilion. From here the concert could be enjoyed while sampling chicken salad, followed by Madeira cake, both courses enjoyed with champagne. Champagne was Marigold's favorite drink, but it was inclined to go a little to her head, so tonight she was particularly resolved not to drink more than two glasses. It was a resolution that was not to be adhered to for long.

The June evening was warm and balmy, a tenor and soprano were singing duets, and the supper was excellent. Rowan seemed oblivious to the effect his bride had upon everyone. He made her smile by recounting amusing stories, one of which made her laugh outright, since it concerned a plump but odious fellow she had detected in the act of relating her supposed past to a group of companions. The story revolved around the ice that had been used to chill the champagne they were drinking. Such a precious item was not easily acquired, and the management of the gardens had procured it the previous month from a vessel from Iceland that happened also to be patronized by Messrs Gunter, the famous confectioners of Berkeley Square. It seemed that the Gunters considered the entire cargo to be theirs, and from all accounts there had been a most unseemly quayside fracas. Insults had been hurled, tempers had flared, and the representative from Gunter's—to wit, said plump and disagreeable tittle-tattler—had been deposited ignominiously in the Thames.

Laughing made Marigold feel infinitely better, and Rowan smiled at her. "There, their clacking tongues do not seem so bad now, do they?"

"Not quite."

"You will be a nine days' wonder."

"They clearly think you have been duped by a designing trollop."

"Trollop? Good heavens, is that what you are?"

"Don't tease me, for we both know what's being said."

"And we both know it will have to be *unsaid* when my lawyers unearth the truth. Pay society no heed tonight, Marigold, for tomorrow we will be at Avenbury Park in the depths of Wiltshire, far away from spiteful, inconsequential tongues."

She was curious about his country seat. "Tell me about Avenbury Park."

"What do you wish to know?" he replied.

"Well, how old is it? Is the park large? What is the surrounding countryside like? Anything really."

"Parts of the house date back to the twelfth century, but it was mostly rebuilt and enlarged during the reign of Henry VIII. The park is considerable, and boasts a natural lake, which is a rare thing in an area of chalk downs. The gardens are formal, in the Tudor style, and part of the henge runs through it—by henge, I mean the great circle of prehistoric standing stones and surrounding water-filled moat for which Avenbury is famous."

"Percy told me the village is built actually inside the henge. Is that true?"

"What a tiresome mine of information is Master Percy Bysshe Shelley. Yes, it's true. The village and the house are within the stones, but not at the center. That position is occupied by a small area of common land and a particularly ancient oak tree."

"Who put the stones there? The druids?"

He exhaled slowly. "Rustics no doubt attribute them to giants or the arch-fiend, but the truth is that no one knows. In my opinion the Avenbury circle, Stonehenge, and so on, *predate* the worshippers of mistletoe. I do not doubt that the druids used them, indeed I know they did, but they did not create them. And please don't take this conversation as a signal to bring up the subject of the curse yet again."

"I promised not to, just as you have promised to tell me when you're ready."

"And I will stand by that."

He poured her a third glass of champagne, which she wouldn't have touched were it not that at that moment she at last saw Alauda. Rowan's loathed mistress was with her husband, and they had encountered Sir Reginald Crane and his wife. Sir Reginald's clothes were quite subdued for once, because he would not have been allowed in unless he conformed. His nose, however, was far from subdued, being rather red and swollen from its ordeal with the snuffers. Lady Crane, a flat-chested woman with a pronounced lisp, wore a mauve silk gown that clung unbecomingly to her bony figure. Beside a beauty like Alauda, she was at a decided disadvantage. Marigold's archenemy was glorious in a bright yellow muslin that was so fine it afforded tantalizing glimpses of her magnificent body. Her raven hair shone with diamonds, her fan wafted elegantly to and fro, and her tinkling laughter carried clearly. The elderly Earl of Fernborough was a short man, slender and dapper in formal black. He was a notoriously ruthless devotee of gaming hells, and had ruined many a less fortunate man. His amours now exceeded those of his wife, although at the outset of the marriage he had been faithful.

As Marigold watched, Lady Crane suddenly pointed toward the supper box, and said something. By the way Alauda's smile vanished, Marigold knew she had just learned of the new Lady Avenbury. After tossing a thunderstruck glance toward the supper box, Alauda made some excuse to her husband, then hurried away toward the long, less well-lit avenue known as the Dark Walk. There she paused, looking long and hard at Rowan before disappearing into the enticing shadows.

Like Marigold, Rowan had become aware of his mistress's presence, although he pretended he had not. Marigold willed him not to go after Alauda, but she was disappointed. He tossed his napkin onto the table, and then rose. "If you will excuse me for a moment, I have something to attend to."

Marigold couldn't look up at him. "By all means," she said quietly.

If he noticed anything amiss in her response, he gave no sign of it as he left the box. Marigold remained motionless as he followed Alauda into the Dark Walk. She was hurt by the swiftness with which he'd responded to his mistress's silent command. Maybe it was the champagne that caused the bewildering succession of emotions that now rushed through her, from resentful anger to keen pain. She knew she was being foolish, because as he'd already pointed out, she'd known all along about his liaison with Alauda.

Gradually a fiercely determined light entered in her green eyes. The new Lady Avenbury would not—*could* not—let an assignation take place right under her nose without at least taking some token action. This was *her* marriage, Rowan was *her* husband, and his private arrangements *were* her concern! To perdition with Alauda!

Trembling, Marigold drank her champagne, folded her napkin, and placed it on the table next to his. Then she got up and hastened after them.

Chapter Eleven

There weren't many people in the Dark Walk, and the noise of the main crowds soon faded behind as Marigold hurried into the shadows. Trees whispered overhead, and the night was brightened by the soft but inviting glow of little lanterns. There were high-hedged paths leading off on either side, and leafy alcoves overhung with roses. Whispers and giggles could be heard in the darkness, but Marigold paid them no heed, for she knew Rowan and Alauda would be much further from public view. When she and Rowan had taken a general stroll on first arriving, her attention had been drawn to a subterranean grotto by a fountain. Something in the way he'd glanced at the entrance of the grotto told her that this was the one at which he and Alauda had begun their liaison. If the guess proved wrong, she'd search all over until she found them.

There were fewer and fewer people around as the gentle murmur of water sounded ahead, then the path led into a circular paved area surrounded by tall shrubs. In the center of this area stood a statue of Neptune, where water danced in the light from pink and green lanterns, and directly opposite, lit by more lanterns, were the shell-studded steps leading down to the grotto. She paused. Apart from the sound of the water, everything was quiet, then she thought she heard Alauda's voice coming from below.

For a moment discretion almost had the better part of valor, but champagne warmed her veins unwisely. Feeling the way she did about Rowan, and loathing Alauda as she also did, it was clear that sooner or later there had to be a confrontation between wife and mistress. Better to get that particular unpleasantness over with as quickly as possible. She walked resolutely toward the entrance, but as she reached the steps, what she heard brought her to a dismayed halt.

Alauda's voice had become more clear, echoing strangely. "You've broken your word to me, Rowan."

"What word?"

"About this midsummer. You swore that when Fernborough visits his brother in Ireland, I could come to stay with you at Avenbury."

"Alauda, you asked if you could come to Avenbury at that time, but I didn't agree."

"Nor did you say no! Rowan, I *must* be with you then!" cried Alauda.

"Why such urgency?"

"I—I just want to be with you."

"Well it's out of the question now, is it not?"

"Because of *her*!" replied Alauda with a considerable amount of venom. "Oh, Rowan, in that creature you've made a *mésalliance par excellence*. Due to the bride, the name Avenbury is a laughingstock here tonight."

"Alauda, if anything is being said of my bride, it is because of your family's vindictive tittle-tattling."

"No, Rowan, it is because of *her* lack of character. Why have you done it? She isn't a beauty, and she has a thirteen-year-old son."

"Maybe I love her, or had that not occurred to you?"

"Do you?" When he didn't reply, Alauda went on. "Please tell me this whole thing is a jest."

"Marriage is never a jest," he replied.

"Except when it is never a marriage at all. Is that it? Has she been gullible enough to make a *second* false marriage?"

"I've already told you I don't regard marriage as a jest, so I really don't know why you should think I would fake such a thing."

"Will you at least deign to tell me how you met her? I imagine she sought you out in order to relate my supposed sins?"

"As you relate hers? As it happens, we met by accident at the Spread Eagle in Windsor."

There was a startled silence, then, "The Spread Eagle?"

"Yes." He laughed. "Where the wheel turns."

"What do you know of that?" Alauda asked quickly.

"What do *you* know of it?" he countered with sudden new interest.

Alauda drew back swiftly. "Nothing."

"I don't believe you. What is the wheel, Alauda?" he demanded more forcefully.

"I've already said that I don't know anything about it. I—I've just heard Falk and his friends speak of it now and then. I presumed it was some society or other."

The explanation was so patently fabricated that Marigold knew Alauda was lying. She was sure Rowan must have known too, but he didn't press the matter any further. Alauda quickly returned to the matter of his marriage. "So you think dear Marigold met you by accident, do you? Oh, Rowan, it's clear you don't know her yet. She's a designing strumpet, and knew you might be there that night, because I confided in her that you had an appointment at Windsor. I know how those things drag on, and that when that happens, you use the Spread Eagle."

Marigold's eyes widened incredulously. Confided? Alauda would rather swallow hot coals than confide anything in her!

Rowan thought much the same. "Alauda, you have just spent the last quarter of an hour telling me what you think of Marigold, so I cannot imagine you wishing to *confide* in her."

"I did!" Alauda protested. "Rowan, I felt sorry for her because neither Merlin nor Falk treated her well."

Marigold's fury simmered. Felt sorry for her? Alauda was the worst of them all!

"But you *did* treat her well?" Rowan inquired lightly.

"Of course, although to be sure she wasn't in the least grateful. She is a viper, Rowan, as you will soon discover to your cost."

Marigold leaned back against the wall of the entrance, so angry she could have rushed down into the grotto and slapped Alauda for her lies.

Alauda went on. "Is Marigold my match between the sheets?"

"You don't really think I'd tell you anything like that, do you?"

"If she is my match, and if you do indeed love her, you wouldn't be here with me now." Alauda gave a low laugh. "Besides, I already know the answer to my question. Merlin told me she was cold and unimaginative, the equivalent of bedding a codfish."

Rowan called a halt. "Enough, Alauda. I've humored you sufficiently regarding my wife."

"But—"

"No, Alauda."

Alauda's voice swiftly took on a seductive tone. "Do you still desire me, Rowan?"

"What man could fail to desire you?"

"Then make love to me now," Alauda breathed.

All went silent, and Marigold knew they were kissing. At first she was fixed with dismay, but it was soon swept aside by renewed anger. Were they going to make love, safe in the belief that his foolish bride was waiting meekly in the supper box? Suddenly the robin fluttered out of the shadows and perched on the step beside her. He puffed out his chest, and his eyes shone in the lanternlight as he looked up intently at her. He gave a single chirrup, and once again she knew he was urging her to do something. But what? It wouldn't do for Rowan to find out that his bride had followed him, so how could she bring the clandestine meeting to an end without revealing her presence? Like the robin, inspiration winged from nowhere. Lady Crane's distinctive lisping voice would be easy enough to imitate in the echoing surroundings of the grotto. Without a second thought, Marigold cupped her hands around her mouth.

"Alauda? Alauda, you'd betht know the earl is therching for you. Oh, I think I hear him calling! For heaven'th thake beware!" Then she ran behind the fountain to hide.

After a moment Alauda emerged, pausing at the entrance to glance around, then gathering her yellow skirts to hurry away toward the Dark Walk. It was only when Rowan followed a moment later, that Marigold realized her mistake, for how on earth was she going to reach the supper box before him? Her triumph sank into dismay. Why hadn't she thought more carefully? That last glass of champagne had a great deal to answer for! Alauda was bound to discover that Lady Crane had not called out the warning, and if Rowan's bride wasn't in the supper box when he returned, he was certain to put two and two together.

Trying desperately to think up a plausible excuse for leaving the box, she followed in the others' footsteps. There was no sign of either Rowan or Alauda as she reached the Dark Walk, and the scattered pools of light and shade made it hard to tell anything. Gathering her skirts, she began to run toward the Grand Walk, but then, just as the first fireworks dazzled the night sky, Rowan's voice arrested her.

"And where, pray, have you been, madam?"

She whirled guiltily about as he emerged from an arbor she had just passed.

Chapter Twelve

Marigold's sense of having been caught in the act was so keen that she didn't know what to say. Rowan came a little closer, his hazel eyes raking her face in the light from the fireworks. "Well?" he prompted.

"I—I decided to walk a while," she answered lamely.

"I would have thought we walked sufficiently earlier on. Besides, you were running."

At last an answer occurred to her. "You had been gone so long, I became bored. Then I thought I saw Lord Toby Shrike approaching, and didn't wish to be his target again, so I left the box. I was just strolling in general when I suddenly realized how long I'd been away, so I started to hurry back."

"I thought Shrike had wisely left town."

"Then maybe it wasn't him. One Bond Street lounger is very much like another."

"Which is the last thing any of them wishes," he murmured, toying with his lace cuff while still studying her.

Rockets and fireballs exploded across the night sky, and she used them as a distraction. "Aren't they lovely?"

"If one cares for that sort of thing."

"Don't you?"

"Maybe I have seen too many."

"You consider yourself jaded?"

The question clearly amused him. "Yes, right now I probably am," he replied dryly, then offered her his arm. "Let us return to the box."

Relievedly she slipped her hand over his sleeve, and they strolled back toward the Grand Walk. There was a crush by the orchestra pavilion, where nearly everyone seemed to have congregated to watch the fireworks. In the supper box, Madeira cake and another bottle of champagne had now been placed upon the table.

Rowan refilled Marigold's glass, and although she knew she shouldn't, she was still in such a fluster of nerves that she sipped a little more. Bursts of color sparkled against the night sky, and there was delighted applause, but although most people's gaze was turned skyward, Marigold's scanned the crush for Alauda. She soon saw the Earl of Fernborough by the orchestra. He was openly importuning the soprano as she rested prior to singing again when the fireworks display was over. At last Marigold picked out Alauda, who was once again with Sir Reginald and Lady Crane. As Marigold watched, Lady Crane shook her head at something Alauda said, but then said something behind her fan and nodded toward the box. Alauda turned, and by the furious look on her face, Marigold knew that if nothing else, Lady Crane had observed her following Rowan into the Dark Walk. It was all up, Marigold thought in dismay, for at the very least Rowan would learn that far from waiting long enough to become bored, she'd left straightaway! Her attention was drawn back to Rowan as he suddenly proposed a toast.

"To us, my lady."

"To us, my lord."

As their glasses clinked together, he looked curiously at her. "Is something wrong, Marigold? You seem a little, er, distracted."

Was it better to tell him now, rather than wait for him to find out through Alauda? But as she hovered on the brink of confession, a lisping female voice greeted them loudly from the entrance to the box. "Why, what a pleathure to come upon you again, Lord Avenbuwy, Lady Avenbuwy. Are you enjoying the fireworkth?" It was Lady Crane, who had with her not only a very reluctant Sir Reginald, but Alauda too.

Rowan rose swiftly to his feet, and ignoring Sir Reginald, inclined his head at the two ladies. "Lady Crane, Lady Fernborough."

Lady Crane, who was clearly taking malicious delight in forcing Rowan and Alauda to face each other in front of Marigold, pushed open the door of the box, and came inside. "My lord, I underthtand that Lady Fernborough and your new bwide are alweady acquainted."

"Indeed they are," Rowan replied.

"I wath jutht telling dear Alauda that I haven't left Thir Weginald'th thide all evening, tho I cannot imagine why she thought I had." Lady Crane looked maliciously at Marigold as she spoke, and the latter's heart sank.

Rowan feigned not to understand. "I beg your pardon, Lady Crane? I'm afraid I don't quite follow the significance . . . ?"

Sir Reginald gave his wife an appalled look, for he was afraid her tongue was about to embroil him in Lord Toby's recent fate. Lady Crane knew she'd gone far enough. "Oh, la, I don't thuppose it weally matterth," she murmured disappointedly.

Marigold's thankfulness was such that she almost gave a gasp of relief.

Alauda was annoyed that the moment had come to nothing, so decided to try to make Marigold look foolish. "Why, dear Marigold, what a shock your news is, I vow I did not expect you to emerge so neatly from the jaws of disaster."

By now Marigold's initial shock had subsided, and once again the champagne urged her into battle. "Disaster? What on earth do you mean, Alauda?"

"Why the debacle of Merlin's will, of course."

"Ah, yes, the *faked* document," Marigold replied amiably.

Alauda's lips twitched. "Hardly that, my dear."

"Oh, but Falk admitted it, Alauda."

"Well, with your reputation at stake, no doubt you are forced to say such things."

"If it ever comes to that, Alauda, I will be sure to consult with you, for if anyone knows what it is to have one's reputation in jeopardy, you do." Marigold's smile could not have been more sweet. "May I say how very lovely you look tonight? What material is your gown? I vow it is so transparent it must be Madras muslin."

Alauda flushed. "Transparent?"

"Well, one can see a great deal of your, er, form."

"I think you exaggerate," Alauda replied icily. "Besides, it isn't Madras muslin, but Swiss. I wouldn't stoop to something as cheap as Madras."

"Really? Well, whatever the price, vibrant yellow is definitely your color, for it is so very conspicuous, is it not?" Marigold's trill of laughter was a cruel imitation of Alauda's. "Why, I believe that if all the illuminations here were to be extinguished, we would still be able to see by the glow of your gown!"

Alauda looked murderous. "I'd hardly call it vibrant, but then fashion was never of particular interest to you, was it?"

"To be truthful, I fail to see why it should be of such intense concern to any woman of intelligence. Why on earth should one slavishly follow every new mode? I'm reliably informed that to a gentleman, a pretty ankle is a pretty ankle, whether it peeps from beneath ten-year-old gray flannel or the latest plowman's gauze. Is that not what you said, my lord?" She turned suddenly to Rowan as she said this last.

He gave her a mixed look. "Yes, my lady, that is indeed what I said," he replied, even though they both knew he hadn't.

Looking daggers at Marigold. Alauda lapsed into a heavy silence. She'd come off worse in the skirmish, and she knew it.

Lady Crane knew it too, and laughed a little embarrassedly. "Why, la, Lord Avenbuwy, I declare thith eveningth fireworkth are the motht thplendid ever, don't you agwee?"

"They are excellent indeed," Rowan murmured.

Emboldened, Marigold decided it was time to fix upon Sir Reginald, who had been steadfastly avoiding both her gaze and Rowan's. "Good evening again, Sir Reginald," she said. "I hope you and Lord Toby were able to find supper somewhere the other night? You left the Spread Eagle so hurriedly that I thought I had imagined you there in the first place."

Sir Reginald gave her a sickly smile. "I, er, yes, Lady Avenbury. We ate at the George and Dragon."

"How is your poor nose?"

Invisible daggers shot from his eyes, for it was quite clear how his nose was. "It will do, madam, it will do." He glanced out of the box, and gave a glad cry. "Why, Fernborough is waiting by our box, so I believe our supper must be ready!"

Without a word, Alauda turned and left. Lady Crane gave another embarrassed laugh. "Why, la," she declared a little foolishly, and made much of extending her hand for her husband to present his arm. Sir Reginald duly obliged, and they too left the box.

Marigold exhaled. "What a very disagreeable few minutes," she said.

"Much enlivened by your notion of humor," Rowan replied, resuming his seat.

"At least I have one. Alauda's was noteworthy for its absence."

He sat back, and ran a fingertip slowly around the rim of his glass. "You can hardly expect her to be pleased with the situation."

"Am I to sympathize with the odious creature? She is a snake, and just behaved very badly indeed. So did Lady Crane."

He looked shrewdly at her. "Are you seeking an argument, my lady?"

"Do you enjoy being the bone of contention?" she countered.

"Is that how you see me?"

"It appears to be the role in which you cast yourself."

"It isn't, believe me."

"But, sir, if you intend to keep a wife and a mistress who abhor each other, you are *bound* to be the bone."

"You are still wrong. Now, I don't intend to pursue the matter any further." He poured her a little more champagne.

Marigold hid her anger from him, for if ever any man ever wanted to have cake *and* eat it, that man was Rowan, Lord Avenbury! He intended to continue seeing Alauda, and at the same time he intended to bed his wife. She smiled sweetly, and pushed the plate of Madeira cake toward him. "Do have some, sir."

Her smile didn't falter as he took a slice, nor did it waver as she recalled Alauda's scathing words in the grotto. *Merlin told me she was cold and unimaginative, the equivalent of bedding a codfish.* A codfish? Well, if that was what Lord Avenbury thought his new bride would be, he was going to be very surprised. It was too long since she had been loved, and she was attracted to him in a way she wished she was not. Tonight he was going to be hers, and she meant to enjoy him to the full. He was not the only one who could have the cake and eat it. Still smiling, she took a slice as well.

Chapter Thirteen

It was gone midnight as Marigold stood alone on the wrought-iron balcony of her bedroom. She and Rowan had been back from Vauxhall Gardens for half an hour, and now she was waiting for him with a shameful degree of excitement. The last glass of champagne had sealed her foolishness. This was her wedding night, and she was about to spend the intimate hours of darkness with a husband she hardly knew, but who had already come to mean far too much to her. He was a tantalizing enigma, a man with magic in his eyes and fate in his touch. He was almost other-worldly, yet only too worldly as well, and she knew she was a fool to be falling in love with him, but on this occasion folly was proving impossible to resist.

She gazed down at the moonlit garden, where silver roses bloomed and diamonds danced in the fountains. Silver and diamonds? She smiled at such fanciful metaphors, but then she was seeing through a champagne glass—brightly! An owl called in the cherry tree at the bottom of the garden, and for the first time she noticed that mistletoe grew on one of the branches. Mistletoe, the sacred plant of the druids. Suddenly the night seemed cooler, and she drew back into the room.

Her small apartment consisted of a main bedroom, a dressing room containing wardrobes and a washstand, and a mirror-walled anteroom that opened onto the landing. The furniture was upholstered in bluebell velvet, and the walls were hung with pale yellow-and-white silk. The sumptuous four-poster bed was draped with a pagoda canopy of dainty white muslin, and the gray marble fireplace was particularly beautiful. An ormulu clock ticked on the mantelpiece, where ornaments with intricate crystal droplets caught the candlelight. It was all very elegant, and she liked it very much, especially as it looked out over the delightful gardens, unlike Rowan's apartment at the front of the house.

A lighted candelabrum stood upon the dressing table, its flames swaying idly in the barely perceptible draft from the garden. She saw her reflection in the cheval glass in the corner, and paused to consider what she saw. Beneath the voluminous white silk, her figure was firm and reasonably curvaceous, although hardly memorable, and at least her complexion didn't suffer the bane of freckles. She supposed her eyes might be considered handsome, they were certainly large, very green, and shaded by blessedly dark lashes. Her eyebrows were dark too, not the pale reddish hue that all but disappeared when viewed from more than a few feet away. Her only true asset were the red-gold curls that fell loosely about the shoulders of her nightgown, but good eyes and copper gold hair alone would never make her Alauda's equal. She looked at the mirror. "*You* are the one who will be with him tonight, not Alauda," she reminded herself.

Suddenly the clock chimed the quarter hour. It was the time Rowan had said he would come to her. She hastened to stand by the candle, for she knew how the flame would burnish her hair and outline her figure more becomingly through the thin white silk of her nightgown. Tonight she had no shame. She heard the anteroom door open and close, and then there was a discreet tap at the door of the bedroom itself. "Marigold?"

"Please come in."

He entered the room, and went to place the lighted candle he carried on the mantelpiece. He wore Turkish slippers, a maroon paisley silk dressing gown that was tied loosely at the waist, and his dark hair was tousled. He turned, his glance sweeping over her. "Well, here we are, madam."

"Here we are indeed, sir."

"Marigold, it is now my turn to offer a way out. There is still time for you to change your mind about being Lady Avenbury. Are you sure you wish to continue?"

She was taken aback. "Why do you ask?"

"Tonight at Vauxhall you were the object of much staring and quizzing. Maybe it has made you pause to think twice."

She was unsure of him. "Or maybe *you* are the one who has thought twice, sir."

He smiled a little. "My feelings have not changed, Marigold, although I confess to finding this situation somewhat novel."

"Novel?"

"It is very strange to find myself with a wife."

"Come, sir, you have often found yourself with a wife."

He smiled again. "*Touché,* but never my own."

"Am I so very different?"

"It is the situation that is different."

"For you maybe."

His eyes flickered away. "Ah yes, I must not forget that this will be the second wedding night you have known."

"The second wedding night, and the second husband, indeed only the second man, for until now Merlin was the only one. Whereas you, sir, have no doubt lost count of your conquests."

"I wouldn't exactly say lost count."

"Then let us settle for the fact that you are very experienced indeed, whereas I have only Merlin with whom to compare you."

"You think I mean to compare you with others?"

"With one other, perhaps."

He drew a long breath. "You do me an injustice, Marigold."

"Do I?" She wondered if he could have put his hand on his heart in that moment, and sworn that the word "codfish" had not passed his mind!

Humor glinted in his eyes. "Let us be clear here, my lady. My, er, activities have never been in a marriage bed, *you* are the one who has experience in that respect."

"Then you, sir, will be the one who benefits, will you not?"

He raised an eyebrow. "That is a very forward thing to say, Lady Avenbury."

"How do you know I'm not a very forward woman? Maybe I am completely abandoned."

"Are you?"

"That is for you to discover."

"Is it indeed. Very well, Marigold, come here and let me begin this investigation." His voice was very soft as he held out a hand.

She went to him as if in a dream, linking her arms around his neck and then stretching up to kiss him. He put his hands to her waist as her lips moved seductively over his, but as the tip of her tongue teased his, he slid his arms fully around her. The kiss brought her to life. Her pulse quickened, and her body began to ache for the consummation that enticed so exquisitely through his warmth. She pressed closer, and was conscious of his arousal. She moved against the firm, hard masculine contour, and exulted in the sensations she had craved so long. It was like awakening after a long, long slumber.

At last he drew his head back to look into her big green eyes. "Champagne certainly releases your inhibitions, Marigold," he breathed, gently untying the ribbons of her nightgown and slipping it from her shoulders so that it fell to the floor at her feet.

"But I am a forward woman, sir," she whispered. Not a codfish, never a codfish. . . .

He gazed at her in the candlelight. "You are a very surprising woman, my lady," he replied, then suddenly lifted her into his arms and carried her to the bed. He laid her on the silken coverlet, and then took off his dressing gown. He wore nothing beneath it, and she thought his lean, muscular body was perfect. There were dark hairs on his chest, leading down to the forest at his groin, from where his maleness sprang readily. Oh, how readily. Excitement flamed through her, and she reached up to him. He sank down into her arms, body to body, mouth to mouth. Kiss followed kiss, and their caresses grew more passionate and intimate. She wanted him to enter her fully, but he tantalized her, sliding his virility to the threshold, but no further. Then, just as she thought the excitement was unendurable, at last he pushed into her. Magnificent sensations scintillated over her entire being, bewitching waves of pleasure that lit her soul like the fireworks she'd watched earlier. She clung to him, arching with the intensity of her release. His strokes were long and leisurely, extending her pleasure through his own climax, and then more.

Afterward her body was warm and trembling as he drew her close to him. She felt sated and drained at the same time, and it was wonderful. She had missed this pleasure, lain awake at night longing for it, and suddenly it was hers again. Tears sprang unexpectedly to her eyes.

He leaned up in concern. "What is it?" he said, gently pushing a damp curl of her hair back from her forehead.

She hardly dared look at him, for fear her foolish love would shine too bright. "I've been so lonely," she whispered.

For a moment she thought she saw pain in his eyes, but then he pulled her into his arms again, and rested his cheek against her hair. She could no longer see his eyes, but thought his body shook, as if he were fighting back tears of his own. But she could not be sure.

Chapter Fourteen

The next morning she awoke to find herself alone in the bed. Rowan had only just left her, for the sheets were still warm where he had lain. She stretched luxuriously. How wonderful she felt, so relaxed and content. It was as if the years had peeled back, and she was sixteen again, and so in love with—and loved by—Merlin. No, it was far, far better than that. She closed her eyes and remembered the night that had just passed. How many times had Rowan kissed her? How many times had he stroked and caressed her? Oh, too many to possibly count, but every moment had been exquisite. They still hardly knew each other, and yet had indulged in such passionate lovemaking that she blushed to think of some of the intimacies they had shared, intimacies she wished to share with him over and over again. And today they were to leave for Avenbury Park, where they would be alone together for as long as they wished. . . .

The clock chimed eight, and her eyes opened again. Suddenly she no longer wanted to lie there, so she got up to put on her apricot muslin robe, then she went out onto the balcony. The scent of honeysuckle was as sweet and refreshing as the night before, and the fountains played in the sunlight. The mistletoe shone golden among the green cherry leaves, horses stirred in the mews lane at the foot of the garden, and an occasional voice carried as the grooms went about their business. She flung her tangled hair back, and took a huge breath, but then the birds fell curiously silent.

Expecting to see a cat, Marigold looked down into the garden again, but instead saw a stealthy human movement by the wicket gate that gave access from the stables to the garden. Alauda's maid, Lucy, hurried to the cherry tree, then stretched up to push a piece of paper into a crevice in the trunk. The robin hopped along a branch, his head cocked as he watched the paper being carefully tucked out of sight. Lucy, a plain girl with straight brown hair and freckles, glanced nervously toward the house, but not up at the balcony, then gathered her fawn linen skirts to hurry back to the gate. After a moment the birds began to sing again.

Marigold was filled with dismay the moment she recognized the maid, for until that moment she had managed to put Alauda from her mind. Now reality swept back with a vengeance. Rowan may have spent last night with his wife, but his mistress was still there. Suddenly Rowan himself emerged into the garden directly below her. He carried his top hat and gloves, and was dressed in a pine green riding coat and cream breeches. As he ran a hand through his hair and walked quickly down between the rosebeds, his watching wife knew he would stop first at the cherry tree. Tears stung her eyes as he did just that, reaching up unhesitatingly to take the note from its hiding place. He was just reading it when suddenly a groom came through the wicket gate and almost walked into him. Rowan shoved the note hastily into his pocket as the groom begged his pardon, then hurried on toward the house. Rowan proceeded out of the garden to the stables, and a moment later Marigold heard him ride away along the mews lane. But the note, which he thought he had put securely in his pocket, had fallen onto the path, and lay there in the shade of the cherry tree.

Marigold had to know what it said. For modesty's sake she donned her nightgown beneath her robe, then hastened from the room. She was careful that no one saw her slipping down through the house, then out past the kitchens, where the servants were about their breakfast. She hardly noticed the fragrance of the garden as she hastened down the path toward the speck of white by the cherry tree. Swiftly she retrieved it, then pretended to examine some of the newly forming fruit on the cherry tree. She glanced back toward the house, but there was no one around, so she moved beneath the shady branches, from where the fountains would also obscure the view from the house, then she smoothed the paper out to read what was written there.

"R. Please do not leave for the country today as planned, for I must see you tonight. *Je t'adore avec tout mon coeur. A.*"

More tears stung Marigold's eyes. Would he respond to this entreaty? Yes, of course he would. . . . Suddenly a gust of wind got up from nowhere. She shivered as from a perfectly still morning, a strong draft of almost chill air stirred over Mayfair. Her gaze was drawn up through the branches toward the golden bough of mistletoe as it swayed seductively. Then there was a fluttering sound, and the robin came to perch close by. The wind died away again as swiftly as it had arisen, and he gave a little warble, and puffed out his red breast.

"What shall I do now, Robin?" she asked him. He chirruped, then suddenly flew down to the hand that held the note. He was so light she hardly felt him as he began to peck angrily but ineffectually at the paper, as if it offended him too. She smiled sadly. "I think you know how I feel, don't you?" she murmured. He looked intently at her, as if urging her to something, and gradually an idea began to come to her. She had parted Rowan from Alauda last night at Vauxhall Gardens, and she'd keep them apart again now! And since Alauda thought it was clever to resort to forgery, her lover's new wife would take a leaf from the same unethical book! The robin flew off with a defiant burst of song, and Marigold gathered her skirts to hurry back to the house, again being careful that no one saw her.

She went to Rowan's study, and searched for paper that resembled as closely as possible that which Alauda had used. Then she smoothed out the original note, and sat down to fabricate one of her own, copying Alauda's writing. It took several attempts, but at last she achieved a satisfactory result. "R. Do not alter your plans after all, for F. has announced we are to attend Holland House tonight. Remember always that I love you. A."

Marigold studied it for a long moment. Was it convincing? Yes, the more she read it, the more she felt it would perform the necessary task. If Rowan received this, he would still leave for the country, and Alauda would wait in vain tonight. And serve the doxy right! Smiling a little wickedly, Marigold returned to the garden to put the original note back where it had fallen, so that Rowan wouldn't know it had been found. Then she made her way back to the house with her forgery, but when she reached the kitchens this time, she made her presence known. The servants were still seated comfortably around the table, enjoying an overlong breakfast in their master's absence, and they started guiltily as she appeared in the doorway. The butler hurried to her. "My lady?"

"I was just about to walk in the garden, when someone's footman arrived that way with this note for his lordship. Will you see he gets it the moment he returns from his ride?"

"Er, yes, my lady." The butler glanced down at the note. He clearly suspected from whom it may have come, for his face went distinctly red and uncomfortable.

She feigned a little puzzlement. "Isn't it a little unusual for footmen to deliver notes to the rear entrance?"

"It, er, does happen occasionally, my lady," he replied awkwardly.

"I see." She turned to go, but then hesitated. "I've changed my mind about walking in the garden, and wish a hot bath to be prepared."

"Certainly, my lady."

With a serene nod of her head, she walked away.

Marigold sank into the rose-scented water. Her hair was twisted up loosely on top of her head, and she leaned back against the soft pink cloth which was draped all around the shaped bath. She was being attended by her new maid, Sally, a dainty, dark-haired girl, half French, and very clever indeed with hair. To Sally, the new Lady Avenbury appeared the picture of relaxed contentment, but Marigold's heart was pounding nervously. She knew Rowan had returned from his ride, but she had yet to see him. Had he received her forged note? Had it deceived him? Maybe he'd realized whose hand had really penned it . . . !

His tread was at the door. He knocked. "Marigold?"

At her nod, Sally hurried to answer. She bobbed a quick curtsy to him. "Please come in, my lord," she said, then went out, closing the door behind her.

Hardly daring to meet his gaze, Marigold sank a little lower in the water. Suddenly her apprehension moved on two levels, for apart from her sleight of hand with the notes, she was self-conscious about last night. As he crossed the room toward her, she couldn't tell anything from his face.

His hair was windswept from his ride, and he loosened his neckcloth as he halted by the bath. "Good morning, Lady Avenbury." His tone conveyed nothing.

"Good morning, Lord Avenbury," she replied, wishing she could read his face more than she could, but in spite of their night together, he remained closed to her.

"I trust I find you well?"

How stilted and formal the words sounded. Were they the prelude to an angry confrontation? Her heart quickened uneasily, but somehow she managed to reply lightly. "As I hope I find you?"

To her relief he smiled. "Then may I presume you are ready to face our journey to Wiltshire?"

Triumph coursed invisibly through her. "You may indeed, sir."

"I felt the urge to ride in Hyde Park. I hope you didn't mind me leaving you asleep like that?"

"Why should I mind?"

"Because it may not have seemed appropriate for you to awaken alone."

She lowered her eyes. "I do not expect you to behave like an adoring husband, sir, for I realize this is a marriage of convenience."

"So it is."

"I still intend to defeat the curse by being your wife this time next year," she said determinedly.

"You expect in vain, as you will realize when you arrive at Avenbury Park. There are portraits of every Lord Avenbury, and each one is a young man because none of them survived long enough to be painted in middle age." He anticipated her next question. "I swear to tell you everything as soon as we get to Avenbury." Then he turned to go, but hesitated at the door. "Breakfast will soon be served. I would like it if you joined me."

The change of subject was so deliberate, that for a second she couldn't reply. But then she found her tongue. "I would like that too."

"Good."

She couldn't let him leave without saying more about the night they'd shared. It was foolish to feel so embarrassed about it. He was her husband now, and she was no shrinking virgin. "Rowan, about last night . . ."

"What about it?" he asked, returning to her.

She looked up into his eyes, and then quickly away again in dismay as her brief surge of courage faded. "I was a little abandoned. You must forgive me, I—I fear champagne goes to my head," she said feebly.

He smiled. "I certainly will not forgive you, in fact I sincerely trust it wasn't just the champagne. Marigold, I found it exceeding agreeable to have such an ardent wife."

She colored. "You are a very skillful lover, sir. A woman would need to be oddly cold not to respond," she said. A codfish, in fact, she added silently.

"It wasn't the champagne, and I think you know it."

Her cheeks were very pink. "Yes, I do."

"You thoroughly enjoyed our wedding night, did you not?"

"It would be pointless of me to deny it, when every minute last night proved otherwise."

"As it would be equally pointless of *me* to deny that I find you one of the most perfect lovers I have ever known."

"I—I am?" Her eyes widened.

"Why are you so surprised? Surely you sensed as much?"

She longed to know how she compared with Alauda, but knew it would not be wise to ask. Besides, why remind him of his mistress at a time like this? Picking up her sponge, she squeezed warm, rose-scented water over her shoulders and breasts. "You forget how long it had been since I last shared Merlin's bed," she said then.

"I'm certainly reaping the benefit. What a fool Merlin Arnold must have been," he added, watching the water trickle over her skin.

"He didn't make me feel as wonderful as you did last night," she said frankly, her courage returning a little.

He bent down to draw a fingertip across one of her nipples. "You're very tempting right now, Marigold," he said softly. A thrill of anticipation warmed her, and her nipple tightened at his touch. He went on. "Have you ever shared a bath?"

"Shared . . . ? No, I haven't." But I'd like to, oh, how I'd like to. . . .

"It's very pleasing, very pleasing indeed," he murmured, pulling off his neckcloth, and then sitting down on a nearby chair to take off his footwear.

"But what of the servants? Sally may return!"

"Every servant in London knows better than to open a door behind which newlyweds may be ensconced." He tossed his coat, shirt, and waistcoat aside, and then undid the buttons of his riding breeches.

It was not long before he stepped into the bath with her. The scented water splashed over the sides as they made love again, and at the ultimate moment, Marigold was so swept away in ecstasy that she cried out.

A maid who was feeding the birds in the garden glanced up at the window, then giggled and ran inside.

Chapter Fifteen

The journey from London had been tiring. Now it was late evening, and sunset's long shadows stretched across the countryside. Marigold's head lolled against the carriage's rich green leather upholstery as she gazed out at nothing in particular. She wore a forget-me-not blue velvet spencer over a white muslin gown, and an artificial knot of the same flowers adorned the underbrim of her straw bonnet. Blue ribbons were tied beneath her chin, completing a fresh but fashionable appearance of which she was very well pleased. Privately she again thanked the capricious lady of fortune and fashion who had so providently canceled her order.

Opposite her, Rowan lounged on his seat. He wore a dark mustard coat and beige breeches, and a brown silk neckcloth burgeoned above his brown-and-beige striped waistcoat. His top hat and gloves lay beside him as he too gazed out of the window with a faraway look in his eyes. They had talked a lot at the beginning of the journey, and had eventually fallen into a companionable silence. The Wiltshire scenery was now one of sweeping chalk escarpments, almost bare of trees, and rich river valleys, like the one through which they now drove. It was very beautiful and mellow, and not at all the place for anything so dark and wicked as an ancient druidic curse. The carriage negotiated a bridge, then the road swept sharply away to the north, skirting the eastern end of an escarpment toward a neighboring valley. The escarpment now blocked the sun's fading light, and everything became suddenly more dark.

Rowan glanced out as if looking for something. At last he saw it. "The gates of Romans at last. It's only another two miles now."

She looked out too, and saw a sharp turning between high hedges. She caught a glimpse of plain stone-pillared gates, then the carriage had driven on too far. "Romans is a rather odd name," she said.

"There are remains of ancient fortifications on the escarpment, and it has always been believed that they are the remains of a Roman fort. The house is just below the summit, and the eastern reach of the lake is at the foot of the hill. The lake is about two miles long, and curves around the foot of the escarpment from Avenbury Park."

"It must be a very isolated house," Marigold said, thinking of the escarpment.

"Yes, but originally it was just a hunting tower for the Norman lords of Avenbury, then in later medieval times a house was added. About thirty years ago my father decided to improve it into a gentleman's residence, but due to the construction, a rather awkward feature had to remain. The only internal staircase is very steep, narrow, twisting, and unsafe, especially for ladies, and the only solution that didn't involve tearing the whole place down was to construct a great balcony around the upper story, with an external staircase at the back."

"You mean, that's the only comfortable way upstairs or down, even in winter?" Marigold asked in astonishment.

"So it seems. It's inconvenient, but although all tenants are informed, it doesn't seem to deter them. They take the place because of its situation."

"Does Romans belong to your estate?"

"Yes."

"Who lives there?"

"No one, it's been empty since the last tenant left in the autumn." He sat forward to look up toward the shadowy escarpment. "That's odd, I could swear I saw lights."

She craned her neck to look. Romans itself was impossible to make out, but the faint glow of lighted windows gave its position away. "Yes, I see them too."

He sat back. "My agent must have found a new tenant."

The carriage descended into the new valley, where the sun's last rays lay in banded lines. Marigold's first glimpse of Avenbury village could only be described as eerie. She was ready to see the famous standing stones, but wasn't prepared for the reality of a place so steeped in mystery it was second only to Stonehenge. The light was strange, sometimes rich beams of crimson and gold sunset, sometimes deep shade, and Marigold felt almost spellbound as she gazed out of the carriage window. A summer mist was beginning to rise, adding so much to the air of mystery that when she saw a strange tall shape at the roadside, her imagination carried her away into thinking it was a very tall man shrouded in a long cloak. The form loomed so suddenly out of the gathering shadows that her instinctive fear was of a highwayman, but then she saw it was a standing stone, and a primitive shiver of fascination ran through her.

Rowan's voice made her start. "Behold the first sentinel of Avenbury."

"It—it gave me quite a shock," she said, thinking how foolish she must sound.

Rowan smiled. "The stones are carved from local sandstone. There are boulders of it scattered all over this part of the world, and they should properly be called sarsens, but because from a distance they resemble flocks of sheep, they're called gray-wethers." He smiled. "Yet another piece of useless information from my endless store."

She smiled too. "It isn't useless information, I find it all very interesting."

The carriage drove on, and another stone appeared, taller and more lozenge-shaped than the first. It stood on the inner bank of a water-filled moat about twenty feet wide, and curving away into the mist beyond, all lining the moat, stretched more stones. She had been told the henge enclosed the village and much of Avenbury Park, as well as the small common that stood at the actual center of the circle, and as the carriage drove on, she saw this was indeed so. When the common came into view alongside, she saw ghostly sheep grazing on the close-cropped, lawn-like grass. There was a mystical atmosphere, as if echoes of the far-forgotten past were still sounding faintly in the modern air.

Rowan spoke again. "I see Avenbury already begins to exert its mystery upon you."

"Yes, it does." She gave him a rueful smile. "I had quite a shock when I saw that first stone. I thought it was a highwayman."

"Something so modern? I would have thought that at the very least you'd expect a druid."

"I'm afraid not."

"How very pragmatic you are."

"That's the nature of this particular beast," she replied.

"And a very agreeable nature it is too," he murmured.

Smaller stones now lined the road as if it were a processional way, and then she saw cottages, a steepled church, and an inn, with a lantern hanging outside. The village had grown around a crossroad, at which the carriage turned west. Almost immediately, Avenbury fell away behind, and the common land appeared again. Marigold gave a start as Rowan reached up with his cane to rap loudly on the carriage roof. The coachman immediately applied the brakes and reined the team in.

Donning his top hat and gloves, Rowan flung open the door, and alighted. The mist swirled around him as he turned to extend his hand to her. "Come, it's time to answer all your questions."

She slipped her fingers into his, and stepped down. About one hundred yards away, in the very center of the henge, was the ancient oak tree Rowan had mentioned. It was surrounded by an almost protective inner circle of much smaller stones, which were blue instead of the gray of the great circle, and its leafy shadow was so dark and long that it disappeared into the mist that rolled very slowly in from the moat and the lake at Avenbury Park. Someone whistled, and she turned. A boy and his dog were rounding up the sheep, to drive them into shelter for the night.

Rowan began to lead her toward the tree, but then she halted as a duck flew overhead. It quacked several times, and she gasped. "I'm *sure* that was Sir Francis! He makes a very distinctive noise."

Rowan raised an eyebrow at such a fancy. "Marigold, the lake in the park is full to the brim with ducks of every shape and size, and I promise you that one mallard sounds exactly like another. Besides, why on earth would Sir Francis come here?"

"I don't know, but I still think—"

"Please, Marigold, right now ducks are the last thing on my mind."

He pulled her hand over his sleeve again, and they walked on. The grass was soft beneath their feet, and as they passed through the small circle around the oak, the leaves rustled as a breath of air swirled the encroaching mist. She was reminded of that moment by the cherry tree, but this time there was no sign of Robin.

Rowan halted beneath the outspreading branches, then leaned back against the tree trunk. "First, I'll tell you all I know of the curse. It commences with a legend. Before men, there were birds, who were all under the protection of Taranis, the god of thunder—"

"Taranis?" Marigold interrupted. "Why, that's the god Perry and Bysshe were trying to raise."

"No doubt because of Bysshe's dratted volume of Stukeley."

"Yes, I think it was. Anyway, forgive me for interrupting. Please go on."

"Right. One day Taranis grew bored, and to amuse himself he turned some of his birds into people. That is how the human race is supposed to have begun. Anyway, in the sixteenth century, long after Taranis had faded into folk memory, a man came here to Avenbury who, with a dozen followers, secretly celebrated the old god's rites again. This man was named Aquila Randle, and he was a doctor, philosopher, alchemist, and druid. His druidic power is said to have come from his possession of a potent talisman known as the anguinum, through the use of which the entire village fell under his influence."

"Anguinum?" Marigold had never heard the word before.

"It's also known as the serpent's egg or druid's stone, but I have no idea what it actually is, or was."

"Go on."

"My ancestor, the first Lord Avenbury, had a beautiful sister called Jennifer, and Randle wanted her as his wife." Rowan smiled, and said almost as an aside. "She really was very beautiful. A portrait of her was recently rediscovered in an attic at the house. Anyway, that is incidental. Randle used the anguinum upon Lord Avenbury, forcing him to do his bidding, but Jennifer not only despised and feared Randle, she also loved a handsome young squire by the name of Raddock. She begged Randle to release her, but he refused, so she threw herself on her brother's mercy. At first Avenbury resisted her pleas, but then his wife, who was with child at the time, begged him to reconsider, and because he loved both women, he agreed to let Jennifer marry Raddock instead. Randle was furious. He arranged a terrible druid ceremony at the dawn of midsummer, right here by this oak, which is a particularly sacred tree because of the mistletoe growing on it. Oak is a very hard wood, and mistletoe rarely chooses it, preferring softer trees like apple. That's by the by. Where was I? Oh, yes, Randle's druid ceremony. Using the anguinum, he imposed a spell on the village, so that those few who were not entirely converted to his beliefs would not awaken, then he compelled Jenny and Raddock to come to him. He meant to marry Jenny, kill Raddock, then lay hands upon the Avenbury title and lands by ridding himself of Lord Avenbury as well, but the latter realized what was happening, and came with a force to break up the ceremony. His armed intervention not only resulted in the immediate deaths by drowning of thirty-five of Randle's druids, but also the fatal injury of thirteen more. The moat around the village has four evenly placed causeways that to this day provide access to the henge—we drove over one when we arrived—and Lord Avenbury stationed his men at these strategic points so the druids couldn't escape, except by jumping into the water, which is very deep. There was panic, many drowned because they became entangled in the water lilies that have always grown here, and which are my family's emblem. To make Randle's dismay complete, he lost the anguinum in the confusion. This resulted in Taranis's magic being somehow reversed, so that not only did he and his twelve remaining followers become birds again, but also Jennifer and Raddock. She became a wren, and Raddock, naturally enough, a robin. They are supposed to be birds to this day."

"Why 'naturally enough' a robin?" Marigold asked quickly, her mind beginning to race.

"Because the old English word for a robin is a raddock. It's somewhere in Shakespeare."

"Jenny Wren and Robin Redbreast," she murmured. Plain common sense told her it was mere coincidence, and yet how could she ignore Robin's decidedly unnatural persistence? Or the fact that he had a wren with him that day at Eton? She pulled herself up sharply. She was behaving like an impressionable miss!

Rowan went on. "Randle still had sufficient power left to punish Lord Avenbury by decreeing that none of his line would live beyond their thirty-fifth birthday—thirty-five for the druids who drowned—and that the thirteenth lord—thirteen for those druids who received fatal wounds—would die at midsummer dawn. Randle vowed to find the anguinum again, and with the final lord's death to return to take the Avenbury title and inheritance for himself. He also vowed to turn Jennifer back into a woman, so she would become his bride after all. His curse delivered, he and his companions flew away."

Before he'd finished, Marigold had drawn back in dismay. "The thirteenth and last lord? But *you* are the thirteenth!"

"Yes, and this year my thirty-fifth birthday falls on midsummer day."

A chill tremor went through her. "But that's barely two weeks away!"

"Yes."

Chapter Sixteen

Marigold felt cold as she remembered what Rowan had said at the Druid Oak. *Let me assure you that my demands for your favors will cease before the end of this month* . . . She searched his face in what was left of the light. "Do you really in your heart of hearts believe all this, Rowan?"

"About Taranis and his birdmen? No, I think that is sheer fantasy. But about Randle's curse? Yes, I do."

The reply stung her. "How monstrously unfair of you! How could you wed me and say nothing? When I made my marriage vows to you, I did so in good faith, but you've believed all along that you are about to die!"

"My vows were made in good faith too, Marigold."

"Were they? I think not. Did you pause even once to consider me? You've used me quite heartlessly, being quite content to see me widowed twice in as many months! Didn't it matter how I'd feel when I found out? And what of Perry? He already likes and trusts you immensely, and you like him, yet you're blithely prepared for him to lose you as well."

"Marigold, as I recall, you were only too willing to accept the particular helping hand I extended. You would have clutched at a straw, but I offered far, far more than that, and when the moment comes, you will inherit everything. What I've done is provide for you and Perry for the rest of your lives. You should be thanking me, not berating me."

"Has this marriage really been such a coldly calculated contract for you? Don't you feel any warmth toward me at all? I know I do toward you, especially after last night, and—and this morning." She flushed as she remembered the shared bath.

"Don't mistake desire for love. I desire you very much, and you desire me, but we do not love each other."

She hid the pain his words caused. "I made this bargain thinking I only had Alauda to contend with, but it seems I must battle the supernatural as well."

"You do not need to battle anything. Marigold, I thought I'd made it clear—"

"I thought I had too," she interrupted. "I don't believe in your curse, Rowan, and I intend to make you realize I'm right. So I mean to do battle with whatever stands in my way."

"Marigold—"

Again she interrupted him. "Midsummer day has always been for celebration, for flowers, dancing, and merrymaking, not for the dark deeds of a defeated old magician from the time of Henry VIII. Aquila Randle is *not* going to reach across the centuries to take you from me! Two marriages is enough for anyone, and I don't intend to be available for a third!"

He took her arms gently. "Flattered as I am by your spirit and vehemence, you *must* face facts. The first Lord Avenbury was heartbroken over losing his sister, and to show his defiance he built Avenbury Park within the circle, but he, his wife, and baby son died of the plague before it was completed. The second Lord Avenbury was his younger brother, who was fallen upon by robbers and murdered. And so it goes on, without exception. All of them died on or before their thirty-fifth birthday."

"You are going to be the exception that proves the rule," she said obstinately. She wouldn't accept this, she *wouldn't*!

"But the precedent is there twelve times over," he said patiently. "Think about it, Marigold. If the head of every generation in your family had without fail succumbed to the terms of an ancient damnation, wouldn't *you* think it highly likely you'd follow suit? Yes, of course you would."

She struggled for something suitably defiant to say, but the words wouldn't come, and after a moment he released her to put on his top hat. "I've answered everything you need to know, and now, as the light has all but gone, I think it best if we complete our journey, mm?" he said.

"So there is nothing you want from me?" she whispered.

"Only your warmth."

"You have that."

He removed the top hat again, and looked deep into her concerned green eyes. "And you have mine. Marigold, I have more than one reason for offering you marriage. To begin with, I want to restore the reputation Falk Arnold and his conniving lawyer stole from you, and although you may not have enjoyed Vauxhall Gardens, the truth is that our alliance *will* be a nine days' wonder. By the time you return to town, you will be regarded as all that is respectable. Another of my reasons is that I believe Castell Arnold, and all that goes with it, rightfully belongs to Perry, which is why I have put my own lawyers on the business of finding proof of your first marriage. My third reason is that I consider you and Perry to be far worthier recipients of my own inheritance than a bully of a second cousin twice removed who now lives with five 'wives' in Madras! And thirdly, I like you very, very much."

Tears sprang to her eyes. "Oh, Rowan, I'm so glad you've explained at last, for I could not understand why a man like you would want a wife like me."

"A wife like you? Why do you never do yourself justice? *Any* man would like a wife like you."

She reached up impulsively to kiss him, and for a sweet moment his arms moved around her beneath the mistletoe. Then she mastered her tears, and drew back to smile at him. "Well, now that you have this particular wife, you had best know that nothing you've said about the curse will make any difference to her. She will fight every second of every day to keep you, and if old Randle thinks it's going to be easy to take you away from her, or get his hands on poor Jennifer, or step neatly into your place, she'll see that he is well corrected."

He smiled. "Oh, Marigold, you are a very remarkable woman."

"Or a very mulish one?"

He laughed. "Well, possibly, but delightfully so."

"Just one thing more . . ."

"Yes?"

"What do the servants at Avenbury Park know of the curse?" She needed to know the atmosphere awaiting them.

"Nothing."

"Nothing?" She was astonished. "How can that possibly be? According to you, every Lord Avenbury has—"

"Well, when I say 'nothing,' I mean that my father and his father before him were at pains to play the whole thing down. I have been careful to continue in the same vein. Society is barely aware of it. I behave as if there is no such thing as the curse."

"Which there isn't," she declared firmly.

"Whatever you say, my dear," he replied in the infuriating tone of a tolerant husband. Then he donned the top hat again, offered her his arm, and they began to walk back toward the carriage.

Suddenly Marigold heard a familiar chirrup coming from the tree. Glancing quickly back over her shoulder, she saw Robin Redbreast and Jenny Wren looking down at her from the mistletoe, and Jenny began to sing her plaintive song again. But then the song changed to the imperative tic-tic- tic of all wrens. Marigold's breath caught, for although Rowan clearly heard only a bird's call, she distinctly heard a young woman's imploring voice. "Help us, Marigold! Help us, please, before it's too late!"

In that heartstopping second, Marigold knew the birds really were Jennifer Avenbury and her lover, Squire Raddock. And if that were true, then so probably was the curse. A wave of dismay washed over her. She didn't want to believe any of this, but so much apparent proof couldn't be ignored. Nor could her determination to protect Rowan be ignored. A warlike glint lit her eyes. She wouldn't give up easily! She'd fight for him, and for Jenny Wren and Robin Redbreast. In fact, she'd fight for them all until her very last breath! Her fingers tightened protectively over Rowan's sleeve, and she walked on at his side without saying a word.

Marigold was still shaken but determined a few minutes later, as the carriage neared the lodge at Avenbury Park. She had never believed in the supernatural, yet she was being forced to accept that there was such a thing. Ever since Robin's first appearance on the day of Merlin's will, she had become more and more embroiled in events she still only partially understood. One thing she did understand, however; if she didn't fight for what mattered, she'd be swept helplessly aside. Maybe she'd be swept helplessly aside anyway. . . .

She glanced out as the carriage turned through gilt and black wrought-iron gates that were topped by the heraldic water lilies of the lords of Avenbury, and she gave a start as the lodgekeeper blew a horn to warn the house that Lord and Lady Avenbury approached. She composed herself, for in a few moments she would have to meet all the servants, well, most of them anyway, for some of the kitchen staff would be busy preparing a suitable repast. Word had been sent ahead from London to warn the staff of Rowan's visit with his new bride, whose new maid, Sally, would have arrived about an hour before as well, so the servants were well primed to hurry out to greet their master and new mistress.

Marigold lowered the carriage window, and looked all around, her eyes so used to the virtual darkness that she could see quite a lot, especially as for some reason the mist had not yet enveloped anything here. Lights shone ahead, and at last Avenbury Park house came into view. Even at the edge of night, she could see that it was beautiful. Rambling, built of stone, and gabled, it had magnificent mullioned windows, wisteria-covered walls, and a jutting stone porch. Peacocks called in gardens that were filled with finely clipped topiary bushes, formal rose beds, and sweet-scented herbs. At the end of the gardens she could make out the moat and line of standing stones, and beyond that a tree-dotted lawn that swept down to a reed-fringed lake. The shining expanse of water disappeared into the mist, which advanced discernibly toward the house, as if it had suddenly realized its mistake.

At the sound of the lodgekeeper's trumpet, hundreds of waterfowl had been startled into the air, flying noisily out of the vapor, but as the carriage drew up at the house, the flocks began to settle again, their complaining cries echoing as they descended once more into the silvery shroud. For a second Sir Francis crossed Marigold's mind again. Was he really still plaguing the boys at Eton? Or was he here at Avenbury? Like Perry before her, she was *sure* she recognized that quack, and after everything else she'd been compelled to accept tonight, why not a supernatural duck as well? Marigold shivered, and drew back into the vehicle as Rowan prepared to alight.

The servants stood in a welcoming line, their faces lit by the lanterns held by several of the footmen. Another lantern had been lit beneath the porch, and its glow fell upon the wisteria, which was in full bloom, its flowers hanging like countless bunches of lilac-blue grapes. The butler came to lower the carriage rungs and open the door on Rowan's side. His name was Beech, and he was a plump man in his late forties, with rosy cheeks and an unexpectedly luxuriant head of straight salt-and-pepper hair which he tied back with a black ribbon. He wore a plain charcoal coat, and dove gray breeches, and the button of his blue waistcoat strained across his ample belly. He had a pleasing smile, and Marigold liked him on sight.

Rowan stepped down and greeted everyone, before turning to assist her down as well. Then her introduction to the Avenbury Park servants commenced, but as each footman bowed and each maid bobbed a curtsy, she was conscious of their curiosity. They would have learned a little from Sally, but not a great deal, since the maid herself did not know much, and they were clearly wondering how their master had suddenly been snapped up. Was it love at first sight? Was his new bride no better than she should be? Had he got her with child? Oh, their silent queries were legion, and not very well concealed on some faces.

At last the formalities were over, and Rowan escorted her beneath the porch into the candlelit house. Marigold found herself in a fine Tudor hall, with a stone-flagged floor upon which was laid a wine red carpet that was flushed to warm crimson by the light. On the carpet stood a long, very old table upon which were arranged three polished copper bowls filled with roses from the gardens. A magnificent oak staircase led up to a half landing, then split into two to the floor above. The carved stone fireplace was ornamented with Rowan's water lily badge, and so was the stained glass of the magnificent oriel window that dominated the western wall. Twelve portraits were evenly spaced around the oak-paneled walls, one for every previous Lord Avenbury. Each one was of a young man.

Rowan turned to Marigold. "Welcome to Avenbury Park, my lady," he said, then handed his top hat, gloves, and cane to the butler, who had hastened to take up a position by the table.

"It's a very beautiful house, Rowan."

"I'm glad you approve."

"How could one not?"

He nodded toward the oriel window. "I wish we'd arrived about an hour ago. At sunset, the light streams through the stained glass, and lies like jewels over everything," he murmured, almost absently.

"Are you about to wax poetic, sir?" she said lightly.

He smiled. "It has been known, madam, it has been known."

The waiting butler cleared his throat discreetly. "Begging your pardon, my lord, my lady, but will you require dinner?"

Rowan nodded. "I fancy so, Beech, although only a cold supper. We ate very well on the way at the Bear at Hungerford."

"Mrs. Spindle always has your favorite marbled ham in readiness, my lord."

"Excellent."

"My lord, my lady." The butler bowed, but as he turned, there was a sudden cacophany of shouts, screams, and frantic quacks from the direction of the kitchens. Then a door opened, and the uproar became much louder. A mallard drake erupted into the hall, pursued by a small gray-haired woman in a sober brown linen dress, starched white apron, and mobcap, brandishing a meat cleaver above her head with murderous intent. Other servants followed, and there was pandemonium as the terrified drake took to its wings to flap desperately around the ceiling.

Marigold pressed her hands to her mouth in dismay, for this time she was certain beyond all shadow of doubt that it was Sir Francis. As she watched, the panic-stricken mallard flew straight into an iron chandelier above the staircase, and its volley of frantic quacks was abruptly silenced as it fell to the stairs in a shower of feathers.

"Ha!" declared the small woman triumphantly, as she began to mount the staircase, cleaver at the ready.

Chapter Seventeen

N o!" cried Marigold. "Oh, no! Please!
The woman paused, and her face changed as she realized Lord and Lady Avenbury were witnessing the scene. The cleaver was hastily concealed behind her back, and she gave a rather embarrassed curtsy. "Begging your pardon, my lord, my lady . . ." The other servants, excepting Beech, melted prudently back to the kitchens.

Rowan looked at Marigold, and then at the woman. "What is the meaning of this, Mrs. Spindle?"

The cook bobbed another uncomfortable curtsy. "By your leave, my lord, I was about to prepare the bird for tomorrow's dinner. I thought that with a little gooseberry sauce, it would be the very thing for your first full day home. You see, I sent Whitebeam down to the lake earlier, but he didn't bag anything, so when this one just walked into the kitchen bold as brass a few minutes ago, well . . ." She shrugged, and didn't finish.

Marigold closed her eyes. Eat Sir Francis with gooseberry sauce? It didn't bear thinking about.

Rowan exhaled slowly. "Very well, Mrs. Spindle, but please take the wretched creature back to the kitchens in order to do the deed."

Sir Francis began to stir, and then gave a strangulated shriek as the cook's skinny fingers closed eagerly around his neck. Marigold caught Rowan's arm desperately. "Please don't let her kill him, Rowan!" she begged.

He groaned. "Oh, don't tell me you think *this* is Sir Francis as well!"

"I don't just think, I *know*. Please let me have him." Sir Francis's cries were choked, his little webbed feet paddled the air, and his wings flapped as he strove to escape the cook's unexpectedly viselike grip. Marigold fixed Rowan with her most imploring gaze. "Please! I'm begging you, Rowan!"

Rowan gave her a quizzical look, but nodded. "Oh, as you wish. Mrs. Spindle, please give the duck to Lady Avenbury."

The cook blinked. "But, my lord . . ."

"Do as I say, if you please."

"Yes, my lord."

Mrs. Spindle came disappointedly down the stairs, with Sir Francis still struggling for his life, and Marigold hastened to rescue him. The planned dinner was reluctantly surrendered, and the drake collapsed relievedly into the arms of the new Lady Avenbury. The cook shuffled bemusedly. Was his lordship's bride touched? She cleared her throat. "Would goose do instead tomorrow, my lady? Or mayhap a fine capon?"

Sir Francis's head came up indignantly, and he fixed the cook with a look of absolute outrage, Marigold spoke hastily. "No birds at all, Mrs. Spindle," she said, stroking the affronted mallard's head.

"No birds? But I'm famous for my birds, my lady," the cook protested.

Sir Francis's bill clacked as if he were momentarily rendered speechless by such openly murderous bragging, but then he let forth a decidedly vituperative broadside. Fowl language indeed, thought Marigold, as she was obliged to raise her voice above his racket to reply to the cook. "I assure you that I do not care to eat anything feathered, Mrs. Spindle."

"As you wish, my lady," Mrs. Spindle replied a little stiffly.

Sir Francis subsided, clearly satisfied that his neck—as well as those of some of his fellow birds—was now completely safe from the cleaver, but his ireful gaze remained upon the cook. If he had his way, it would clearly be Mrs. Spindle who was served up with gooseberry sauce!

Rowan nodded at the cook. "That will be all, Mrs. Spindle."

"My lord, my lady." Mrs. Spindle curtsied again, and hurried away toward the kitchen. Marigold was anxious not to get off on the wrong foot, and so called quickly after her. "Mrs. Spindle?"

"My lady?" The cook turned.

"Your choice would have been truly excellent. You were not to know I do not like to eat birds." Sir Francis gave a sour quack, and Marigold closed his bill with her hand.

The cook was mollified. "Will rack of Wiltshire lamb do instead tomorrow?"

"Yes, thank you."

"I will serve you the finest lamb you have ever tasted, my lady. And tonight, you shall taste my marbled ham. It's always been a favorite with his lordship."

"I look forward to it, Mrs. Spindle."

The cook hurried on her way, and Beech followed.

Rowan immediately turned to Marigold. "Since when do you not like to eat birds? I seem to recall that at Vauxhall you enjoyed a large plate of chicken and salad."

Sir Francis's head rose until he was eye to eye with Marigold, but she promptly pushed him down again. "That was then."

Rowan looked at the duck. "Why are you so certain it is the same mallard?"

"I just am."

"I have to admit it has the same obnoxious temperament. May I inquire what you intend to do with it?"

"Do with it?"

"Well, you pleaded for its life, and now you have it. What next?"

"I . . . Well, I suppose I'll just let him go. I'll do it now."

Two footmen were still unloading the carriage, and looked around in astonishment as the new Lady Avenbury emerged with a duck in her arms. Sir Francis wriggled as Marigold took him in both hands and made him look at her. "Maybe Bysshe did raise you in a demonic circle after all, for to be sure you aren't an ordinary drake. Anyway I want you to go away. Go back to Eton, or wherever it is you come from. If you stay here, Mrs. Spindle may forget herself after all!" Sir Francis muttered something derogatory beneath his bill as she placed him on the gravel, so she shooed him crossly. "Don't be so ungrateful. Go on, off with you," she said. He shook his tail, tweaked a flight feather or two, then suddenly took to the air, but he didn't turn for London, instead he disappeared into the gloom in the direction of the lake. Marigold listened to his diminishing wing beats, then went back into the house.

Rowan was still waiting, leaning back against a table with his arms folded. "Is it done?"

"Yes."

"Excellent. Now then, is it safe to conduct you around the house while we await supper?"

She smiled. "It *was* Sir Francis, you know."

"Whatever you say, Marigold."

"Are you humoring me, sir?"

"Probably. Come." He held out his hand.

As Marigold was shown room after room of the mansion of which she was now the mistress, she thought Avenbury Park was truly the finest house in England. It was grand, yet intimate, irregular, yet a magnificent harmony. She adored everything, from the rich dark oak paneling and exquisite Flemish tapestries, to the ornately carved Tudor furniture and fine old paintings. It was a house in which she could be very happy; if only . . .

At last they approached the dining room, which opened off the hall. Beech was waiting at the heavily carved door, which he flung open to reveal the room beyond. As they entered, a longcase clock in a corner chimed the hour. A five-branched candelabrum stood upon the gleaming table, and provided the only light. The walls of the room were dark paneled like the rest of the house, and portraits of past ladies of Rowan's family gazed down from gilded frames. There was a ham salad supper awaiting them on the gleaming table, with crusty fresh-baked bread, peaches from the glasshouse, and a bottle of white wine that was very cold from the cellar. Everything was arranged amid glittering crystal glasses and highly polished cutlery, and there were more flowers, marigolds, in honor of Lord Avenbury's new bride. Marigold smiled, for it was a welcoming touch which she appreciated, but she was still concerned for Sir Francis. She turned to the butler. "Beech, I trust the duck did not come back again?"

"No, my lady."

"Oh, good," Marigold replied with relief, for she knew only too well that her instructions to the cook regarding feathers would not make the slightest difference to what might be set before the servants themselves.

Beech hastened to belatedly draw the green velvet curtains at the east-facing French windows, that in daylight must face toward the common and the oak tree. After shutting the night out and seeing they were both seated, the butler withdrew with studied tact, leaving the newlyweds to their intimate *dîner à deux*.

Mrs. Spindle's marbled ham was delicious, as no doubt would have been her duck with gooseberry sauce, and in spite of Marigold's deep concern over what had happened at the oak, she enjoyed her first meal at Avenbury House. It was afterward, while she and Rowan were discussing how some fashions changed very little, that he drew her attention to a portrait that was well lit by the candles on the table. It depicted a woman in black, holding a baby in swaddling bands. Apart from the baby, the woman was reminiscent of Mary Tudor. Rowan smiled. "The first Lady Avenbury could appear at a funeral now, and not look out of place. Don't you agree?"

"The first Lady Avenbury? Is that who it is?" Marigold immediately got up and went closer. "Why is she wearing black?"

"Don't you remember what I told you by the oak? She, her husband, and the baby all succumbed to the plague. Lord Avenbury died first, and she was said to have been so griefstricken at his death that her baby son was born prematurely. They survived him by one month, before they too fell victim to the pestilence."

"How sad." Marigold was about to return to the table, when another portrait caught her eye. It was at the very edge of the candlelight, and was a full-length likeness of a young woman in a russet gown, and if the first portrait was like Henry VIII's unhappy elder daughter, Mary Tudor, this one was very like that same king's ill-fated second queen, Anne Boleyn. Going closer, a chill sensation of inevitability passed over Marigold, for the young woman was standing among marigolds, and her hand was raised, with one finger outstretched. On that finger was perched a robin with white feathers in its wings.

Rowan followed her gaze, and identified it rather reluctantly, or so she thought. "That is the lost portrait of Jennifer Avenbury. I fear it has yet to be properly cleaned."

Marigold held her breath as she gazed at it. The background, which was dimmed by nearly three centuries of smoke and grime, was divided in two, each half separated by twined marigolds. On one side was depicted the Avenbury circle, with the central oak tree surrounded by white-robed figures, druids presumably; on the other side was the lake, with waterfowl rising in a cloud as they had done when the carriage arrived. Some of the background was almost entirely smoke-darkened, but she could still see the important features. Jennifer Avenbury had a pale, heart-shaped face, with brown eyes that gave no hint of her character. She was pretty, at least Marigold thought she was, for it was difficult to tell from likenesses of that period. Her tawny hair was parted in the middle, then swept back beneath a pearl-studded headdress that was of a darker shade of russet than the richly decorated velvet and brocade gown. There were two necklaces around her neck, one a short golden chain from which hung an oval sapphire and pearl pendant, the other longer, so that its pendant, the jeweled initials J and A, rested against the gown's stiff bodice.

She turned excitedly to Rowan. "It must be an allegory, for it contains most of the elements of the legend and curse. The only person who seems to be missing is the first Lord Avenbury. Please bring the candles, I'd love to see more detail." As he brought the candelabrum over, she couldn't help noticing that he had the air of one who wished the painting had remained in the attic, but she didn't comment. "Why do you think she's standing in marigolds?" she asked, studying the painting.

"It may not mean anything. Perhaps she simply liked them, after all, they were a particularly favorite flower in those days."

She glanced curiously at him. Why was he so intent on playing down the portrait's significance. "Is that your honest opinion?" she inquired after a moment.

"Can you say I'm wrong?" he replied, not answering the question. Had he said "Let's talk about something else," his manner could hardly have been more pointed.

She decided to be direct. "What's wrong, Rowan? Why don't you want to discuss the portrait?"

"Marigold, until now *you've* been the one who has dismissed everything as chance or coincidence, but now I detect a definite volte-face. What happened to your absolute conviction that the legend and curse is all nonsense?"

"Perhaps I'm open to debate after all," she said after a moment.

He gave her an oddly disappointed glance, as if she'd failed him in some way.

"Have I said something wrong?" she asked anxiously.

"No, of course not. Marigold, the curse isn't a subject I enjoy discussing."

"Nor is it one you can ignore."

He gave her a wry look. "Especially when you're around, it seems," he murmured.

"I can tell that this portrait is important to everything, so please help me look at it," she entreated.

"You, my lady, are a very difficult woman," he said resignedly. "Very well, let us subject every brushstroke to a microscope." He held the candle really close, and they both gazed at the painting.

Almost immediately, Marigold gave another gasp. "There's a wheel lying among the marigolds! Why put it there, I wonder?"

"Heaven alone knows." He gave her a sideways glance, guessing her thoughts. "If you're wondering about what happened at the Spread Eagle, I suggest you stop. What possible connection can there be between that nonsense and the Avenbury curse? I don't think any significance can be attached to the wheel in this, any more than there can to the marigolds. Your imagination has the bit between its teeth. Why, earlier you even tried to drag that odious drake in it all."

"Because I think he is part of it. Rowan, there are mallard drakes in the portrait too. See? There, among the waterfowl on the lake. Are you going to tell me *they* happen to be Jennifer Avenbury's favorite too? And look here, there's also a spray of rowan in the grass! Oh, the more I look, the more strange things I discover. See the white-robed druids in the background? The one with an arm extended has black feathers instead of a left hand. Why is that, do you think?"

"Heaven alone knows. All right, I admit that you're right, there are things in the portrait which cannot with honesty be unconnected with the legend and curse, and if the wheel mentioned at the Spread Eagle had something to do with it—"

"It does. Don't you remember the little picture of the robin?" With the same white wing feathers as my Robin . . ."

"I've already bowed to your superior comprehension," he replied.

She smiled, and resumed her inspection of the portrait. "These white-robed figures remind me of a painting at Castell Arnold. Anglesey was a druid stronghold in Roman times, and—" She broke off as another intriguing thing caught her attention.

"What have you seen?" he asked quickly.

"Something else that connects the Spread Eagle with all this. You told me Falk Arnold was among those who frequent the inn, didn't you? Well, this druid here with the staff is the very image of him!"

Rowan leaned to look. "Good God, so it is." Then he drew back, as if the likeness to Falk wasn't the only thing he had suddenly perceived. He went to put the candelabrum down on the table. "Marigold, this may be something or nothing, but I think I should mention it. Do you remember I mentioned the occasion at White's when Falk was in his cups, and would have been thrown out but for Merlin? Falk claimed that one of his ancestors had been denied his rights by one of my ancestors?"

"Yes, I remember."

"Well, the figure you've singled out as being like Falk, is supposed to be Aquila Randle."

Marigold's lips parted in amazement. "What are you saying? That Randle may have been Falk's forebear?"

"Not *saying* exactly, but certainly wondering."

Marigold gazed at the portrait again. "So, at White's, Falk could have been referring to Randle's defeat by the first Lord Avenbury?"

"It's all conjecture, but . . ." Rowan shrugged.

"Rowan, when you told me the story of the curse, you said Randle's parting vow was that he would return to see the thirteenth and last lord die, that he would marry Jennifer after all, and that he would take your title and inheritance." She lowered her glance. "Falk has recently acquired a taste for stealing inheritances," she added quietly.

"Marigold, it's one thing to speculate that Falk may be descended from Randle, quite another to hazard that he may be about to take up the cudgels on Randle's behalf."

"Oh, believe me, it would be on Falk Arnold's behalf, not Randle's," Marigold replied dryly. Her gaze wandered back to the druid with the staff. The painting was less distinct now that the candlelight was further away, but even so she thought the figure was her unamiable brother-in-law to a T, so much so that the artist might have painted it quite recently instead of several centuries ago.

Rowan looked at the figure as well, and then made another rather reluctant observation. "Randle didn't spell his name the usual way. There's a specimen of his signature on some document in my lawyers' keeping. He signed himself R-a-n-d-o-l, which I've just realized is an anagram of Arnold."

Marigold gasped. "So it is!"

"More than that, the obsession with bird names extends to Randol as well, for Aquila is Latin for eagle."

"And Arnold means eagle power." Birds, always birds. Falk, Merlin, Peregrine, Alauda, Shrike, Crane, Robin Redbreast, Jenny Wren, even Sir Francis! She lowered her eyes, recalling Jenny's plea at the oak. *Help us, Marigold! Help us, please, before it's too late!* Now that so much had seemed to be shown in the portrait, should she tell Rowan about Robin and Jenny? She decided she would. "Rowan, after all this, I can't help accepting that there really *is* something strange in progress after all, maybe even that the curse is—"

He broke in quickly. "Please don't say anything more, don't think anything more, don't look for anything more!"

His unexpected vehemence took her aback. "Barely an hour ago you were exhorting me to believe!"

"I know, but I don't always say what I mean, or mean what I say."

"Rowan, I may usually be practical and always in search of a logical answer to everything, but there isn't a rational or natural explanation for all this, therefore we have to enter the realms of the irrational and supernatural."

Suddenly he put his finger gently but firmly to her lips. "I know, Marigold, but can't you see that I need you to be strong and scornful? That's why your volte-face feels almost like betrayal to me."

"Betrayal? Oh, but—"

"In twelve days it will be midsummer, and in the meantime I need you to argue, to pour disdain upon it all, to make me hope the whole business is a nonsense. Please, Marigold."

His vulnerability in that moment was so affecting that tears sprang to her eyes. She loved him so fiercely that to defend him she would have faced Satan himself. She would certainly confront whatever lay behind this portrait!

Slowly he removed his finger from her lips, and kissed her. Then he smiled into her tear-washed eyes. "Don't cry, my lady, for the night—and our marriage bed—awaits. Come." He took her hand and led her from the room.

Chapter Eighteen

Marigold awoke the next morning with Rowan's arms around her. Outside it was a sunny June morning, and she could hear the peacocks on the lawns. She gazed at the cream velvet bed hangings, and the tasseled golden ropes that tied them back to the dark carved oak posts. They were in her apartment, the one that was always set aside for the lady of the house; Rowan's apartment was a little further along the passage, and occupied the prime position above the main entrance.

She snuggled closer to him inhaling his warm masculinity, and putting her lips to the soft hair on his chest. Oh, this was paradise, and how wonderful the night had been, making love with him until the small hours before falling asleep in an embrace. Heaven help her, she loved him to distraction, and at a moment like this she didn't want to think about anything threatening, but she knew she must, for as he had pointed out, there were only twelve days to midsummer. She tried to be her usual sensible self, finding a commonplace explanation for it all, but it didn't work. How could it, when a robin followed her from Anglesey, and a wren spoke? And when so much could be read into a mere painting? She rested her cheek against Rowan's chest, and closed her eyes. If she accepted that it was really happening, she also had to accept the curse, but for Rowan's sake, she knew she must hold her tongue. Last night his vulnerability had cut into her heart like the sharpest knife, and if she could spare him any pain at all, she would.

Rowan stirred, and his arms tightened around her. "This is a very pleasing awakening, my lady," he murmured.

"I find it so too, my lord," she whispered.

"I still cannot believe that Merlin Arnold was so great a fool as to desert your bed," he said softly, pulling her on top of him, so her red-gold hair tumbled forward over her shoulders, and her nipples brushed his chest. He put his hand up to run his fingers through her hair.

She felt him hardening and pressing between her legs, and closed her eyes with pleasure. *Let these moments never end. . . .* But the moment did end, indeed it was shattered by an urgent knocking at the door. Her eyes flew open with dismay, and Rowan looked irritably toward the sound. "Yes?"

"It's Beech, my lord. Please forgive the intrusion, but I *must* speak with you."

"Can't it wait?"

"I fear not, sir."

"Oh, very well, I'll see you in her ladyship's dressing room directly."

"My lord."

Rowan sighed, and then looked up at her. "The pleasures of the flesh must wait, I fear," he said, putting his hand to the nape of her neck and pulling her mouth down to his. Then she rolled reluctantly aside as he flung back the bedclothes, and grabbed his dressing gown. She then drew the bedclothes warmly around herself, then watched as he went through into the adjoining dressing room, leaving the door ajar. She heard the ensuing conversation.

"What is so important that I must be disturbed, Beech?"

"My lord, I would not presume, but the situation is, er, delicate."

"Delicate?"

"The landlord of the Royal Oak has come running to report an overturned wagon at the village crossroad, and—"

"Beech, with all due respect, I fail to see how this can be termed delicate."

"I must relate it all, for you to understand, sir."

"Oh, very well. What about this wagon?"

"It's carrying the luggage of a lady who is about to stay with her brother, the new tenant of Romans."

"So there *is* a new tenant? I wondered when I saw lights there yesterday."

"Oh, yes, my lord, the agent arranged it all a week or so ago."

"Go on."

"The tenant is expecting a large party of guests, his sister included, and she sent her belongings ahead by this London carrier, a very vulgar and quarrelsome fellow by the name of Starling. Anyway, it seems he missed the sharp turning to Romans, and only realized when he reached the village, so he tried to turn his wagon, but it overturned, and spilled its entire load. Naturally, the villagers hurried to help, but instead of showing gratitude, the fellow leveled a shotgun at them and vowed he'd shoot anyone who so much as came a step closer."

"Good God."

"It's true, my lord. And there he sits now, refusing to let anyone near, and saying that the only persons with authority to say who can and cannot handle the property are the lady herself, who has yet to leave London, or her brother at Romans."

"Well, I trust someone has had the sense to send word to Romans?"

"Yes, my lord, but the gentleman was out. A message was left, but that was an hour ago. The crossroad is completely blocked, other traffic cannot pass, and tempers are running high. The innkeeper fears someone could be killed, and that you are the only person to whom this lunatic may listen."

"Who in heaven's name *are* these people I have at Romans?"

But butler cleared his throat. "This is the rather delicate point, my lord," he replied.

"How so?"

Beech's voice dropped out of Marigold's hearing. There followed a brief silence, and then Rowan answered. "Very well, I will be ready directly."

"My lord."

Beech left the dressing room, and Rowan returned to the foot of the bed. He seemed a little unsettled. "Marigold, I fear I must go out to deal with an incident in the village. After that I have estate matters to attend to, and will breakfast as I can. I should be free by the middle of the afternoon, but trust you will be able to amuse yourself in the meantime?"

"I am well able to amuse myself, my lord," she replied, wondering greatly about the tenant of Romans and his sister.

"I will send Sally, and give instructions that your breakfast is to be served here. Then you may do as you please, for you are now mistress of this house." He turned toward the door, then paused to smile back at her. "Be assured that I have not forgotten our unfinished, er, business."

She smiled back, but when he'd returned to his own apartment to dress, she pondered the overheard conversation. Why had the butler believed the identity of the new tenant was too delicate for the ears of Lady Avenbury? What's more, why did Rowan apparently think the same?

Sally came as promised with a breakfast tray of scrambled eggs, toast, and tea, and while Marigold ate in bed, the maid laid out the clothes they decided upon. Marigold had finished breakfast, washed, had her hair combed and pinned, and had begun to dress in a black-spotted white muslin morning gown when she heard a faint tapping at the bedroom window. It was Jenny Wren. Marigold glanced quickly at Sally. "That will be all now, Sally, I can finish myself."

"Very well, madam." The maid bobbed, and hurried away.

Marigold immediately opened the casement. "You *are* Jenny Avenbury, aren't you?" she asked, somehow knowing that the wren would understand.

"Yes." To anyone else the wren sounded as if she called tic-tic-tic, but Marigold heard the spoken word. Jenny hopped closer. "Help us, help us, please."

"But how?"

"Come. Come now."

Jenny flew to the walnut tree that grew outside, where Marigold saw Robin was waiting. "Come where?"

"Ride, ride," called Jenny.

Marigold nodded. "All right, I'll get ready."

"Quick, quick."

Without calling for Sally again, Marigold dressed as quickly as she could in her riding habit. Word was sent to the stables to prepare a horse for her ladyship, and within ten minutes she was hurrying down to the hall in her sage green habit and brown hat, her white gauze scarf floating behind her. A groom had saddled a fine roan mare and brought it to the front of the house, together with a horse of his own, indicating an intention to accompany her.

"I will not require an escort, thank you," she said, as he helped her to mount.

"But, my lady, you don't know your way around."

"I know enough to ride one way and then retrace my tracks. I'll be quite all right."

"Well, if you're sure . . ." he said doubtfully.

She kicked her heel before he could deliberate further, and the mare scattered the gravel of the drive as she rode swiftly away. In a moment Robin and Jenny were flitting from tree to tree beside her. "Quick, quick," sang the wren.

At the lodge the lodgekeeper snatched off his hat respectully on seeing who rode past. "Good morning, my lady."

"Good morning," Marigold called back.

For some reason she expected the birds to lead her toward the village, but instead they went in the opposite direction. "This way, this way," Jenny urged, skimming low over the road as it crossed one of the four causeways that gave access over the wide moat. Almost immediately the birds left the road and turned toward the escarpment around the foot of which Marigold and Rowan had driven the day before. The land began to rise steadily out of the valley, and after a while she reined in, unable to resist the temptation to look back at Avenbury.

The scene below was laid out like a patchwork, with the great henge easy to pick out as it swept around the village and the common. The water in the moat shone in the sunlight, and the standing stones seemed almost white. The little flock of sheep grazed again near the great oak, watched over by the boy with his dog, and the mellow sound of the church bell echoed through the shimmering summer air. At the crossroad in the village, she could see how the overturned wagon was blocking the way.

Her attention moved to Avenbury Park. The house was a jewel in the filigree of its formal Tudor grounds, and the standing stones and moat had been skillfully blended into the design of elegant formal flowerbeds and topiary trees. A wooden bridge led over the water to the lawns that swept gently to the serpentine lake, which she could now see wound eastward along the foot of the escarpment. She noticed a small boathouse among some weeping willows, and a jetty where a flat-bottomed skiff was moored. The reedy shores were ideal for the immense variety of ducks and other waterfowl that had converged on one of the few stretches of water in this chalky region. As she watched, something disturbed the birds, which rose in a noisy flock, then settled again a little further along.

Robin and Jenny were impatient. "Hurry, hurry! Must see!" cried the wren, swooping low above Marigold's hat.

"See what?" But the two small birds flew swiftly on, and she had to urge the mare after them. Where were they taking her? What were they so anxious she should see?

Chapter Nineteen

The escarpment air was sweet with the scent of wild thyme, and blue butterflies danced above sward that was lavishly sprinkled with wildflowers. Sandstone boulders were dotted around, and did indeed look like sheep, Marigold thought, conceding that to call them graywethers was actually very appropriate. A few windblown hawthorns and the occasional rowan tree had found root in the thin layer of soil that covered the white chalk, and clumps of yellow gorse bloomed here and there. Skylarks tumbled high above, their wonderful bubbling song rippling across the warm mid-June sky. Oh, how criminal to name someone as disagreeable as Alauda after such a glorious songbird, Marigold thought as she continued to follow Robin and Jenny.

It wasn't long before she realized the birds were leading her toward the eastern end of the escarpment, where Rowan had told her there were ancient fortifications believed to have been a Roman camp. The closer she rode to the edge of the summit, the more oddly undulating the land became, and at last she saw that the dips and rises in the land were linear earthworks created countless centuries before. Whoever occupied this site would not only have found it easy to defend, but also a superb lookout point. Robin and Jenny dipped down into a hawthorn bush that grew out of a tumble of graywethers right at the edge of the descent, and when she reined in next to the bush and looked down, she saw she was directly above the house and former hunting tower called Romans.

The grounds were flanked by curtains of trees that stretched right down to the foot of the escarpment, but the house enjoyed a fine uninterrupted view. It was a three-bayed stone building, with a fine wrought-iron veranda extending all around the ground floor. A matching balcony surrounded the floor above, and the original square, ivy-covered hunting tower still rose sturdily from one end. The incline from here on the summit down to the house was very steep indeed, but the quarter of a mile or so from the house to the valley was much more gentle, with open grounds and a long drive that curved down to the road along which she and Rowan had driven the evening before. Just visible beyond one of the curtains of trees, was the eastern extremity of the lake, and a jetty like the one at Avenbury Park. To the rear of the house, just before the steepness of the incline became too great, there was a small walled apple orchard, with a white summerhouse where someone was seated. It was a gentleman, but all she could see were his gleaming top boots and the newspaper he was reading.

Hoofbeats carried on the air, and she looked down the drive to see a horseman riding slowly up the drive. She immediately recognized Rowan. As he disappeared from her view at the front of the house, Robin and Jenny hopped urgently from branch to branch of the hawthorn bush. "Follow us! Follow us!" the wren urged in her odd tic-tic tones, then she and the robin flew down the hill toward Romans.

Marigold gazed uneasily, down the steep slope. Was it safe to attempt to ride down? The answer was definitely not, so she hurriedly dismounted to tether the mare to the bush. She stole one last glance at the house, and was in time to see a maid hurry into the orchard to tell the man in the summerhouse that Lord Avenbury had called, then she began to clamber down the incline.

"Quick! Quick!" called Jenny.

"I'm doing the best I can!" Marigold protested through clenched teeth as she slithered a little. The rest of the descent proved just as fearsome a scramble, and she slipped once or twice, leaving grass stains on her riding habit, but at last she was by the orchard wall, in which was set a sturdy but weatherbeaten wooden door she hadn't noticed from up the hill. The door was so overgrown with ivy and weeds that it had clearly not been opened in years, but Robin and Jenny fluttered to the top of the wall above it, and the wren urged her again. "Come here! Come here!"

"I can't go through *that*!" Marigold whispered back. It was all very well for them, they could fly!

"Look through! Look through!"

Look through? It was a solid oak door! But then she saw a hole where a small knot had fallen out, and she put her eye to it to peer into the orchard. The view was very restricted, only a few of the apple trees and part of the summerhouse, and although she couldn't see him, she could hear Rowan's voice. It was raised in anger, but she couldn't make out what he was saying. Of the other man she heard and saw nothing at all, although Rowan was plainly speaking to him. At length there was silence, and she caught a brief glimpse of Rowan striding away. The man in the summerhouse called mockingly after him. "You cannot win, Avenbury! I'm invincible!"

Marigold started with shock. Falk! So this was what Robin and Jenny were so anxious she should know! Her heartbeats quickened uneasily, and she drew back from the spyhole as if the door had suddenly burned her skin. She leaned against the wall, her thoughts in a whirl. What was Falk doing here? Then she remembered the overturned wagon. The new tenant's sister. Alauda was coming here too! Was that what Rowan would have learned if he'd kept the assignation requested in the note? It was certainly why Beech had felt it prudent to tell Rowan in private about the "delicate" matter of his new tenant's identity.

Suddenly there were two small squeaks of fear, followed by the whir of little wings, and she looked up sharply to see Robin and Jenny flying away. They fled up the hillside into a dense hawthorn tree, and disappeared. Marigold straightened warily as she heard the beat of much larger wings. A dark shadow passed over her as a black carrion crow landed where the smaller birds had been. It tilted its glossy head to gaze down at her, then began to flap and caw loudly. Fearing Falk would come to investigate, Marigold gathered her cumbersome skirts and began to hurry up the slope as best she could, hoping to reach the shelter of the hawthorn bush, but the crow followed, fluttering directly overhead, still giving its loud, croaking calls.

Long before she reached the bush, she heard someone trying to push open the door in the orchard wall. The ivy resisted for a while, then suddenly gave way, and the rusty hinges complained as the door was shoved roughly. Its hinges groaned as it swung out from the wall, then Falk emerged, and his eyes shone as he saw her clambering up the steep hillside about fifty feet above him. The crow immediately pulled away toward him, and disappeared over the wall into the orchard.

Falk smiled thinly. "Well, well, if it isn't Lady Avenbury. Congratulations on your second marriage, my dear. Clearly I underestimated you." She was so rattled to find herself confronting him, that her voice seemed to have frozen. He enjoyed having her at a disadvantage. "What a pity your union with his lordship is doomed to be brief. Still, no doubt you will make the most of your few remaining nights together."

Such words could only remind her of the white-robed figure with the staff in Jenny's portrait. *Was* he connected in some way with Aquila Randol? She had to probe. "Doomed? Few remaining nights? Oh, Falk, surely you don't believe that old tale about a curse?"

"It's no tale, my dear, as I imagine you well know by now."

"I pay no heed to such superstitious nonsense, and I must say I'm rather surprised at you, Falk."

"Play the cynic all you wish, Marigold, it's immaterial to me."

"Why are you so sure I'm *playing* at anything?"

"Because it has been my mission to find out," he replied.

"Mission?"

A pale smile twisted his lips. "You may have thought to outwit me by marrying Avenbury, but it will avail you of nothing. There will be no gain for you, my dear, whereas *I* . . ." He allowed the sentence to die away meaningfully.

"Whereas you what, Falk?"

"You'll soon know."

She felt a chill touching her skin, and pulled herself together angrily. He was toying with her, and she didn't seem able to best him. Somehow she had to convince him she was a stronger, cleverer opponent than he'd thought. She met his gaze full square. "And you will soon know that my second marriage will not only be far happier than my first; but will also endure for far longer. Rowan isn't doomed, nor am I playing the cynic." Oh, brave, defiant words . . .

Falk's eyes became virtual slits. "So, the cards are on the table, are they? I knew on the day of the will that you were not quite what you pretended to be, but be warned, although you may have the power, it is as nothing beside mine. I will crush you if you presume to oppose me."

The power? What power? "Are you so certain you can defeat me?" With a huge effort she forced herself to keep meeting his gaze.

He found this amusing. "Certain beyond all doubt," he said softly. "Someone may have filled your head with your own importance, but whoever it was mistook your small ability for something far greater."

His confidence was frightening. She longed to run away, to put as great a distance between them as possible, but she knew she had to face him out. *He* had to be the one to bring the meeting to an end. He continued to look at her. "Well, my dear, aren't you going to congratulate me?"

"Upon what?"

"My forthcoming midsummer marriage. The shortest night is appropriate for joyous celebrations that will go on from dawn to dawn. Don't you agree? You may be sure that you and Avenbury are invited. Oh, and my nephew Peregrine, of course."

Uneasy thoughts skimmed alarmedly through her mind. "Who is the bride?" she asked, although she was sure she already knew the answer.

"I will leave you to guess, my dear."

"Jenny Avenbury?"

Slowly he took a silver snuffbox from his pocket, and made much of flicking it open. "My, my, I certainly did misjudge you, didn't I?"

What else could she believe now except that she and Rowan had been right to connect him with Aquila Randol? "Was Randol your ancestor?" she demanded bluntly.

"Why, Marigold, what an unending source of wonder your perspicacity is proving to be. Perhaps I begin to understand my brother's infatuation after all." As he applied a little snuff to each nostril, his eagle ring caught the sunlight.

"You won't succeed in whatever it is you're planning, Falk. I will see to that."

He chuckled. "The time has come, and nothing can turn it back. Just remember that I have warned you not to tamper with things that are beyond your capabilities and understanding."

"And I now warn you. Leave my husband alone, or you will find out you have underestimated me more than you think," she replied. She was amazed at herself. Inside she was little more than jelly, so where on earth was she finding her nerve?

Her manner suddenly annoyed him intensely, and he struck back with words that hurt her more than even he could have hoped. "His ring on your finger means nothing, my dear, for it is Alauda that he loves and she will be here later today. You will see little of him then, of that you may be certain." He smiled as for a moment she couldn't hide what she felt, then he turned to go back into the orchard. He spoke again without looking back at her. "Oh, yes, be on your guard for the crows in these parts, they're rather large and bad-tempered, and can be quite a hazard." He stepped into the orchard, and dragged the door to again.

Marigold stared down at the torn ivy, which continued to tremble after the door had closed. Her mouth was dry and the small of her back damp with perspiration, but there was still something steely inside her. He had to be defeated, and there were twelve days in which to do it! Twelve days! Grabbing her skirts, she scrambled inelegantly up to where she'd left her mount, and hauled herself with difficulty onto the sidesaddle. There was no sign of Robin and Jenny as she urged the mare back to Avenbury.

Chapter Twenty

When Marigold arrived back at Avenbury Park and handed her mount to a waiting groom, she saw Rowan leaning on the bridge at the bottom of the formal gardens. He did not seem to have heard her return, for he was gazing pensively down at the water, his top hat swinging idly between his hands. There was something unapproachable and remote about him in that moment, and she hesitated. What absorbed him to such an extent? The curse? His confrontation with Falk? Or the fact that his mistress would soon be nearby? Whatever it was, his wife needed to speak to him about what had just happened at Romans. Hoping that what he said would allay her fears about Alauda, if not about Falk's connection with the curse, she smoothed her rather rumpled riding habit, and walked toward him.

Two peacocks moved out of her way, their beautiful tail feathers dragging through some sweet-smelling herbs, so that the fragrance was released. Bees hummed drowsily in the roses, and beyond the bridge and the gently sloping lawns, the lake shimmered in the summer heat. The waterfowl were peaceful, floating upon the waveless surface, or sleeping contentedly at the reedy margins.

As she drew closer to the moat, she became acutely conscious of the dark, looming silence of the standing stones, and when she walked between two of them in order to step onto the bridge, she felt as if they were waiting to pass judgment on her. It was an odd notion, and she ticked herself off for becoming ready to believe absolutely anything. Suddenly a peacock flew to the top of the stone to her right, and began to call loudly. It gave Marigold such a fright that she cried out, and Rowan immediately turned. He dissembled as he saw it was she, but not before she saw the shadow of brooding irritability on his face. It was gone in an instant, and he smiled. "And did my lady enjoy her ride?" he asked, coming to meet her.

"Yes, thank you," she lied.

He drew her gloved hand to his lips, and then noticed the grass stains on her clothes. "What happened? Did you fall?"

She didn't want to admit her inelegant scramble down the slope behind Romans, and so told a white lie. "Yes, but it wasn't much, just a lack of concentration."

"Are you all right?"

"Yes, I assure you."

"You should not have gone without a groom, anything might have happened to you." He smiled again, and led her to the parapet.

She looked down at the channel of cool, deep water. The banks on either side were cloaked in flowers, from lupines and delphiniums, to sweet williams, pinks, and nasturtiums. At the water's edge there were exotic rushes and yellow flags. Water lilies, pink and waxy, floated on the moat, and large dragonflies whirred above the surface. It was such a pleasure to the eye, that she did not want to recall that two hundred and seventy-three years ago, fleeing druids had drowned in these watery depths. But the recollection *was* there, and because of Falk, she had to speak of it now. She wanted him to broach the subject of the tenant at Romans, and so tried to prompt him. "Did you accomplish your tasks?"

"Tasks?"

"The overturned wagon, and then the estate business."

"Oh, yes."

She waited for him to mention Falk, but he didn't say anything more. So she tried to prompt him again. "Was the carrier really brandishing a shotgun?" she asked lightly.

"With great vigor, but I managed to soothe him. The wagon was righted, the spilled load collected, and I should imagine he is delivering it all at Romans at this very moment."

Why didn't he mention Falk? Clearly a direct question was required. "Who is the new tenant?" she asked.

"No one I know. His name means nothing to me. Carruthers, I believe."

Her heart sank like a stone. It wasn't Falk's presence he was trying to keep secret, but Alauda's! Why else would he be so unforthcoming? "How strange," she said, "I thought this morning that Beech believed you were acquainted with him. Why else would he think the situation was delicate?"

"I didn't realize you could hear what we were saying."

"Only some of it. Wasn't I supposed to?" She glanced at him.

"It was hardly a secret conversation. Actually, I have no idea why Beech thought it would be delicate." He pointed along the water. "Look, a kingfisher," he said in a deliberate ploy to divert her.

Such determination not to say anything reconfirmed her suspicion about his intentions regarding Alauda. Salt tears burned Marigold's eyes, but she kept them back as she watched the bright blue-green bird dart from the bank into the water, and emerge with a silverfish in its bill. She was hoist with her own petard. How could she now tell him what she'd learned at Romans? To do so would be to expose his lies! Oh, how she wished she'd brought the whole business up at the outset of the conversation, but it was too late now. In a quandary, she leaned over to look at the water again.

Rowan had been watching her profile. "Is something wrong, Marigold?"

"No, of course not. What could possibly be wrong?" Summoning a smile, she faced him again. "You seemed very preoccupied when I got back. What were you thinking about?"

He drew a long breath. "Actually, I was considering your former brother-in-law."

The reply caught her off guard. Was he about to tell her after all? "Falk? Why?"

"It seems we were right to connect him with Aquila Randol."

"Oh?" *I know, Rowan, for I have heard it from Falk's own lips . . .*

"Yes. This morning I received a missive from his lawyers, informing me that he is laying claim to my title and estate."

She looked away, and bit her lip. So that was why he'd raised his voice in the orchard. She thought for a moment. "Rowan, don't misunderstand what I'm about to say, but is it possible that there is an inkling of truth in the claim? I only ask because Falk seems so amazingly fortunate with the law at the moment."

"The claim is baseless as far as I know, but I'm certainly not laughing it off. Legal clarification after a span of nearly three hundred years won't be easy, and the minutest detail will be examined over and over again." He put his hand over hers on the parapet. "But whatever happens, you and Perry will remain secure. I can say this because my title and the Avenbury inheritance are not my only income, so I am well able to provide for you. Falk cannot steal everything from you a second time, I promise."

"Oh, Rowan . . ." In spite of her wretchedness over Alauda, her fingers curled in his.

"This is one case Falk Arnold will not win," Rowan said softly as he pushed a stray curl of her hair back beneath her riding hat. Then he bent his head to brush his lips tenderly over hers.

But tender or not, she knew the gesture meant nothing. He had studiously omitted to say he'd spoken to Falk at Romans less than an hour ago, and thus had not been obliged to mention Alauda's imminent arrival either. The reason seemed painfully manifest. She drew unhappily away, and glanced back toward the house. "I—I ought to write to Perry. He wants to know all about Avenbury Park."

"I have things to attend to as well, so I'll escort you," Rowan said, and offered her his arm. As they left the bridge, the peacock that had startled her earlier, flew noisily away from the standing stone. Rowan gave a rather forced laugh. "Maybe it fears that the stone is about to do a jig," he said.

"What do you mean?"

"Oh, it's a local nonsense. At certain times of the year, all the stones are supposed to uproot themselves and dance around the village. Then they go down to the water to slake their thirst, before returning to their positions." Rowan halted, and so she had to as well. "As a matter of curiosity, touch the stone, Marigold."

"Touch it?"

He nodded. "Some people claim to feel ancient forces. Randol did. I've tried, but nothing happens at all, in fact, I've never come across anyone who actually experienced anything!"

Slowly she reached out. The stone felt cold and unyielding, just like any stone, but just as she was about to take her hand away again, suddenly a sensation of great heat struck through her fingers. She tried to snatch her hand away, but couldn't. The stone seemed to tilt and move, as if the entire henge were revolving. She heard a commotion on the lake as all the waterfowl rose simultaneously. The birds' noise seemed to thunder through her, and everything began to spin. She saw Robin and Jenny, but they were people, a beautiful young Tudor woman in a russet gown, and her dashing lover in a scarlet doublet and brown hose. Jenny extended an imploring hand. "You must help us, Marigold! We need you to save us, save us, save us . . ." Darkness began to close in from all sides.

Rowan's arm was strong around her waist as she swayed. "Marigold?"

The darkness retreated, and the world slowly steadied. It was just a warm June day again. Her frightened eyes fled toward the lake, and she saw the waterfowl settling quietly once more. She remembered what Falk had said. *You may have the power, Marigold, but it is as nothing compared to mine.* Was what had just taken place an example of the power he was referring to? If so, he would certainly be amused—and relieved—that she had no idea how to use it!

"Marigold?" Rowan turned her to face him. "What happened?"

"I—I'm not sure."

"You felt something, didn't you?"

"Yes. The stone suddenly became intensely hot, and then everything began to turn, like one of those merry-go-rounds at fairs. I heard the birds on the lake . . ." Remembering his vulnerability the night before, she made no mention of Robin and Jenny.

"The waterfowl? Yes, something startled them."

It was me, it was what I did when I touched the stone, she thought, recovering apace and deciding to make light of it. "Anyway, I'm all right now. Maybe it had nothing to do with ancient forces, and I just felt a little faint because I didn't eat enough breakfast," she said.

"That must be rectified immediately, come on." He put his arm around her waist again to support her, but then paused to make her look at him. "I didn't frighten you with this business of the stones, did I?"

"No, of course not."

He didn't seem quite convinced. "Are you really sure?"

"Yes."

As they continued toward the house, she glanced back over her shoulder. For a moment it seemed the stones were moving again, but it was only an illusion.

Chapter Twenty-one

Marigold's wretchedness over Rowan's untruthfulness was made all the worse that night, because she slept on her own. She had cried herself to sleep, and now awoke just before dawn to find he'd never come to her bed. She lay gazing at the mantelpiece clock, wondering if he was still out, or if he'd returned and gone to his own apartment. He'd left shortly after dinner the evening before, saying something about assisting his gamekeepers to lie in wait for an organized gang of poachers, and he told her not to stay awake waiting for him. She didn't believe the story about poachers, for she was convinced that Alauda had now arrived, and somehow had sent a message to him. He and his mistress were keeping a tryst, while his heartbroken wife lay on her own in the marriage bed.

As always in the hours before dawn, all problems assumed monumental proportions. Some of them *were* monumental, of course. The curse, for instance. It was surely impossible to overcome, and even though she now knew she possessed an ability of some sort, not only did she have no idea how it could be employed, but there was no one she could ask. Then there was her love for Rowan, which second by wretched second seemed increasingly fated to remain unrequited. There were lesser things too, such as the fake note at Berkeley Square, and the false message from "Lady Crane" at Vauxhall Gardens. Alauda had clearly realized about the latter at Vauxhall Gardens, but until now hadn't yet had a chance to tell Rowan. As to the matter of the note, the first thing Alauda would demand at the tryst would be why Rowan hadn't delayed his departure from London and met her as requested. He would cite the second note, of which Alauda would deny all knowledge, and from there it would be a simple matter to deduce that the forger and the mimic were one and the same! Marigold's stomach churned anxiously. Rowan didn't want his wife meddling in his private life, but meddle she certainly had. What would he have to say to her when he returned?

Suddenly she felt too unsettled to lie there any longer, so she got up, put on her slippers and the pink muslin robe that lay over a chair, then went to the window. It was misty outside, and she could only make out half the garden. The bridge and moat were obscured, and everything was silent. She turned restlessly back into the room. When she couldn't sleep, some hot milk usually worked. Why shouldn't she do the same here? It would certainly give her something to do, and might take her mind off the endless circle of worries. After dragging a hairbrush through her hair, she left her apartment.

The kitchens were deserted, but she soon found the pail of milk standing in water in the stone trough under the sink. Soon she had a relaxing hot drink to take back to her room, but as she emerged into the hall, the dining-room door caught her attention. It stood slightly ajar, and the night light on the hall table reached faintly as far as Jenny's portrait. Marigold hesitated. Had she and Rowan missed something vital the other night? Maybe now, when everything was quiet, she could concentrate more. Catching up her skirt, she went into the room.

The longcase clock ticked slowly as she cradled the glass of hot milk in her hands, and gazed at the painting. "Oh, Jenny, I wish I knew what is wanted of me," she murmured. "I know my help is needed, and I know I have a power, but that is *all* I know! How can I save you and Robin if I don't know what to do?"

Her attention was drawn to a French window that had recently been installed in the wall, between Jenny's portrait and the one next to it. The sound that made her look was the familiar tapping of tiny bills upon the glass. With a gasp, she put down the milk, and went to pull back the heavy green velvet curtains. As she opened the window and went out, the little birds flew off without making any more contact. Puzzled, she gazed through the early dawn light after them. Why had they come, only to immediately fly away again? She glanced around. The window opened on to a balustrated terrace that reached along the rear of the house. There were lawns beyond it, and a path that led past the kitchens and stables toward a ha-ha that separated Rowan's land from the common. A mist had risen again, although it wasn't as dense as on the evening she and Rowan had arrived at Avenbury. A few village lights glowed dimly, and she could just make out the oak tree, around which . . . She stared incredulously, for white shapes were making a slow circuit of the oak, as if in a dreamlike country reel. The stones were dancing! But then she realized it wasn't the stones. *People* were dancing, people like specters in cowled white robes!

Her heart quickened uneasily. Who were they? Jenny's portrait flashed into her mind. Druids? No, that couldn't be, for there weren't any druids now. Or were there? The likeness of Aquila Randol, so very like his descendant, Falk, slipped into her mind as well. Aquila and Falk. Randol and Arnold. The same letters, same bloodline . . . The fear she'd felt at Romans returned, and she wanted to hurry back to the safety of the house, but knew she couldn't. Robin and Jenny had deliberately drawn her out here, and she was as determined to help them as she was to help Rowan. Slowly she walked toward the steps at the far end of the terrace, then down the path, where she began to hurry toward the ha-ha.

But the nearer she drew to it, the more conscious she became of how very exposed the common was. The first breaking of the new day on the eastern horizon lent such an eerie luminosity to the mist, that instead of concealing her, it seemed to make her more observable. Her only chance of not being seen was a small clump of brambles about twenty yards beyond the ha-ha. She climbed down the wooden steps against the retaining wall, went cautiously up out of the dip at the bottom, then peeped toward the oak again. The white figures were still moving in a slow circle, and did not seem to have noticed her, so she bent low to run to the brambles. Once there, she lay on the grass to peep out from beneath the thorny canopy. The strange dance continued, and now that she was closer, she was sure she could hear a low murmuring sound. Were they talking? No, it was rhythmic and repetitive chanting, male voices saying the same few words over and over again. There were thirteen men altogether. A coven? Did druids have covens? No, that was witches, who didn't wear white robes!

Marigold studied the only figure carrying a staff. There was more than just the staff to mark him as the leader of the gathering, for there was a crown of mistletoe around his cowled head, and every now and then she glimpsed the gleam of a golden torque at his throat. She wondered if it was Falk, aping the rites and ceremonies performed by his forebear. The more she thought about it, the more likely it seemed. Falk had commenced moves to purloin Rowan's title and property, and at Romans had openly warned her that her marriage was doomed to be brief. He'd admitted to fully believing in the curse, boasted of his incredible abilities, and hadn't even bothered to deny that it was Jenny he soon meant to marry. What more proof was required? Of *course* it was Falk, and he was here to repeat the ritual of midsummer's day, 1534, and to carry out Aquila Randol's vows of revenge!

Marigold felt chilled to the marrow as she gazed at what was happening by the oak. Who were his accomplices, she wondered? They were clearly the guests he expected at Romans, and maybe one was Alauda. When chanting, the voices all sounded male, but that did not mean there weren't women among them. As she watched, the figures halted, fell silent, and bowed their cowled heads toward the oak. Falk stepped forward and held up his arms, brandishing in one hand the staff, and in the other something small that she couldn't make out. Then he moved to the tree, and used the staff, which was topped with a bronze sickle, to slice off a little of the mistletoe, after which he struck the tree trunk three times. Two other figures then approached him, and one lit a flame from a tinderbox, while the other held out something wrapped in a white cloth. He took the offering and placed it on the grass with the mistletoe, then he accepted the flame and held it to the offering. Marigold prayed it wasn't anything alive, for she knew that the druids were famed for their sacrifices, some of which had been human. But there was no sound as both mistletoe and white cloth caught fire.

She craned forward, and in the process caught her arm on the brambles. The pain made her gasp, and the thorns tore at the delicate pink muslin of her fashionable London wrap. Dismayed, she disentangled herself, and rubbed her arm. She was sure she hadn't made much noise, but suddenly a huge black crow swooped noisily down from nowhere. Flapping and cawing, it snatched at her with its talons, and she tried desperately to fend it off. Her hair and clothes became more and more caught up in the brambles, and soon she was hopelessly ensnared. The figures had all turned toward the disturbance, and to her terror, they began to advance, but then a pistol was fired nearby. The crow shrieked and fell to the grass with a wounded left wing, but managed to haul itself into the air again and fly unevenly away. To her relief, the figures took to their heels in the direction of the road. Then there were hoofbeats as they escaped on horses they had left tethered there.

Shaken, she cast desperately around for the owner of the pistol, but then a door opened at the nearest cottage, and someone with a gruff voice held a lantern aloft and shouted. "What's going on out 'ere! Who fired? Show yourself, or I'll 'ave all 'is lordship's men on you!"

"It *is* his lordship, Hazell, I dropped my pistol. All's well. I'm sorry to have disturbed you." It was Rowan who answered, and she saw him emerging from the dip of the ha-ha, tucking the pistol into his coat. She felt suddenly close to tears.

"Very well, my lord," the gruff voice replied.

Lights now appeared at other village windows as awakened villagers peered out to see what was happening, and Beech emerged from the kitchen garden of Avenbury Park with a lantern and a shotgun. Rowan turned toward him. "There's nothing wrong, Beech, I was a little clumsy with my pistol, that's all." The butler bowed, and withdrew, looking very different in his nightshirt, with his luxuriant hair down past his shoulders.

When all was quiet again, Rowan hurried over to Marigold, and began to gently free her from the unkind hold of the brambles. She was ice-cold with shock, her face was scratched, and her robe now more torn than ever. Tears pricked her eyes as she sat up, and out of nowhere she thought what her mother would say right now. *Marigold Marchmont, you look as if you've been dragged through a hedge backward!* She felt an odd urge to laugh, but then Rowan suddenly gripped her shoulders and shook her.

"What in *God's* name are you doing out here?"

"I—I saw them from the house, and came to see."

"It was a stupid thing to do!" he snapped.

"I didn't think. I thought I was safe here by the brambles."

"Well, you weren't. If I saw you running from the ha-ha, so might they have. As it was that damned crow gave you away. What if I hadn't been close by?"

"Why *were* you near, Rowan?" The question had an edge.

"I was returning to the house and saw what was going on by the oak."

"Returning from where?" she asked, looking accusingly at him.

"Does it matter?" he replied, helping her to her feet.

"Yes, Rowan, it does."

"You know what I've been doing. I've just spent a very uncomfortable night with some of my keepers, lying in wait for poachers who didn't turn up. As I returned my horse to the stables, I saw those fools cavorting in white vestments!"

"You don't really expect me to believe that, do you?" she replied, brushing grass and bramble leaves from her ruined wrap, and then inspecting the scratches on her arms and legs."

"Yes, I do expect it. I'm not in the habit of lying to you, Marigold." He took off his coat and placed it around her shoulders.

She struggled to keep control of herself, but her emotions were all awry and suddenly she couldn't hold back anymore. "Nor are you exactly in the habit of confiding, instead you judiciously omit to tell me things of a *delicate* nature! You've been with Alauda, haven't you?"

He was startled. "Alauda?"

"Don't play the innocent, Rowan. I know she's joining Falk at Romans. Why didn't you tell me?"

"Because I thought it would upset you unnecessarily."

"How thoughtful."

Her acidity angered him. "And how, pray, do you know about who is at Romans?"

"I rode that way yesterday, and saw you meeting Falk in the orchard."

"Did you indeed? Well, that is a fact that *you* omitted to mention, is it not?" he pointed out tersely.

"Because I realized you weren't going to say anything!" she retorted resentfully.

"My sole reason was consideration of your feelings. As to Alauda, I haven't seen her or been in contact with her since the night at Vauxhall. Now, you either accept my word, or you don't."

Marigold looked away. What of the note that was concealed in the cherry tree? Wasn't *that* to be termed contact? A crushing response blistered on her lips, but she forced it back.

He tried to temper his anger. "Alauda isn't at Romans yet, Marigold," he said in a more conciliatory tone.

"Really? Well Falk told me she was arriving yesterday."

His lips parted. "You actually spoke to him?"

"Yes."

"And if he says something, ergo it is the truth, the whole truth, and nothing but the truth. By God, Marigold, your talent at prosecution would pass muster in a court of law!"

"If I'm crossexamining you, sirrah, it is with good cause! For instance, how can you be so very sure Alauda isn't at Romans?" she cried.

"The implication being that I am *au fait* with her movements?"

"Yes."

"Well, you're wrong, my lady. All I know is she isn't at Romans and therefore she must be somewhere else. And how do I know? Because I have had a man watching Romans ever since I discovered who my new tenant is! At sundown last night, Falk was still alone in the house. Will that suffice?"

"Well, clearly at least twelve guests have arrived since then," she replied. "The figure with the staff was Falk, I'm sure of it. Just as in the portrait."

"I think you are right, but I have no idea if Alauda was also there. Marigold, I will not discuss her further. Have I made myself clear?"

"Oh, perfectly."

"God be praised. Now, before we return to the house, I want to see what our white-garbed friends were burning, but you are to stay here."

"Stay here? But—"

Furiously he overruled her protest. "By all the saints, madam, you test my patience and the old words to the full. How does it go? The blithe and thrifty marigold for obedience? As far as I can see, you may well be blithe and thrifty on occasion, but obedient you are not. Now, do as I tell you!"

The outburst startled her into silence, and she remained where she was as he walked away toward the oak. She pulled his coat more closely around her shoulders. It was warm from his body, and smelled of costmary. She watched as he crouched by the curl of smoke that still rose from the grass. Then he stood to stomp whatever it was with his boot, and began to return. He was still some yards away when more hoofbeats broke the dawn, a single horse this time, being ridden at a headlong gallop through the village. There was sufficient light for Marigold to catch a shadowy glimpse of the rider urging his mount toward the lodge. He had disappeared into the mist again by the time Rowan reached her.

"Who could that have been?" she asked as the hoofbeats died away.

"Heaven alone knows," he replied.

She looked at him. "What was being burned by the oak?"

"Just leaves of some sort."

"Mistletoe, yes, I saw it being cut, but what was in the cloth?"

"I've just told you. Leaves."

"More leaves? What sort?"

"It was all ashes, and no one thought to leave an explanatory note," he replied sarcastically.

She flushed a little. "Rowan, about Falk—"

"I don't intend to embark upon that again," he interrupted shortly.

"But I have to tell you something."

"It can keep. Marigold, I'm tired and becoming rather cold, and I don't think you should remain outside any longer either. Mrs. Spindle and the rest of the kitchen staff will be awake by now because it's baking day. She keeps a medicine store and will have something ideal for administering to your scratches. Come on." He caught her hand, and led her back toward the ha-ha. From there they went directly to the kitchens, where lights now shone as the staff went about their duties. The smell of toast and fried bacon swept out as he opened the door and ushered Marigold inside.

Chapter Twenty-two

In the kitchens, Rowan and Marigold were greeted by a very odd scene, although later she had to concede that it was hardly more startling than the sight she herself must have presented, with Rowan's coat around her shoulders, her scratches, and badly torn wrap.

Beech and Mrs. Spindle were bending attentively over an ashen-faced young man whose teeth chattered audibly. Several wide-eyed maids stood nearby, and one of them squeaked in alarm as Rowan opened the door without warning. Mrs. Spindle was startled as well, and dropped the cup of sweet tea she was holding to the young man's lips. It fell with a crash that echoed like a report through the otherwise silent kitchens. Everyone stared at Marigold, who could only imagine what they all thought had been going on outside!

Rowan looked curiously at them all. "What's afoot here? Who's this?" he demanded, nodding at the young man.

The latter scrambled nervously to his feet. He was small and weedy, with damp, spiky hair and drab brown clothes. He was breathing heavily, and his teeth continued to chatter as he gave his name. "I—I'm S-Spiky Blackth-thorn, s-sir."

"That conveys nothing to me," Rowan replied.

Beech cleared his throat. "Begging your pardon, my lord, but he is a messenger, and he had something of a fright on the highway when he was almost ridden down by a large group of riders in white robes. He believes they were ghosts."

"Not ghosts, I assure you," Rowan replied.

"N-not ghosts?" Spiky repeated.

"Definitely not. Just some fools in fancy dress."

Spiky breathed out with relief. "Cor, that's a relief," he muttered, swallowing as he tried to pull himself together.

Rowan looked at him. "You have a message?"

"Oh, yes. It's for Lady Avenbury." Spiky searched in the leather pouch that hung from his belt.

"For me?" Marigold was surprised.

"Here it is, my lady," Spiky said, holding out a rather creased letter.

She took it, and immediately recognized Perry's writing. Oh, no, what had happened? Had he and Bysshe misbehaved beyond redemption? Quickly she broke the seal. It was dated at Eton the previous evening.

> "Dearest Mama.
>
> I was right, it *is* the chicken pox! Bysshe and I have both been struck down, and Dr. Bethel says that as soon as arrangements can be made, we are to be sent home to recuperate. The thing is, Bysshe's family are in Ireland, and their house shut up for the summer. So can he *please* come with me to Avenbury Park? He would dearly like to, and he would be excellent company for me. We promise faithfully not to get in your way, or Lord Avenbury's.
>
> Your loving son, Perry.
> P.S. *Please* say it is all right.
> P.P.S. Did I tell you you were the prettiest bride that ever was?
> P.P.P.S. Sir Francis has gone at last. Horrah!"

That afternoon Marigold slowly retraced her steps toward the ha-ha. The sun was high, and the peacocks called on the lawns. She wore a cherry-and-white gingham gown that was tightened beneath her breasts by a little drawstring, and her red-gold hair was twisted up on top of her head, with several ringlets tumbling over her left shoulder. Mrs. Spindle's balm—marigold, naturally—had soothed the bramble scratches, but it would take a great deal more than that to soothe emotions that were stretched to infinity with wretchedness.

Marigold blinked back tears. She so wanted to believe Rowan about Alauda, but knew he had lied about having no contact since Vauxhall. If he lied once, the law of probability decreed that he most likely lied again now. And there was the added fact that he had gone to his own apartment to sleep. Then, when he'd risen just before noon, he'd taken breakfast alone before going out on his horse. In fact, she hadn't been able to speak to him at all since dawn when he granted permission for Perry to bring Bysshe to

Avenbury Park to recuperate. He still knew nothing of her conversation with Falk, or that she was convinced it was Falk who had led the ceremony around the oak. There were now eleven days to midsummer, and she knew some sort of plan should to be made. She had no idea what, except to persuade Rowan to run away with her, to some secret place where Falk wouldn't be able to reach him.

She crossed the ha-ha, and then walked past the brambles toward the oak, which looked so innocent in the bright June sunshine. The tree rustled gently in the lightest of breezes, and the ball of mistletoe shone golden, looking almost like the oak's heart. She could see where Falk's sickle had sliced off a spray, and on the grass below, scattered quite widely because Rowan had kicked them, were the charred remains of the fire. There was half burned mistletoe, and fragments of the white cloth, which she now saw had contained a marigold flower and rowan leaf. When Robin had brought the same things to her at Castell Arnold, she had glimpsed Falk's fear for the first time. What did it mean? Her heart began to thud unpleasantly, for what other interpretation was there except that Falk's malice was directed at her as well as Rowan? She was in Jenny's portrait, and therefore part of it all!

At that moment hoofbeats drummed urgently toward her. Unnerved, she shrank back against the tree with a frightened cry, but as the sweating horse was reined in within a foot of her, she saw Rowan looking down at the telltale remnants of marigold and rowan, and then into her wide eyes. The mettlesome horse danced around excitedly as he held a hand down to her. "I thought to spare you the knowledge that they burned our namesake leaves. But that is of no consequence now, for I have come to give you proof about Alauda." He seized her fingers and swung her effortlessly up to sit astride behind him. "Hold on tight, madam, for this is not going to be a leisurely trot!"

She had no option but to grip him around the waist as he kicked his heels, and the horse leapt away toward the road, then west toward the escarpment. It was the same way she had ridden. The thyme-scented air was warm, and she could feel the lithe flexing of his body as he controlled the horse. She pressed her cheek to his back, and closed her eyes. She was angry and hurt by his deception, but oh, how she adored him. Until him, she had never truly known what love could be.

At last Rowan reined in, and she opened her eyes to see they were at the earthworks above Romans. He dismounted, and then held his arms up to her. "Come on." She slid down to him, but he released her the moment she was steady. After tethering the horse to the same bush she had used, he led her to the edge of the escarpment, directly above the house. "Get down on the ground," he said then, getting down himself.

"But—"

"Do you wish to be seen against the sky? Get down!" He grabbed her hand and pulled her to the grass.

Together they peered over. There were a number of people in the orchard, all of them men except Alauda, who suddenly appeared on the upper floor balcony. She wore a bright apricot gown and chestnut spencer, and her raven hair was pinned up beneath a stylish leghorn bonnet. Everyone turned as she called out to them all. "I'm here at last! Oh, *what* a tedious journey!" Then she gave her odious tinkling laugh, and hurried toward the hunting tower end of the balcony, where a wrought-iron staircase descended to the orchard.

Marigold looked at Rowan. "What does this prove? So your mistress is here now, but who is to say she wasn't here last night as well? She may just have driven to Salisbury or Marlborough."

"She may indeed, except that if you look at the front of the house, you will see her traveling carriage being divested of her usual unconscionable amount of luggage."

The carriage was identifiable as Alauda's by its bright sapphire blue lacquer and vivid scarlet wheels. Two grooms and the coachman were examining the wheels, which appeared to have suffered some damage. Rowan glanced at Marigold. "She has just arrived from London, I assure you. I happened to be with my lookout down by the road when her carriage came in sight. It was going very slowly because that wheel was giving the coachman cause for concern. What with that, and the fact that it's a long steep drive up the hill to the house, and the horses are tired, I knew I would have time to get you here. *Now* will you believe me?"

"I—I . . ."

"Perhaps you'd prefer me to draw one of your teeth?"

"Oh, very well. Yes, I believe you."

"Thank heaven for small mercies."

"Do you mean to see her now she's here?"

"No, because I don't intend to go any closer to Romans than we are now. I have informed Falk that his tenancy will not be confirmed, and that I expect my property to be vacated as soon as possible."

"He won't comply."

"Then I'll take a leaf from his book, and resort to legal action."

"He'll rub his hands with glee."

Rowan raised an eyebrow. "We'll see," he replied, then took a pocket telescope from his coat. "My lookout tells me numerous carriages have arrived since sundown yesterday, all with their blinds down, so let's see who the shy occupants were." He trained the telescope on the gathering in the orchard. "Well, I'll be damned," he murmured.

"Who can you see?"

"Look for yourself. You know some of them." He handed her the telescope. She peered through and suddenly the faces in the orchard seemed to leap closer. Lord Toby Shrike and Sir Reginald Crane were there, with Lords Stonechat and Siskin. Judge Grouse of Moorchester was there, along with Archdeacon Avocet and the Reverend Spoonbill. The famous actor, Jonathan Dove, was with Mr. Crowe, the lawyer, and the renowned accoucheur, Sir Hindley Tern, was deep in conversation with the Prince of Wales's friends, Lord Dunnock and Viscount Swallow. She lowered the telescope, and looked at Rowan. "I know all of them," she said.

"Really?"

"They came to Castell Arnold, and I met them from time to time when I was obliged to come out of seclusion to attend some tedious function or other at the castle."

"They are among the highest and most famous in the land, and I've encountered them all at White's in recent months. Few of them are members, they were brought by either Falk or Merlin, and they all made a point of engaging me in conversation," Rowan said softly, taking the telescope and looking through it again. "A surprising aviary, eh? If we exclude Alauda, there are twelve birds, thirteen with Falk himself."

Marigold swallowed. It was just as she had suspected, the white-robed figures were Falk's guests. She hesitated, and then decided it was time to tell him all she knew. "Rowan, I must let you know what Falk said to me. It's very important."

He met her eyes. "If it concerns the curse, as I'm sure it does, I would still prefer not to know. Ignorance is sometimes as close to bliss as one is able to get."

"You can't be an ostrich about this, Rowan, you *must* listen."

He looked away. "Very well, if you insist, but I hear you under protest."

She told him everything that had passed between Falk and her, and at the end, she said, "I'm sure I'm right about it all, Rowan. In eleven days' time, Falk is going to attempt to carry out Randol's vow of revenge, even to somehow transforming Jennifer Avenbury back into a woman, and making her his wife. He boasts of his powers, and maybe he really can do it."

Rowan had listened unwillingly at first, but had gradually become intent upon her every word. Only when she finished, did he say anything. "Much as it grieves me to admit it, I think he is quite capable of transforming birds into people, and vice versa. I fancy the evidence is in the orchard right now."

"Evidence?"

"Look at the lawyer. What do you see?"

Through the telescope, she searched for Mr. Crowe. He and Jonathan Dove were now strolling toward the house, and apart from the fact that the lawyer's left arm was in a sling, she couldn't see anything else particular about him.

"Well?" Rowan prompted.

"I don't know what I'm supposed to be looking for."

"Don't you notice *anything* about him?"

"Only the sling."

"Yes, on his *left* arm."

She looked at him in puzzlement. "I still don't understand."

He pointed to her scratches. "How did you come by these?"

"It was the brambles, and the crow—" She broke off in shock.

"Exactly. The crow I shot in the *left* wing. Think of Jennifer's portrait. One of the robed figures in the background had black feathers instead of a left hand." He paused. "Did you hear what they were chanting at the oak?"

"No."

"May the wheel turn, may the wheel turn," he said softly.

"Oh, that wretched wheel. Apart from it being in the portrait, I can't begin to think what it means."

"There's no mention of such a thing in the legend, not that I know of anyway. Unless, it's the simple business of going *around* the oak."

Marigold considered it, but then shook her head. "I don't think that's it."

"Nor do I, really." Rowan drew a very long breath. "Marigold, I don't simply think the twelve men down in the orchard are Falk's followers, I think they're Randol's as well. They're the twelve devotees who in 1534 were transformed into birds so they could all escape."

Marigold's green eyes widened. "The actual men from the sixteenth century?"

"Yes."

"Which means that Falk Arnold is—?"

"Aquila Randol? Yes."

Chapter Twenty-three

There was a moment of stunned silence as both Marigold and Rowan stared down at the scene below. That Falk might be copying his ancestor was bad enough, but that he might actually *be* that ancestor, was a little too unsettling.

Rowan gave her a quick smile, and put his hand briefly over hers. "Well, I suppose it's no more bizarre than anything else."

"Bizarre wasn't exactly the word that sprang to my mind," she replied.

"Nor really to mine, but it's more agreeable than some of the ones that did."

Marigold glanced at him, wanting so much to tell him about Robin and Jenny.

He met the glance. "What is it?"

"Rowan, I have more to say."

"About Falk?"

"Well, in a way. I've wanted to tell you before, only you wouldn't let me, but now that so much has been said, you really should know the rest."

"I give in gracefully, but let's come away from the edge here. On the assumption that Falk can turn his little nest of feather-headed acolytes into real birds if he wishes, I don't really fancy being swooped upon by the likes of Lord Toby Shrike, who looks as if he would quite enjoy impaling us upon something suitably sharp. There's a little hollow just the other side of these gray-wethers, where we'll be safe from detection." He drew her down into the small dip in the grass, and there took off his coat, loosened his neckcloth, then lay back beneath the heat of the June sun. "Right, now tell me whatever it is."

Cool in her gingham gown, Marigold lay at his side among the wild thyme and other scented wildflowers. She gazed at the flawless blue sky. "Before I met you, I knew something very odd was going on, indeed it started at Castell Arnold when the robin flew out of a rowan tree and caused Merlin's death." She told him everything that had happened since then.

When she'd finished, he gave her a rather wry smile. "Perhaps I should have known too."

"Why?"

"Well, I told you Jenny's portrait was discovered in the attic, but what I didn't say was that it was found because a bird was trapped there, and a footman was sent up to get it out. The bird was a robin, and it lighted on the portrait, which was under a cloth behind an old cupboard. In his efforts to catch the bird, the footman pulled the cloth off, and realized he'd found a lost portrait. The robin then flew out of its own accord, the footman came down and mentioned his discovery to Beech, who told me. I went up to investigate, realized whose portrait is was, and had it brought down."

"Did you see the robin?"

"No."

"If you had, I'm sure it would have had some odd white feathers in its wings."

Rowan plucked a piece of wild thyme, and rubbed it between his fingers. "You know you wondered the other night if that damned mallard was connected with it all? Well, given all that's become clear since then, I've just thought of an amusing coincidence. The first Lord Avenbury was named Francis."

"Really?" She smiled and turned her head to look at him. "Why do you think Jenny can speak to me, but Robin can't?"

"Marigold, the abilities of supernatural birds are a mystery to me," he replied with a slight laugh.

She sighed. "Jenny keeps begging me to save them, but I don't know what to do. All I'm certain of is that I have to be at your side to fight the curse, and that's why marigolds appear in Jenny's portrait. On the day of the will, Robin brought me a marigold and rowan leaf in front of Falk, and I saw for a moment that Falk was alarmed. Now he and his friends have burned the same plants at the oak. He knows that while I'm with you I am a threat to his plans. Rowan, I'm sure I have a strength or power of some sort, for I felt it yesterday when I touched the standing stone, but I don't know what it is or how to use it. Falk is aware of it, but is satisfied that his strength is much greater. He regards me as something of a single candle next to his blazing sun!"

Rowan answered a little teasingly. "Don't belittle yourself,

madam, for Robin and Jenny are relying on your candle. And so
am I, come to that."

"Don't joke, it's not funny."

"All right, let's be serious again. Something puzzles me. Why
do you think Robin caused Merlin's death? After all, it helped
Falk, not you. Because of that single event, he was able to create a
will to suit himself, and take Castell Arnold from Perry."

She suddenly perceived the answer. "By removing Merlin,
Robin freed me to marry you!"

"But it was pure chance that brought us together at the Spread
Eagle!"

"Was it?" She looked intently at him. "You said you stayed there
because your appointment at Windsor Castle took much longer
than expected. Why did it take longer?"

"Well I . . ." He drew a long breath, and then laughed a little
sheepishly. "There was a robin in the Queen's apartment, and her
ladies were having the vapors. It took some time to quieten
things."

"I hazard it was our robin. You see? It wasn't chance after all!"

"All right, I accept that chance probably had little to do with it,
although how it could be foreseen that on such minute acquaintance I would ask you to marry me, I fail to see."

"Rowan, you are the one who has always believed in fate. I'm
in the portrait, and so I have to be here. Therefore you asked me
because you were bound to. And if Robin and Jenny's interest in
me is anything to go by, I'm not meant to be a helpless bystander.
There is something I have to do. Robin and Jenny know I can help.
They aren't ordinary birds, they're supernatural, and Jenny can
speak, so why doesn't she *tell* me!"

"Being supernatural may not mean she actually knows. Maybe
you have to find out for yourself."

She turned her head to look at him. "I'm determined everyone
is to live happily ever after."

He laughed. "As in the best fairy tales?"

"Yes!" she said fiercely. "I'm not going to let Falk and or a miserable old Tudor alchemist dictate *my* fate! Nor yours, nor Robin's
nor Jenny's. Nor Perry's, come to that."

"What a veritable tiger you are, Lady Avenbury."

"I fight to defend what I love and what is mine."

"I know you do."

"I'll fight to keep you from Alauda," she said suddenly, hardly knowing the words were there until they'd been said.

He smiled a little regretfully. "I, er, fear I haven't been entirely fair with you concerning Alauda. The fact is I don't love her anymore, nor is she still my mistress. It's over."

Marigold sat up to stare at him. "Over?" she repeated incredulously. "But, why didn't you tell me?"

"Oh, reasons . . ."

"When did it end?"

"From the moment you told me she was party to what Falk perpetrated at Castell Arnold. How could I love someone who was capable of such spite?" He smiled up at her. "Especially when the victim is so very, very fascinating, being not only an amazing forger, but a gifted mimic as well." He assumed a lisping tone. "Oh, Alauda, Alauda, you'd betht know the earl is therching for you!" Marigold was dumbstruck. Even without speaking to Alauda, he'd *known* it was her? Her stunned silence amused him. "As to the note you composed so carefully, did you really think I wouldn't recognize my own paper and ink? I knew Alauda hadn't sent that second note, but as I had no intention of complying with the first, I fear you labored in vain, Marigold."

"If you wish to make me feel foolish, you're succeeding."

He pulled her back down to the grass, and leaned over her. "The last thing I wish to do is make you feel foolish, Marigold," he said softly, drawing a thyme-scented fingertip gently across her lips. "The truth is, I was flattered by your efforts to obstruct Alauda. No, that's not strictly true, for I'm *still* flattered."

"You're my husband, Rowan, and I didn't intend to share you with her."

"You've never had to share me."

"But I would have had to at Vauxhall Gardens if I hadn't followed you, wouldn't I?" she said quietly.

He shook his head. "No. I know what it may have appeared to you, but in fact I was leading her on, with every intention of informing her the liaison was over. I'm afraid I was punishing her for her treatment of you."

"How astonishingly ungentlemanly, my lord."

"I agree, but in mitigation I offer the fact that I had just discovered how little of a lady she really was."

She smiled, and couldn't resist reaching up to touch his cheek. "Well, my husband, I am a very determined wife. I'm not going to let Falk succeed in *anything* on midsummer day! This legend is mine too, remember? And I only believe in happy endings," she whispered.

He took one of her ringlets in his hand, and parted the strands between his fingers. "I wish I could believe too, but I can't. Marigold, I didn't tell you it was over with Alauda because I was afraid you would feel too much for me, and be hurt because of what I think must happen in eleven days' time."

"I'm going to outshine his beastly sun!" she said determinedly.

"Marigold—"

She broke in. "Anyway, it's too late to prevent me from feeling too much."

"I can only bring you heartbreak."

"That I suffer already, but I would rather endure an age of heart-break because of you, than never have met you at all."

"Oh, Marigold . . ." He put his lips softly to her forehead.

She gripped his arms. "Rowan, if you no longer love Alauda, do you think you will ever be able to love me?"

"Oh, foolish, adorable Marigold, don't you realize that I already do?" he breathed, and bent his head to kiss her.

Her arms slid joyously around him! She loved and was loved, and her heart was so full of happiness she thought it would burst. His kiss became more urgent, and she felt the sensuous brush of his tongue against hers. His scent filled her nostrils, so heady and masculine, so arousing . . . He untied the drawstring on her gown, and her bodice parted to allow his hand to cup her breast. Her nipple was hard and so sensitive to his touch that her breath caught with pleasure. His lips moved from her mouth to her throat, and then down to her other breast. He took her nipple into his mouth, drawing upon it and flicking it with his tongue until she almost cried out with delight.

She felt him drag her skirts up, and then undo the front of his breeches. She held her breath with excitement as he pushed into her, filling her with his entire length. For a long moment he did not move at all, but simply lay joined with her. She felt how he throbbed within her, then he leaned up to look into her eyes. They gazed at each other as he began to withdraw and then reentered. His strokes were long and leisurely, becoming gradually more and more imperative. She could feel herself reaching out toward some-thing wonderful, a doorway into ecstasy. They crossed the threshold together, and were swept up into a glory of emotion and color that was so magnificent that she felt tears on her cheeks.

They lay together afterward, still joined, their hearts beating close, their fingers and limbs entwined. There was complete understanding between them, a shared intimacy so precious that neither of them wished to break it. Love enveloped them both, as warm and glowing as the sun itself.

Chapter Twenty-four

Two afternoons later, while awaiting Rowan's return from some business matters in Salisbury, Marigold walked alone toward the bridge over the moat. Knowing that Rowan loved her gave her a new strength and determination, and she had thought long and hard about what she might be able to do to halt the seemingly relentless march of the curse. Neither Robin nor Jenny had come to her again, so she was no wiser concerning her role, and all she could think of was touching the standing stone again, to see if she could glean some understanding of her power.

The air was very warm and still as she reached the stone. As before, the atmosphere surrounding it was very strange, and so she didn't go too close. First she needed to summon her courage. When she touched it the first time, the experience had not been pleasant, and Rowan wasn't here to catch her if she fell again. She swallowed and bowed her head for a moment, trying to concentrate fully upon what she was about to do. There mustn't be anything to distract her . . . She inhaled deeply, savoring the summer sweetness of all the flowers. Everything was quiet. So quiet. Slowly she stepped closer, and stretched out her right hand to the cold stone.

Almost immediately the searing heat blazed through her fingers once more, seemingly almost to make her one with the stone. The world tilted, as if the sun were about to tumble from the heavens, and she felt the great stone circle of Avenbury begin to turn. The birds on the lake were aroused again, flapping wildly skyward as if upon a secret signal. Their cries were so piercing they seemed to echo through her as she struggled not to lose consciousness. She began to see things. Everything was spinning as blurred shapes came into focus. Robin and Jenny, lovers, their arms entwined, their faces pale with fear. Marigold tried to call them, but she had no voice. She extended a hand. She was holding something, but what it was she did not know. The lovers' faces brightened with desperate hope "Yes! That's it!" cried Robin.

"The painting! The painting!" called Jenny, her voice almost lost in the shrill racket of the waterfowl. "Look at it, Marigold, look at it! The truth is there! We can't tell you more, for you must find the answer yourself. You are the one, only you!"

Robin looked pleadingly at her. "Nine days, Marigold! You only have nine days!"

She longed to ask more, but the lovers were fading again, and all she could do was try to reach after them with whatever it was in her hand. What was it? Why couldn't she see? The whole world seemed to be hurtling around now. Everything was indistinct, and the noise of the birds was so loud that it hurt her ears. The sky began to splinter, and the sun fell slowly through into an awful abyss. The birds' cries reached an earsplitting crescendo as darkness closed in, and she knew no more.

She awoke to find herself lying on the path. Beyond the soaring height of the standing stone, there was an immaculate blue heaven, where the sun shone steadily, and safely. Everything was calm and still, as if nothing had happened, she could even hear a bee on a nearby rose. She closed her eyes with relief, but then they flew open again as something hard jabbed her head. She sat up with a frightened gasp, then laughed at herself because it was only Sir Francis. The mallard was beside her on the path, and had prodded her with his bill.

"Hello," she said, and gingerly put out her hand to touch him. He rattled his bill, and shook his tail.

"I wish you could speak," she said wistfully.

"Quack," he replied sympathetically, and stretched his wings. For a moment she thought he was going to fly away, but he didn't. She glanced at the standing stone, and recalled her vision, or whatever it was that had overwhelmed her. "What was I holding in my hand?" she murmured, to herself. "Robin said it was the right thing, but I couldn't see it."

"Quack," muttered the drake, clacking his bill again.

"And Jenny told me I must find the answer in the painting, but Rowan and I have looked and looked at it. I'm sure there's nothing more to see." Catching her skirts together, she got to her feet, but as she tried to walk back up the path, the mallard deliberately waddled in front of her, almost tripping her up. Then he stood up

as tall as he could, so that he looked very long and thin, and he
gave her a look that could only be described as highly indignant. It
was very plain he wanted something of her.

She hesitated. "What is it?" she asked.

"Quack," he replied, then stretched up to pull at her skirt with
his bill. She was reminded of a child that wanted to be picked up.
Was that what he wanted? Uncertain, she bent to him, and when he
didn't back away, she gathered him into her arms. It was exactly
what he wanted, for he made a satisfied little noise, and shuffled
comfortably. This was definitely *not* an ordinary duck, she
thought, as she carried him toward the house.

She encountered Beech as she went inside, and his eyes
widened when he saw Sir Francis, but he bowed his head respectfully. However, a young housemaid who was just emerging from
the dining room was startled because the mallard gave a loud, suspiciously mischievous quack. Dropping her duster, the girl fled toward the kitchens.

Marigold halted and gave Sir Francis a shrewd glance. "You
enjoyed doing that, didn't you?" His bill rattled, almost as if he
were sniggering, and she studied him. "Just how much do you
understand, mm? Your ability to convey your feelings with a
single quack is quite amazing." He gazed back at her, and after
a moment she carried him to Jenny's portrait. Was there something that she hadn't noticed before? After a while, she sighed.
"Well, sir, I'm supposed to find the solution, but every time I
look, I only see what I've seen before," she murmured to the
drake.

Sir Francis became restive. He wriggled and squirmed, began to
quack very loudly and seemed quite upset. "Do be still," Marigold
chided, and was rewarded with a highly indignant glare, so she put
him down on the floor. Ruffled and somewhat peeved, he gave her
another very dire look, then fluffed his feathers, and waddled
along the room. When he was about twelve feet from her, he
turned and directed a vocal broadside that more than conveyed his
displeasure.

"You're quite impossible," Marigold declared, becoming more
and more certain that he understood far more than any mallard
should.

His response was something very like a derisory snort, but
then she forgot all about him as through the far window she saw
a carriage coming along the drive. It wasn't very grand, indeed

it was a rather old post chaise, with an equally old postboy seated on the lead horse. As she looked, one of the chaise windows was lowered, and Perry leaned out. With a glad cry, she gathered her skirts and ran from the room. She positively flew across the hall, and out beneath the porch just as the chaise rattled to a standstill.

Perry flung the door open and leapt down to run to her. He was pale and clearly far from well, but his delight on seeing her again could not have been more warm. He hugged her tightly. "Oh, Mama! How good it is to be with you again!"

She laughed. "Instead of conjugating Latin verbs and applying your dubious intellect to mathematical problems?"

"That's not fair!"

"No, but it's probably true." She turned as Bysshe climbed down as well.

He had been pale before, and was more so now. He gave her a sheepish smile. "Good afternoon, Lady Avenbury."

"Hello again, Bysshe. May I call you Bysshe?"

"Oh, please do."

"Well, I'm afraid Lord Avenbury has gone to Salisbury, but he will be back this evening. In the meantime, I don't know how unwell you both are. Do you wish to retire to your rooms to rest?"

To her surprise they both nodded. They must indeed be ill, she thought. "Very well, I'll have Beech show you the way. Come inside. Would you care for some refreshment?"

"Just a drink of cordial," Perry said, and Bysshe murmured his agreement.

As they entered the house, the boys paused to gaze around the hall. A shine of anticipation crept into Bysshe's eyes. "Oh, gosh, this place is magnificently atmospheric," he breathed. "First those standing stones, and now the very house where the Avenbury curse—"

"Bysshe!" Perry gave him an angry look. "Have a little tact!"

Bysshe blinked, and then looked apologetically at Marigold. "Forgive me, ma'am, I—I didn't mean . . ." His voice died away as something caught his eye in the dining room doorway. It was Sir Francis, who didn't make a sound, but just gazed at the two boys.

Perry looked too. "Oh, no! Not *you* again!" he cried. Sir Francis responded with a quack that verged on the smug.

Bysshe sighed. "We didn't bring him with us, ma'am, truly we didn't!"

"I know. He arrived at the same time as Lord Avenbury and me, and was very nearly served up on a platter."

"Pity he hadn't been," Perry muttered.

The mortified quack with which this remark was greeted made Marigold certain Sir Francis could understand. That being so, she was equally certain he was part of the puzzle. Each time she'd touched the stone, the birds on the lake were involved. And they were in the background of the portrait.

Bysshe turned helplessly to Perry. "What are we going to do with him? He's such a pest, he's bound to get in the way of—" He broke off sharply, and glanced a little guiltily at Marigold.

"In the way of what?" she asked.

"Oh, nothing really."

"Not experiments, I trust?"

"Oh, no, ma'am," he replied earnestly.

"Perry?"

Her son was all innocence too. "Certainly not, Mama. We don't intend to attempt any experiments at all."

"So we aren't going to be treated to more satanic circles, electrified doorknobs, and the like?"

"No, Mama."

"See that is so." But she was still mistrustful. They were a little *too* angelic. "What exactly have you brought with you?" she asked, seeing the footman carrying in several large trunks.

"Lots of books," the boy replied together.

They still looked furtive, she decided, and the obvious reason was something concerning the curse. Better to nip any schoolboy schemes in the bud, she decided. "Very well, sirs, if it is only books, they had better not deal with the foolish legends surrounding this house. If I discover either of you in any mischief on the matter, you will be on your way back to Eton *tout de suite*. Is that clear?"

"Yes, Mama."

"Yes, ma'am."

She turned to Beech, who waited dutifully nearby. "Show Master Perry and Master Bysshe to their rooms, Beech, and see they are served some cordial."

"My lady. Come this way, young sirs," the butler said, and bowed to the boys.

As they followed him, Sir Francis waddled across the hall and then fluttered up the staircase behind them. Marigold heard Bysshe's stifled exclamation of annoyance, but neither boy tried to shoo the mallard away. Clearly they were resigned to his tenacity. Sir Francis was a demon indeed when it came to doing as he pleased.

Chapter Twenty-five

It didn't take long to find out what Perry and Bysshe were up to, indeed it became clear that very night, although at first all seemed well. Rowan had returned from Salisbury, and he, the boys, and Marigold dined together. During the meal, there was no indication of approaching trouble, although the relish with which both boys devoured Mrs. Spindle's superlative cooking made their claims to illness seem increasingly specious. Rowan and Marigold remained at the table afterward to discuss everything yet again, and for a while Perry and Bysshe stayed with them, but then decided instead to adjourn to the adjacent billiard room, which also opened onto the terrace. There was still no hint of what was to come when they returned to the grand parlor at about eleven o'clock to say good night, and then retire to their beds. But schoolboy plans were afoot, as was soon to be revealed.

In the meantime, Rowan and Marigold's intensive dining room debate continued. The curse was raked over, then raked over again. She told Rowan about her second experience at the standing stone, and they tried to decide what form her supernatural ability actually took, but all it seemed to be was a susceptibility to visions or hallucinations. Having failed to pinpoint the power's form, they turned their attention to the painting, but although they scrutinized it for well over an hour, they perceived nothing new. Jenny's "answer" remained infuriatingly elusive, and they concluded that if there was a hidden message or clue, it was so well concealed it had been rendered impossible to find!

Sir Francis was with them, having flown onto the table after it was cleared. Once again he'd settled beside Marigold, and neither she nor Rowan made any attempt to remove him, because it was always easier to let the mallard do as he pleased. And speak as he pleased as well, for their conversation was constantly punctuated by his bill rattling and decidedly bellicose chuntering. He didn't seem at all pleased with either of them, fixing first one then the other with his bright eyes. Occasionally he gave a snort that was so disparaging that at last Marigold confided in Rowan her suspicion that the drake understood what they were discussing.

"I'm beginning to think the same," Rowan replied dryly, "and by his attitude I'd say disagrees with us!"

"I think he's definitely part of all this," Marigold said then.

"A very opinionated part."

She smiled. "Maybe, but all the same . . ."

Rowan nodded. "I concede the point. You've been right about him all along, although I still cannot imagine who he is."

"The first Lord Avenbury?"

With an emphatic quack, Sir Francis stretched his neck to look long and hard at them both.

"Well, I suppose it's as feasible as everything else." Rowan gave a rueful grin. "I must be unique. It isn't every nobleman in England who can claim descent from ducks and wrens!"

"A very exclusive genealogy," Marigold replied, and then bit her lip as without warning tears sprang to her eyes. "I—I can't believe we're joking about it."

Sir Francis rattled his bill soothingly, and rested his head against her arm. Rowan took her hand, and smiled again. "Our web-footed friend doesn't want you to cry, my darling, nor do I. It's always better to smile than weep. Come on now, let's recapitulate everything we know, or think we know."

Taking a deep breath to compose herself, Marigold stroked the drake while she and Rowan went over the whole puzzle again. They were not to know that schoolboy ears were pressed to the door, or that schoolboy eyes widened more with each startling revelation. Sir Francis knew though, for he looked toward the door, but he didn't raise the alarm.

At last the two boys drew well away from the door, and whispered together. They had been about to secretly leave the house when they'd commenced eavesdropping, now they went quietly to the front door, and slipped out into the summer night. The moment they'd gone, Beech emerged from the shadows at the top of the stairs, and hurried downstairs to follow. He tracked them around the side of the house, and watched as they ran past the terrace toward the ha-ha, and then to the common. He waited until he was sure they were intent upon examining the ashes by the oak tree, then he hastened back into the house to tap urgently upon the dining room door. "My lord?"

Rowan glanced around from the portrait. "Yes?"

The butler came in. "Begging your pardon, my lord, but I think you and her ladyship should know that the young gentlemen have been listening at this door, and have now gone out to the oak tree."

Marigold was dismayed. "Listening?"

"Yes, my lady."

"Do you know for how long?"

"No, my lady. I only saw them for a moment, before they slipped away outside."

"Then they may have been there for some time?"

"Yes, my lady."

Marigold looked unhappily at Rowan. "Heaven knows how much they may have heard."

"Well, it's done now," he replied, and nodded at the butler. "Thank you for informing us, Beech, it's much appreciated."

"My lord. Do you wish me to bring the young gentlemen back to the house?"

"No, leave it with me."

"My lord." The butler bowed and withdrew.

As soon as the door closed behind him, Marigold rose agitatedly from her seat. "Oh, Rowan, what if they heard everything we said?"

"Then what's done is done."

"But what we were saying is so utterly outlandish!"

Rowan smiled, and got up to go to her. "My dearest darling, I think our Eton invalids wallow in the outlandish! In fact, I'd go so far as to suggest they're so steeped in the amazing and unlikely, they'd be disappointed by the mundane. I don't recall hearing any frightened gasps at the door, do you? No one came rushing in tearfully, or collapsed with the vapors. No, the little monsters lapped it all up." He put his arms around her.

"Do—do you really think so?"

"I know so. Well, no doubt we will now be obliged to discuss it all with them, for to refuse to do so would be a little absurd. Actually, that might be a good idea," he added, and Sir Francis clacked his bill.

Marigold glanced at the mallard, and then at Rowan. "Discuss it with the boys? Oh, I don't know . . ."

"My darling, Bysshe's huge interest in the occult and so on

might prove useful." Sir Francis quacked, and nodded his head. Rowan indicated the drake's response. "He thinks it's a sensible notion."

"Well, I suppose . . ." Marigold smiled. "I'll go along with whatever you decide."

"Good, because the first thing I intend to do is teach them both a lesson for snooping upon other people's private conversations." He kissed her nose, then went to get her shawl from her chair. "Come on," he said as he placed it gently around her shoulders.

"Where are we going?"

"To your bramble refuge." He ushered her to the French windows, and Sir Francis immediately fluttered down to accompany them. Rowan turned with a frown. "Not you, I want things quiet, and you've got far too much to say for yourself!" he breathed, trying to gently push the drake back inside with his boot. Sir Francis gave several highly indignant squawks, then took to his wings over Marigold's head. "Damn and blast him!" Rowan cursed, watching the mallard disappear toward the village. "I vow that when I next have duck à l'orange, I shall eat it with considerable relish!"

"I don't think I shall ever be able to eat duck again," Marigold said.

"I intend to make a point of it," Rowan replied with a quick smile. "Come on, let's give our young friends a small fright." Taking her hand again, he led her along the terrace.

The lawns behind the house had been scythed that day, and the night air was scented with cut grass as they made their way toward the ha-ha. There was no mist, and the moon was out, so they could see the boys using sticks to poke the ground at the foot of the oak, presumably to inspect the charred remains of the druids' fire. Rowan and Marigold kept low as they negotiated the ha-ha, then hurried to the brambles, where they lay down to peer through the thorny branches. Marigold glanced at Rowan. "What are you going to do?" she whispered.

In answer, he nodded toward the moat, where it left his land and skirted the common. "Look," he said softly.

She saw what appeared to be faint blue flames hovering above the water, and she shrank closer to Rowan. "What is it?"

"*Ignis Fatuus,* will-o'-the-wisp, jack-o'-lantern, call it what you will. It's only marsh gas, and used to appear quite frequently here, but over the past year or so I've had the moat cleared out, and only that one stretch remains. I didn't expect to see it now, but it's most convenient to my purpose. Ah, our young friends have espied it!"

She watched as Perry shook Bysshe's shoulder, and pointed toward the weird blue flames. Bysshe turned to look, and Rowan immediately cupped his hands to his mouth and called out in a horribly hollow voice. "Behold, the flames of hell!"

The boys froze, and then shrank together, glancing around in all directions.

Rowan grinned at Marigold. "Let's see how much Coleridge they know." He cupped his hands again. " 'Like one, that on a lonesome road, Doth walk in fear and dread, And having once turned round walks on, And turns no more his head; Because he knows, a frightful fiend Doth close behind him tread.' " He emphasized the frightful fiend part.

The boys clung together in terror, then as one began to dash back toward the house. Rowan waited until they had just passed the brambles, then he shouted out. "He's behind you! Run! Run!" With shrieks, they fled even faster, stumbling over the ha-ha, and then kicking up their heels toward the kitchens, where welcome lights shone. Rowan laughed out loud. "There go our brave occultists!"

"Oh, Rowan, that was cruel. The poor things were frightened out of their wits," Marigold said sympathetically.

"Serves them right for eavesdropping. Anyway, I've had my revenge, so now we will go and reassure them." He got up, and held out his hand to her.

She accepted, and he drew her to her feet, but then slipped his arms around her. "First I will have a kiss," he said softly.

She gladly surrendered her lips to his, sinking against him as naturally as if she had spent her entire life with him. They had known each other for so short a time, yet were completely one. Her mouth softened beneath his, her lips parted, and as his body pressed to hers, she felt desire stirring hungrily through her. She also felt the physical proof that the erotic hunger was shared.

He drew back, and smiled in the darkness. "I trust we will be soon abed, my lady," he murmured, holding her against his urgent loins.

"I trust so too, my lord," she whispered back, closing her eyes as delicious feelings danced over her warm skin.

His lips sought hers again, and they kissed for a long, long moment, then he gently released her. "You tempt my base male nature so much, I am liable to give in and take you right here and now, but I think our unfortunate young diabolists require our presence."

"Yes."

"I love you, Lady Avenbury."

"I love you, Lord Avenbury."

They walked arm in arm back to the house, and followed the boys into the kitchens, where they came upon a repeat of the scene with Spiky Blackthorn. Mrs. Spindle was just handing glasses of water to the two white-faced boys. Maids and footmen had gathered around, but Beech was seated calmly in his favorite chair, reading a newspaper as if nothing untoward had occurred. The butler had guessed what had happened, and so was totally unmoved by tales of a "frightful fiend" creeping around outside.

Perry gave a cry of relief when he saw his mother. "Mama! Oh, Mama, Bysshe and I have had a dreadful scare!"

"I know," she replied.

"You—you know?" His eyes fled from her to Rowan, and then back again. Bysshe looked at them as well, and rose slowly to his feet, belatedly suspicious of trickery.

Rowan raised an eyebrow. "So, gentlemen, it seems you are frightened of marsh gas. I'm disappointed you really thought it was hellfire." As their faces flamed like the fire in question, he went on. "Nor, it seems, do you know your Coleridge very well."

"Coleridge?" repeated Perry.

" 'Like one, that on a lonesome road, Doth walk in fear and dread, And having once turned round walks on, And turns no more his head; Because he knows, a frightful fiend Doth close behind him tread.' "

Bysshe's face was a picture of embarrassment. "It—it was you, sir!"

"I fear so. Well, not entirely me, I have to say a certain ancient mariner helped a little."

Perry looked quite sick. "You had us well and truly, sir," he said.

"I know, so let that be a lesson to you not to listen in on what does not concern you."

They glanced at each other, hugely dismayed to have been found out. Bysshe recovered first. "You know we did that, sir?"

"Yes. Beech was good enough to tell me."

As the boys gave the butler dark looks, Rowan wagged his finger. "Beech is not at fault, sirs, *you* are. May I ask how much eavesdropping you did?"

"Quite a lot, sir," Perry confessed ashamedly. "In fact, I—I'd say we heard most of your conversation."

"I see." Rowan looked from one boy to the other. "As I understand it, gentlemen, you are both supposed to be recuperating from chicken pox, but I have to say you seem hale enough to me. Mayhap you should be dispatched back to Eton first thing tomorrow."

They were appalled. "Oh, no!" they cried in unison.

"Can you think of a good reason why not?" Rowan inquired.

Bysshe nodded. "Yes, my lord." He glanced at the listening servants, and then dropped his voice to a stage whisper. "I'm sure I can be of assistance with all those birds, in fact, I'm quite an, er, ornithologist."

"I rather wondered if that might prove the case," Rowan replied, glancing at Marigold. "Very well, sirs, we will discuss the matter at the breakfast table. Tell me, how did you convince Dr. Bethel you had chicken pox? Flour on your faces, red ink for spots, and feigning sleepiness?"

Bysshe gave a shamefaced grin. "Something like that," he confessed.

"Hmm. Well, to bed with you, sirs."

They obeyed with alacrity.

Chapter Twenty-six

Breakfast proved a very lengthy affair. Sunlight streamed into the dining room, the French windows stood open, and the scent of coffee, toast, and crisp bacon hung in the air. All eyes were fixed upon Jennifer Avenbury's portrait. The boys hadn't been able to offer further suggestions, so it seemed like an impasse. If only Jenny would come, and say something more, Marigold thought as she stroked Sir Francis. The mallard had wandered in from the terrace, and once again settled on the table beside her. For a while he had added his usual derogatory comments to the discussion, grumbling beneath his bill, and sighing now and then in a long-suffering way. No one paid him any heed, and at last he tucked his head beneath his wing and went to sleep.

The boys had indeed listened at the door for a long time the previous evening, for there was nothing they did not know about the situation. Nor, it had to be said, was there anything they did not take in their stride; but then, apprentice demonologists had to be made of stern stuff, except perhaps when unnamed but frightful fiends might be in the offing. Marigold eventually felt she had to say something about their calm acceptance of it all. "Aren't you two in the least dubious about this? After all, it isn't every day that someone tells you sinister druids are at work, and that a lawyer can transform himself into a large black bird, or that a talking wren is really an sixteenth-century woman."

Bysshe answered her. "Begging your pardon, ma'am, but Celtic mythology is full of birds and shape-shifting. The children of Lir were turned into swans, Branwen trained a starling to speak so she would be rescued, the singing of birds could suspend earthly time, Rhiannon's birds were harbingers of the Otherworld, ravens were oracles . . . Oh, it's endless."

"So are stories about fairies and ghosts, but do you believe them?" she asked.

"I don't disbelieve. Until there is proof that they do not exist, I have an open mind," Bysshe replied.

Rowan smiled. "That's fair enough. So tell me, sir, what is your theory concerning this wheel business? We could only think that it was something to do with going around the tree."

Bysshe thought for a moment. "Well, the wheel is a favorite Celtic symbol. Everything the druids and Celts did was connected with the yearly cycle, which may be viewed as a circle . . . or wheel, I suppose." He glanced around at the others.

Perry sat forward. "So the stones here and at Stonehenge are a circle, but may also represent a wheel? Is that what you're saying, Bysshe?"

"Well, I'm not exactly saying, I'm just guessing. The druids thought the sun was at its weakest in midwinter, and its strongest in midsummer. That's why they placed such importance on sunrise at midsummer. Their rites and so on were intended to encourage the sun—and thus also themselves—to be strong for another year. Some people suggest that Stonehenge was built so that the first rays of that sunrise fall exactly on something in particular, perhaps a certain stone. When Perry and I were at the tree last night, I noticed that the mistletoe on it grows on the side facing sunrise at this time of the year. I calculate that on midsummer day, the first rays will fall directly onto that mistletoe. If I'm right, it would be regarded as particularly auspicious. You see, mistletoe and oaks were very holy to the druids, so the oak tree on the common would have been particularly venerated."

"Aquila Randol certainly thought so, and in his form as Falk Arnold, he still does," Rowan observed.

Perry looked at him. "Sir, do you really think Uncle Falk is Randol?"

"Yes, Perry, I do."

Bysshe had been deep in thought, but then his eyes cleared and he looked excitedly at them. He held up a hand to tick the items he listed. "Let me sum it all up. Perry's uncle has only recently started all this, hasn't he? All of a sudden, after years of failure, legal ventures have begun to go his way. Believing himself unbeatable, he has commenced proceedings to gain your lordship's title and estate. On top of that, at dawn on midsummer day, he intends to turn Jennifer Avenbury back into a young woman in order to marry her, and finally he means to make certain of your lordship's death. Forgive me, sir, but I have to say it."

"That's quite all right," Rowan replied.

"Then it can only mean he's found the lost anguinum," Bysshe declared emphatically.

They all stirred, for the anguinum had been quite forgotten. Sir Francis took his head from under his wing, and gazed intently at Bysshe. Rowan sat back. "Damn, the druid's stone had quite slipped my mind," he breathed.

Bysshe went on. "An anguinum gives its possessor awesome supernatural powers, as well as complete success in all legal matters. I'd stake my life Perry's uncle has it again."

Marigold nodded. "You're right, Bysshe. It explains everything. Mr. Crowe told me Falk was unassailable in court. He also said it was quite impossible for me to win if I challenged Perry's father's will."

"It's the anguinum all right," Bysshe declared. "All we have to do is steal it, and his power will be destroyed."

Rowan gave him a wry look. "Is that all there is to it? Why, it's so easy, I'll toddle off to Romans right now, knock on the door, and ask him if he'll kindly hand it over. I fancy pigs would fly as well as birds before he obliged!"

Marigold sat back. "But Aquila lost it here at Avenbury, so when on earth did Falk find it? He's been at Castell Arnold for months and months, certainly since well before his first success in the courts."

Bysshe grinned. "Maybe he flew down here one night," he said. "But somehow no one thought it was funny, not even Perry. Indeed it was such a disagreeable thought that Bysshe himself stopped grinning, and lowered his eyes.

Marigold had been thinking. "Bysshe, you just said 'an' anguinum. Does that mean there's more than one?"

"Oh, yes. Not all that many, but certainly more than one. One folktale has it there were six."

"And this is something Falk is bound to know," Marigold murmured thoughtfully.

Rowan glanced at her. "What are you thinking?"

"Just that he may wonder if I have one, or part of one. I haven't, of course, but something certainly happens when I touch one of the standing stones." Her gaze went to Jenny's portrait again. "Is the anguinum depicted somewhere?" she wondered aloud.

Sir Francis gave a disgusted snort, and got up. Then, after stretching one wing then the other, he flew down from the table.

Rowan raised an eyebrow. "Our drake friend doesn't seem to think it is," he said, watching as Sir Francis waddled to the French windows, then flew away.

Marigold sighed. "He never agrees with *anything* we say," she complained.

Perry buttered himself another slice of toast. "I say, Bysshe, what on earth does an anguinum look like? It's all very well to say we have to steal it, but first we have to know what we're looking for."

"Well, it's about the size of a billiard ball, and is bright red in color."

Marigold gasped. "Yes, Falk *does* have such a thing! I've seen it!" She described those moments after the reading of Merlin's will, when Robin had pulled Falk's handkerchief from his pocket in order to dislodge the round red ball.

Bysshe's eyes shone. "It will be at Romans right now."

"Which brings us back to the tricky point of how exactly we're going to lay our hands on it," Rowan observed, toying with a table knife.

Perry sighed, and Bysshe looked thoughtful.

Marigold felt so helpless. "There *has* to be a way."

Bysshe nodded. "And it must be achieved before dawn on midsummer day. Everything will happen then. We have eight days." He glanced at Rowan, and then quickly away again.

No one said anything for a few moments, then Perry took a huge bite of toast. "Bysshe and I will think of something," he said with his mouth full.

Marigold frowned at him. "Aren't manners required at Eton?"

"Sorry, Mama," he said, swallowing hastily and then exchanging a meaningful glance with Bysshe.

Late that night, when all was quiet the two boys again slipped stealthily from their rooms, and down through the house. They had given up waiting for Rowan and Marigold to retire for the night, and had decided to commence a very risky venture anyway. Bysshe carried a rather battered old canvas shoulder bag with something heavy inside, and Perry a bundle of white robes made from their bedsheets. Keeping their eyes peeled for Beech, they paused at the bottom of the main staircase, then tiptoed to the great parlor door, which stood ajar, in order to peep inside. Marigold was seated on a sofa in the silver-spangled silk gown she'd worn for dinner. Her red-gold hair was pinned in a knot, and her earrings sparkled in the candlelight as she looked up at Rowan, who leaned over her from behind. He wore a navy blue velvet coat, gray waist-coat, and cream breeches, and was smiling tenderly into her eyes. The boys drew back to a discreet distance. "Gosh, they're very, er, dewy," Bysshe whispered.

"Immensely," Perry agreed.

"Do you think we'll ever be that soppy?"

"About each other?" asked Perry with a wicked grin.

"No, stupid, about a woman!"

"Of course not, we're too sensible," Perry replied. "Come on, let's get on with this."

They hurried to the main door, and then out into the moonlit night. Their steps rustled on the gravel as they ran down through the gardens. They glanced back constantly to see if anyone had no-ticed them, but there was no one at any of the windows. At last they reached the bridge and then paused. "I think we've escaped unnoticed," Bysshe breathed, putting down his heavy bag and then gazing intently back along the path.

"I think so too," answered Perry, thrusting one of the makeshift druid robes into his friend's hands.

They both dressed hastily, then pulled their cowls over their heads. Bysshe gave a nervous smile. "As we were going down-stairs, I felt as if old Beech would jump out from the shadows at any moment."

"Well, he didn't. Come on, it's rather open between here and the boathouse, so we'll have to make a dash for it."

Perry turned to run again, but Bysshe suddenly caught his arm. "No! W-wait a moment . . ."

"What's up?"

"Oh, it's stupid really, but I'm a bit afraid of water at night. I used to frighten my sisters by telling them a giant tortoise lived in our lake."

"A giant *what*?"

"Tortoise."

"Is that the most fearsome thing you could think of?" Perry scoffed.

Bysshe blushed in the darkness. "I know it sounds silly, but, yes, it was."

"Wouldn't a ten-legged lake monster with a taste for tender little girls be better? Or a hundred-foot-long water snake that comes up the drainpipe to swallow them whole while they're asleep?"

Bysshe looked at him in horror. "Oh, *don't . . .*"

Perry grinned, and put a fond arm around his friend's thin shoulders. "I say, you really are frightened of water, aren't you?"

"I—I believe that one day I will drown."

"Stuff and nonsense. Look, are you coming with me or not? We went to a lot of trouble making these robes, and pumping the servants about Romans, but if you're scared to come, I'll go alone."

"I—I'll come."

"Good. So let's get on with it."

They ran as fast as they could down the gentle slope toward the lake, and at last reached the shelter of the weeping willows and the boathouse. Out of breath, they leaned thankfully against the boathouse. Perry grinned. "We must be quite mad!"

"Totally."

"But if we manage to steal the anguinum from Uncle Falk . . ."

"We'll be heroes indeed. Come on, let's get the skiff."

They ran to the jetty, and hurriedly undid the mooring rope. Within a minute or so they had begun to pole themselves away from the shore, but it wasn't long before they realized how very visible they were in the moonlight, so they maneuvered the skiff into the reeds at the water's edge. It was much more difficult to make progress now, but at least they weren't so easy to see, either from Avenbury Park, or from Romans when they reached that end of the lake.

Back at the house, Beech hurried unannounced into the great parlor. "Forgive the intrusion, my lord, but the young gentlemen have gone out again!" he said breathlessly.

"Out? Where?" Rowan came around the sofa, and Marigold sat forward in concern.

"One of the maids was just drawing curtains at an upper window when she saw them on the garden bridge, although she wasn't sure it was them at first."

"Wasn't sure? Why on earth not?" Marigold was uneasy.

The butler was reluctant to respond, because he knew she would be upset by the answer. "Well, my lady, they were wearing white robes."

She stared at him in dismay.

"Where are they now?" Rowan demanded.

"They've taken the skiff onto the lake, sir."

"Oh, no . . ." Marigold pressed her fingers to her mouth.

Beech shuffled awkwardly. "One of the footmen says that Master Bysshe questioned him most particularly about Romans earlier this evening. I fear that is where they are going. The maid said they started out on open water, but then suddenly made for the reeds near the shore. She thinks they realized how the moonlight was shining on them."

Marigold rose agitatedly. "They've gone to get the anguinum."

Rowan sighed. "Oh, wouldn't they, just," he murmured.

"We must stop them, Rowan!"

He glanced at Beech. "Have my horse saddled, I'll bring them back."

"My lord." The butler turned to hurry away again, but Marigold called him back.

"Wait a moment, Beech."

"My lady?"

Rowan turned to her. "My darling, they have to be stopped and brought back."

"I know, it's just—"

"Each minute counts, Marigold. The reeds will hamper them, and the skiff can't be poled very swiftly anyway, so if I go by road, I should reach the jetty at Romans before they do."

"Won't you be seen?" she asked anxiously, remembering how the open lawns in front of Romans afforded a clear view down to the eastern shore of the lake.

"That's a chance I'll have to take. Which is more important? The risk of the iniquitous ornithological den catching the boys or spotting me?"

She looked swiftly at the butler. "Two horses, Beech."

Rowan shook his head. "No, Marigold."

"I won't stay behind."

"Marigold—"

"You'll have to lock me up," she warned.

"Don't tempt me," he replied, but nodded resignedly at the butler. "Two horses," he said.

"My lord." Beech hurried out.

Rowan glanced down at his evening clothes. "These won't do for riding, nor will your gown. We must change."

"But my riding habit is being attended to after I got it in a mess the other day."

His glance moved over her jewelry and silver gown. "Well, diamonds and spangles might be a little-eye-catching in moonlight, so either you stay here, or you must change. Don't you have a gown that isn't too costly?"

"I have a green lawn chemise gown that was in my traveling portmanteau when we met."

"It will have to do. Come." He held out his hand, and together they hurried from the room.

Chapter Twenty-seven

The moon shone brightly upon the water, and the reeds rustled a little in the soft night breeze as Perry and Bysshe struggled to pole the unwieldy skiff around the lake's edge. They had a fright when two very large, very bad-tempered swans flapped their long wings and hissed threateningly about three feet from the craft. The swans were already much put out with humans because earlier that day Alauda had shooed them forcefully from their sunny spot on the Romans jetty; the fact that the boys had disturbed them again now made them more grumpy than ever. The boys were relieved when they had put some distance between themselves and the disagreeable birds, whose hissing abuse could still be heard for some time after the skiff had been poled past.

After that, the only birds the boys expected to hear were the waterfowl stirring uneasily as the skiff went by, but then from the far side of the lake there came an only too-familiar sound. Perry stopped poling, and glanced across. "Listen, Bysshe."

Somewhat out of breath, Bysshe leaned on his pole. "Listen to what?"

"It's Sir Francis."

Both boys listened. Sure enough, the mallard's peculiarly distinctive cries echoed across the moonlit water, punctuated now and then by the calls of other water birds. Bysshe gave a low laugh. "It almost sounds as if he's making a speech. I went to the House of Commons once, and saw Mr. Pitt addressing Parliament. If those other birds aren't saying 'Hear! Hear!' I'll eat this pole!"

Perry grinned. "Sir Francis may be many things, but Mr. Pitt he certainly is not! Come on, let's get moving." He put pressure on the pole to push the skiff forward again.

Bysshe glanced up at the sky as he too began to pole once more. "I say, the moon's about to go behind a large cloud, so we'll be able to go out in the open again."

"Thank goodness. If we have to stay in these wretched reeds, it will be dawn before we get there," grumbled Perry.

As soon as the moon slid from sight, the boys maneuvered the skiff back onto clear water. Able to again set the direct course they'd intended from the outset, they poled as heartily as they could for Romans, which was now just visible around the foot of the escarpment. There were lights at many upper windows, but no one to be seen as the skiff was made fast at the jetty. Bysshe gathered the heavy shoulder bag, and then he and Perry ran to the shelter of the nearest tree. There were to be another ten vital minutes before Rowan and Marigold arrived.

Moving from tree to tree, the boys managed to get within fifty feet of the front of the house. At the last tree, Bysshe thankfully put the shoulder bag down, and together they peered around the trunk. The downstairs windows were all in darkness, and by the number of illuminated windows on the balconied upper floor, Falk and his guests had only just retired for the night. Luck was with the boys, for Falk appeared at the window of his room, which was about midway along the house. He loosened his white silk neckcloth, and removed his black evening coat, then he flung open the French windows, and stepped out onto the balcony. He placed his hands on the rail, and to the boys' dismay seemed to be looking directly down at their hiding place, but then he looked up at the sky for a moment, before turning and going back inside. They saw him moving around the room, and knew he hadn't noticed anything amiss.

Perry glanced at Bysshe. "Phew, that was nasty."

Bysshe nodded. "I thought we'd been spotted."

"So did I."

"I say, was your father really like his brother?"

"To look at, yes, but apart from that I hardly knew him. What I knew I didn't like. He was always under Uncle Falk's thumb, that's for sure, and Mama says he changed a lot from the man she married."

Bysshe pulled a face. "I don't like my papa either." He peered up at the balcony again. "Well, I guess that's the room we have to reach, but I do wish it was at the back of the house. Now we'll have run around the back, get up the outer staircase, and go all around the balcony. Lord knows how many other rooms we'll have to pass. What if some of them come out and catch us?"

"Don't even *think* that! Look, it can't be helped. We know from the footman that the steps at the back are the only ones, so once we've got it all going, we'll have to do some sprinting. And then pray." Perry grinned, but then became a little anxious. "Are you absolutely sure this will work?"

"Of course!" Bysshe replied indignantly.

Perry glanced around the tree again, this time toward the old hunting tower, where a lantern was fixed to a corner of the ancient stonework. Beyond, appearing as mere shadows, were the stables and coachhouse. Romans was a small residence for so many guests, so many of the carriages were drawn up in the open. The horses were in a paddock beyond, and there was no sign of any grooms, or even stable boys.

Bysshe drew a long breath. "Well, let's get to it then, before we lose our nerve." Hauling the heavy bag onto his shoulder again, he bent low to race across the sloping lawns toward the hunting tower. Perry was at his heels, and when they reached it, they pressed back into the arched ivy-draped doorway. They leaned breathlessly against the iron-studded door, which hadn't been opened in years. The light from the corner lantern shone on the carriages' gleaming paintwork and highly polished brass. The horses in the paddock could be heard now, stamping occasionally, or snorting.

Bysshe took the bag from around his shoulder, and crouched down to open it. He took out the only thing it contained, a very large jar of gray powder, and grinned at Perry. "Seventy-five per cent saltpeter, fifteen per cent charcoal, and ten per cent sulfur, equals the very best gunpowder."

"For heaven's sake be careful with it!"

"It won't explode without a flame."

Perry was still anxious. "Bysshe, are you really certain you know what you're doing? I mean, it's one thing to blow up an old tree stump at school, quite another to do the same to someone's carriage!"

"The big bang is just the same," Bysshe replied with relish. "Now then, which carriage shall we choose?"

"The blue one with scarlet wheels. It's Aunt Alauda's," Perry replied without hesitation, for he knew how proud that unpleasant lady was of her elegant conveyance.

"Consider it done," breathed Bysshe, then looked at the old bag. "This is expendable, I fancy. It's so battered I kept dreading the jar would fall through it. I'll blow it up as well." Putting the empty bag over his shoulder again, he moved toward the vehicle in question, carefully pouring the powder in a steady line as he went. He arranged the bag on its side where the trail directly led beneath Alauda's carriage, and then laid the jar on its side inside it. When he was satisfied nothing could go wrong, he hurried back to Perry. Both boys pressed back in the doorway again, and Bysshe gave a nervous laugh. "I say, I never imagined I'd do something like this. It's quite an adventure, eh?"

Perry glanced slyly at him. "It beats a moldy old giant tortoise!"

"If you ever mention that at school, I'll never speak to you again," Bysshe threatened, wishing he'd never confessed.

"I won't tell."

"You'd better not." Bysshe took a bottle of lucifers from his pocket, extracted one, then held it up until it ignited. "Right, get ready to run." He touched the lucifer to the trail of powder, and as a flame began to race along the ground, the boys took to their heels around the tower to the back of the house. There they crouched beneath balcony staircase, and put their fingers in their ears. Their hearts pounded, and the moments seemed to hang, then suddenly there was an explosion that shattered the night. Flames leapt into the darkness, and there was uproar. Grooms, coachmen, and stable boys poured from their cramped quarters behind the coachhouse, and doors were flung open on the balcony. Men shouted, especially Falk, and footsteps rang down the steps. Then Alauda's screams were added to the confusion. Her light steps hastened overhead, and the boys caught the fragrance of her perfume as she hurried down the steps to see what could have befallen her precious carriage. She was in her nightgown, and her glossy dark hair was in curling papers that bounced up and down as she disappeared around the corner.

As soon as she'd gone, Perry and Bysshe hurried up to the balcony, around the end of the house furthest from the mayhem. The fire had now spread to the carriages on either side of Alauda's, and there was chaos as men tried to pull the remaining vehicles to safety. Bysshe had been so lavish with his gunpowder some of the flames were higher than the house, and the hillside behind, beneath the earthworks, was illuminated by the leaping orange light. No one glanced up and saw the two white-clad figures creeping into Falk's room.

Rowan and Marigold had just arrived at the jetty and found the deserted skiff, when the explosion rent the night. Their horses shied, and Rowan reached across to steady Marigold's, then glanced up at the house. "Damn Bysshe and his gunpowder," he breathed.

"Is that what they've done? Oh, what if they're caught?"

Rowan suddenly saw the boys edging along the balcony. "There they are! They're audacious, I'll say that for them."

Marigold's heart sank. "They're not audacious, just very foolish and reckless! Oh, Rowan, they can't possibly hope to get away with this!"

They watched the boys enter Falk's room, and as the curtains were drawn, Rowan looked at Marigold. "You stay here, I'll go see if I can get them out before anyone realizes they're there."

"I'm staying with you," she replied firmly.

"Marigold, I would feel far happier in my mind if I knew that you at least were safe."

"Please, Rowan."

"Oh, my lady, in you I've acquired a very difficult woman."

"You and Perry mean everything to me, so you can't expect me to remain here kicking my heels! It's not fair."

He caught her hand, and smoothed her palm briefly with his thumb. "Very well, but we'll have to be careful. There are two ways to the steps at the back of the house, one is between the tower and the stables, the other is from the orchard. The first is clearly out of the question, so it has to be the orchard, which means getting in through the door in the wall. I only hope Falk neglected to push the bolt back across after speaking to you the other day. Come on, if we stay in the trees, we'll be able to ride most of the way." He urged his horse into the narrow curtain of woodland that edged the lawns. Marigold followed, and they had just reached the door in the orchard wall when the moon came out, adding its silver light to the leaping glow of the fire.

They dismounted, tethered the horses to the ivy on the wall, then tested the door. To their relief, it opened, albeit with a rusty groan that seemed inordinately loud in spite of the uproar by the fire. Once in the orchard, Rowan led the way toward the steps, but then froze beneath one of the apple trees as Alauda, being comforted by her maid, Lucy, suddenly appeared around the end of the house. Lucy was trying to soothe her mistress's sobs. "There, there, now, my lady. You come back to your bed, and I'll bring you a warm drink to calm your poor nerves."

"My carriage, my beautiful carriage." Alauda wept.

"I know, my lady, I know," the maid said sympathetically.

On the balcony, maid and mistress would have gone around the hunting tower end of the house, but a thick cloud of choking smoke billowed over everything, so instead they went the same way around the house as the boys. Rowan cursed under his breath, and then looked at Marigold. "If they were going to go the other way, it must mean Alauda's room is at that end of the house. Now they're bound to go past Falk's room," Rowan said.

"What can we do now?"

"Keep our fingers crossed they don't notice anything amiss. Listen, Marigold, I'm still going to get those young idiots out, but now Alauda is uncomfortably close, I want you to stay here. Is that clear?"

"I—I suppose so."

"I mean it, my darling. If I'm caught on my own, I may be able to bluff Alauda that I've changed my mind about her, but if you're there too . . ."

"I'll stay."

He took her face in his hands and kissed her, then he ducked low beneath the apple boughs and ran toward the steps. She watched him slip along the balcony, then vanish from view. From that moment on, time seemed to stand still. She could hear the commotion at the fire, and the men shouting; she could even hear the frightened horses at the far end of the paddock, but of Rowan, Perry, and Bysshe, she heard and saw nothing. At last she could bear it no more, and hurried to the steps.

Chapter Twenty-eight

Perry and Bysshe were ransacking Falk's room, but so far had found no sign at all of the precious anguinum. Bysshe was just beginning to search beneath the bed when Perry heard a sound outside. He kicked his friend's foot warningly. "Quiet, someone's coming!" he hissed.

Bysshe's head jerked up immediately, and he caught his long hair in the bedsprings because his cowl had fallen back. He was still struggling to free himself when a horrified Perry realized that behind the drawn curtains, the French windows were opening. He pressed fearfully back against the bedpost. Who was it? Please don't let it be Uncle Falk! To his unutterable joy it was Rowan who stepped into the room. "Lord Avenbury!" he gasped. Bysshe exhaled relievedly, and tried again to scramble from under the bed, but gave a yell of pain as he tugged his hair.

Rowan put a warning finger to his lips. "For heaven's sake keep quiet! I've come to get you young fools out."

"But we haven't found the anguinum yet! protested Perry.

"Forget the damned anguinum. Your aunt Alauda has returned to her room with her maid. Come on, we have to get out while we can!"

Perry hastened to obey, but poor Bysshe couldn't move. "I'm trapped!" he cried, squirming as he tried to tug himself away.

Rowan glanced back at the door, which he'd left ajar. All he could hear was the disturbance by the burning carriages. He looked urgently at Perry. "Get him out! And be quick!"

"Yes, sir." Perry wriggled under the bed to see if he could disentangle Bysshe.

As this was going on, Marigold had ascended the staircase to the balcony. She was about to follow everyone else, when something made her go around the hunting tower end of the house. She would wonder ever after whether it had been a premonition or just an incredibly fortunate whim, for it was the saving of them all. At the time, however, it seemed an unnecessarily risky thing to do, for not only did it take her into the choking smoke, but also within sight of those who were trying to extinguish the fire. Anyone might have glanced up and seen her stealing past the rooms by the tower. But no one did, and as she reached the front corner of the balcony, she peeped around just as Alauda's maid emerged from a door two doors along from Falk's.

Another cloud of smoke billowed over the house, obscuring everything for a moment, and when it cleared, she saw Lucy walking away from her past Falk's door, which Rowan had unfortunately left slightly ajar. The maid heard something inside, and after listening carefully for a moment, tiptoed swiftly back to Alauda's room. Within seconds, she emerged again, accompanied by Alauda, who had a small pistol in her hand. Alauda dispatched Lucy to bring assistance from the men at the fire. It would have been simpler to shout for help, but that would have alerted the intruders, and given them a chance to escape. For a moment Marigold feared the maid would come her way, but thankfully the smoke wafted again, and Lucy chose the opposite direction.

Marigold's mind was numb as she watched Alauda advance upon the door, the pistol cocked and ready, for this scrape seemed to be one from which there was no way out at all. Marigold willed herself to think of something, and then she glanced at the first bedroom door, and an idea began to form.

In the room, Perry had at last managed to free Bysshe, and both boys scrambled from under the bed. They pulled their cowls over their heads again, and moved toward the door, where Rowan was waiting impatiently. But then the cold barrel of Alauda's pistol pressed to his temple. "Who are you? What are you doing?" she demanded, not recognizing him in the darkness.

Before he could reply, there was a sudden cry and a scuffle behind him, then the pistol clattered to the floor. He whirled about and saw that Marigold had pulled a pillowcase over Alauda's head, and pinned her arms to her sides. Alauda struggled like a wildcat and screamed at the top of her lungs as she was bundled into the room, where she was forced onto the floor with her back to them all. Her noise was only silenced when Perry took great delight in forcing his handkerchief into her mouth. Then she was securely tied with a silk rope from one of Falk's bedposts. Rowan would then have just left her on the floor, but the boys looked at each other, nodded, and heaved her under the bed like a rolled up carpet. All that could be seen of the Countess of Fernborough were her furiously kicking feet.

Marigold was anxious. "She's sent Lucy for help, so please hurry," she whispered, not wanting Alauda to realize who she was. She went to see what was happening by the fire, and then hurried back to Rowan. "Quick!" she whispered, "Falk's being told right now!"

Rowan retrieved the pistol, then they all ran along the balcony. There was a change in the shouts as Falk and his friends left the fire to attend to the intruders, and it was clear to Rowan that the opposition would reach the steps first. He thought as he ran, then halted around the end of the house to look over the rail. "There's a supporting column here, with a pretty substantial wisteria climbing up it. We'll have to climb down it, then make for those bushes just over there. Come on, there's no time to argue." He almost bundled Bysshe over, then Perry. The boys scrambled down like monkeys, and dove for the bushes. Rowan turned to Marigold. "Now you, my love."

"But—"

"Do it!" He lifted her bodily over the edge, and she had no option but to grab the column and clamber down as best she could. She heard Rowan following, then she was on the veranda below. He jumped down next to her, and they both ran for the bushes, hurling themselves out of sight just as Falk and the other men thundered along the balcony.

Rowan looked urgently at the two boys. "Do you think you can get the skiff back to Avenbury?"

"Yes, sir," Perry answered immediately.

"Take your mother, and moon or not, keep to the reeds until you're around the foot of the escarpment and well and truly away from here, is that clear?"

Perry nodded, but Marigold protested. "Rowan, I would rather stay with you!"

"Not this time, my love, it's far too hazardous. I know that you saved us just now, which you wouldn't have been able to if you'd followed my instructions, but this time I'm charging Perry to do as I instruct. Is that clear, Perry?"

"Yes, sir."

Rowan looked at Marigold again. "So far no one knows who we are. I want it to stay that way, so I have to get the horses because their monogrammed saddles will announce our identities to one and all. Now, please go with the boys."

She wanted to defy him, but knew that this time it would be wrong. Instead she leaned across to kiss him on the lips, then she followed the boys as they crawled out of the far side of the bushes. They ran toward the curtain of trees, and there paused to look back again. Alauda had been freed, and her hysterical fury rang out above the continuing roar of the fire. Then something very frightening happened. With a croaking call, the huge black crow suddenly glided from the balcony, its head turning this way and that as it searched for whoever had dared to break into the house. It flew unevenly, as if its left wing was still damaged, and Marigold knew it was the lawyer. It cast a dark shadow as it glided over the lawns toward the woods, and the trio of fugitives pressed as tightly as they could to tree trunks, being careful not to move until the bird was satisfied there was no one there. Marigold gazed up at it in dismay. What if it saw the horses?

But the rook didn't fly that way. Instead it glided across the lawns toward the other curtain of trees, calling out all the while as if communicating with Falk and the others, who were watching from the balcony. Suddenly the calls broke off on a choked sound, and to Marigold's surprise it began to dive this way and that as if trying to avoid something. The three in the woods strained their eyes to see what was happening, and it was Bysshe who realized. "It's the robin and wren!" he gasped.

Sure enough, Robin and Jenny were harrying the much bigger bird. They allowed it no quarter, swooping again and again, pecking savagely each time they had the chance. Because of its damaged wing, the crow was soon exhausted, and fell to the grass right in front of the house. There it grew in size, changed shape, and became Mr. Crowe once more. He brushed himself down, cradled his damaged arm, and then limped back toward the house. Their mission accomplished, Robin and Jenny had flown hastily away. Marigold soon saw why they were in such haste, for a loud, grating cry—chaek!—came from the balcony as another bird took to the air. It was a small but ferocious hook-billed shrike. Lord Toby!

Bysshe gazed in dismay. "If he catches them . . ."

"He'll impale them on something sharp," Perry finished for him.

"They *must* escape," Marigold whispered.

Bysshe smiled then. "I've just thought, if the wren is Jennifer

Avenbury, Lord Toby won't dare kill her because she's to be Falk's bride."

Marigold breathed out with relief. "Yes, of course . . ."

But Bysshe lowered his eyes. "Poor Robin Raddock doesn't have that protection, though, does he?"

Perry caught his mother's arm. "Come on, we mustn't stay here." He led the way through the trees, and at last they reached the lake. Knowing Falk and the others were still on the balcony, Perry took off his robe, shoved it into Bysshe's hand, then went into the lake. He swam to the skiff, undid the mooring rope, then hauled the little craft ashore and out of sight from the house because of the trees. It swayed as they clambered in, then the boys worked together to pole it away as quickly as they could.

Obeying Rowan's orders, they kept to the reeds, where the night breeze now seemed to rustle everything more menacingly than on the outward trip. Romans was still clearly visible on its hillside, and Marigold looked back to see that the really high flames had been doused at last, although the remains of the three destroyed carriages still burned. Smoke curled up into the moonlit sky, and every window of the house now seemed to be illuminated as the search continued inside. Suddenly she saw the shrike return to the balcony, where Falk and Alauda now stood alone. Falk took something from the bird's bill, and Marigold knew it was either Robin or Jenny. Before resuming his normal shape, Sir Toby gave two triumphant cries. Chaek! Chaek!

As Marigold gazed back in dismay, the firefighters at last overwhelmed the flames. The moon slid behind another cloud at the same time, and everything went very dark. She shivered, sensing something was very wrong. Rowan? As his name came to her, she heard a brief exchange of pistol shots. The reports reverberated along the escarpment, then there was silence. She pressed trembling hands to her mouth, and the boys stopped poling. They all listened, praying to hear the thud of hooves as Rowan made his escape, but there was nothing, only their own heartbeats. No one said a word as Bysshe and Perry renewed their poling, and soon Romans slipped from view.

The rest of the return journey took much longer than anticipated, because Perry's pole snapped and then the skiff got caught up on the reeds, but at last they managed to continue. When they eventually approached the Avenbury jetty, they saw someone waiting with a lantern. It was Beech, and he called out as soon as they were within hearing. "My lord? My lord?"

Perry shouted back. "Lord Avenbury isn't with us! He's riding back!"

The butler lowered the lantern unhappily, and as the skiff came alongside, Marigold saw how pale and uneasy his face was. "What is it, Beech?" she asked, as he assisted her from the rocking craft.

"The horses returned riderless about a quarter of an hour ago, my lady."

Perry looked anxiously at her. "Mama?"

The pistol shots seemed to ring in Marigold's ears as she glanced back across the dark lake. What had happened? For a few moments she found it hard to think, but then found her wits. "Beech, I think his lordship must still be at Romans, either injured or held against his will. I want the head keeper—Hazell, is it?— and as many armed men as possible to ride there. Take whatever horses are needed from the stables. Romans belongs to Lord Avenbury, and I believe that legally the tenant cannot refuse access to the landlord's representatives, even in the middle of the night."

"*Armed* men, my lady?" The butler blanched.

"Yes, Beech. Please do it without delay."

"Very well, my lady." He handed the lantern to Bysshe, then hurried away.

Perry came to put his arm around his mother. "It will be all right, Mama."

"I hope so, Perry, oh, how I hope so," she whispered.

Hazell and his selected men rode out of Avenbury Park half an hour later, and as the hoofbeats died away into the night, the waiting began. Marigold paced up and down in the great parlor, and the boys sat unhappily on the sofa where earlier she had gazed up so lovingly into Rowan's eyes. The mantelpiece clock ticked slowly, and chimed every fifteen minutes. Then, just as the sky began to lighten outside, the riders returned. Marigold ran outside, but the face she prayed to see was not there.

Hazel dismounted. "I'm sorry, my lady. We searched every inch of the house, but there was no sign of his lordship. Nor was there any sign of him along the road. I've sent two men to look on the escarpment, but Mr. Beech said the riderless horses returned by way of the road, so I don't expect them to find anything up there."

"Then where is he?" Marigold cried.

"I cannot say, my lady." The keeper looked helplessly at her.

"We'll search the area again in daylight, but I can promise you he isn't at Romans itself. The tenant offered no objections to a thorough search. If Lord Avenbury is being held there, he is very cunningly concealed indeed. We even searched the cellars and the attics."

"What about the old tower?" asked Bysshe, as he and Perry joined Marigold.

The keeper's face changed. "Well, no, but the door didn't seem to have been opened in a century or more. It was choked over with weeds and ivy." He looked at Marigold. "Would you like us to return now, my lady?"

She shook her head. "It can wait until tomorrow, Hazell. You and the others must be very tired. Thank you for your help."

"We'd do anything for Lord Avenbury, my lady," he replied. Marigold's eyes filled with tears, and the keeper was bold enough to put a reassuring hand on her arm. "We'll find him, my lady, make no mistake of that." Then he turned and led his horse away toward the stables, followed by his companions.

Chapter Twenty-nine

The search recommenced as soon as the sun was up. Hazell and the men started by returning to Romans to search the hunting tower, and—much against Marigold's wishes—Perry and Bysshe accompanied them. At first she firmly forbade the boys to leave Avenbury Park, fearing that something would happen to them as well, but then Bysshe took her quietly aside to explain that Perry desperately wanted to do something positive to show his liking and admiration for Rowan. At that, Marigold fought back tears of pride, quelled her inner fears, and gave her permission. She wanted to join the search herself, but thought it best to be at the house should Rowan return somehow. Not that she really thought he would, for her recently acquired and curiously accurate sixth sense told her he was at Romans, either imprisoned, or under Falk's control.

Throughout the morning the search went on. Falk had made no objection to another inspection of Romans. He and his guests took tea in the orchard, and seemed totally unconcerned as Perry and Bysshe assisted Hazell and the other men to comb the hunting lodge. After that the search widened to the surrounding countryside, which was scoured very thoroughly indeed. The skiff was taken out on the lake, together with several more that were kept in the boathouse, but of Rowan there was no sign at all. He had vanished.

As the hours ticked relentlessly by, Marigold strove to remain calm and composed. She paced up and down in the garden, glancing constantly across the lake or up at the escarpment, praying her sixth sense was wrong, and that at any moment she would see Rowan returning, but he didn't. The searchers came back to Avenbury Park in the middle of the afternoon for some well-earned refreshment. During the makeshift feast Mrs. Spindle provided in the great hall, Marigold overheard something that confirmed her intuition about Rowan being at Romans.

Everyone was trying to enjoy the excellent cheese, Wiltshire ham, fresh bread, and cider, but few had any real appetite because they were all anxious about Rowan, who was held in very high regard by everyone, from the lowest laborer to a gentleman acquaintance who heard of the strange disappearance while halting at the village inn. The gallant band of searchers ate as best they could because they knew they must go out again to continue the search, no matter how hopeless an exercise it seemed. To give herself something to do, Marigold helped Mrs. Spindle and the maids serve the cider, and it was while she was doing this that she overheard a conversation between Bysshe and Perry.

Bysshe helped himself to another wedge of cheese, and then mentioned the door in the orchard wall at Romans. "How anyone gets in and out of it, I really don't know."

"Well, it must be possible, because Mama said Uncle Falk came out through it," Perry replied.

"I wouldn't have thought a man as big and strong as that could squeeze through."

Curious, Marigold put down the jug of cider she was carrying in order to speak to Bysshe. "Why don't you think Falk could get through the door?" she asked.

He looked up with a start. "I didn't know you were listening, my lady."

"I couldn't help overhearing."

"Well, it's just that Perry and I walked around the outside of the orchard this morning with some of the men, and there's a tree growing so close against the door that it prevents it being opened."

Marigold stared at him. She and Rowan had gone through that very door last night, and there certainly hadn't been a tree blocking the way. "What sort of tree was it?" she asked quickly.

They both shrugged, and Perry replied. "I don't know, we didn't look. It was just a tree. Not huge like the oak, more the size of an alder, I suppose. Why?"

"Oh, nothing, it's not important," she murmured.

Bysshe looked curiously at her. "*Did* Falk Arnold get through?"

"Oh, yes," she replied in a dismissive tone, then picked up the jug to resume serving the cider. But her thoughts had quickened. There shouldn't be a tree where the boys said. If there was, it wasn't an ordinary tree. But before she mentioned anything, she had to see for herself, so she waited until the searchers had sallied forth again, the boys included, then she ordered a horse for herself. After changing into her newly laundered habit, she took Rowan's pocket telescope from its drawer in the library, then rode out of Avenbury Park.

The earthworks above Romans were deserted as she tethered her horse where she and Rowan had lain together a day or so before. A day or so? Right now it seemed an aeon ago. She crept to the edge of the slope, then lay down to train the telescope on the wall of the orchard. The door was unobstructed, indeed there wasn't even a bush to block the way. She searched the entire wall, and then returned her attention to the door. Whatever Perry and Bysshe had seen, it wasn't there now. She didn't doubt there'd been a tree, and the fact that it had vanished proved to her that it was a supernatural tree. And what else could it have been but a rowan? But where was he now? Anxiously she raked the house and orchard, but he was nowhere, nor indeed, did she glimpse Falk or Alauda, but some of the others were in evidence in the orchard.

Lord Toby's exaggerated drawl carried clearly on the warm summer air as he lounged on the grass with Lord Siskin and Judge Grouse, and Sir Hindley Tern's equally irritating vowels drifted up with similar clarity from inside the summerhouse as he called to the house for another bottle of hock. Mr. Crowe was seated forlornly on the summerhouse step with a makeshift crutch propped up beside him. The sling on his arm was now accompanied by bandages around his forehead and leg, and he looked very bedraggled indeed, but he received not one iota of sympathy from Marigold, who hoped he was suffering every imaginable discomfort. She wished Lord Toby had suffered a similar tumble during his flight from the balcony, for it would be exquisitely satisfying to see him in the same battered state.

Leaving the small flock at the summerhouse, Marigold moved the telescope toward the house again. A blur of leaves slid before her concentrating eye, but then something made her focus on one apple tree in particular. A gilded birdcage was suspended from a branch, and there was a tiny brown wren fluttering helplessly inside. Jenny! Marigold's breath caught with dismay as she remembered how Lord Toby had returned to the balcony last night with something in his bill. He had caught Jenny and given her to Falk, but what—if anything—had happened to Robin? Oh, please don't let him have been caught to suffer the terrible fate all shrikes accorded their prey! The telescope slipped from her fingers onto the grass, and tears stung her eyes.

At that moment, as if on cue, Robin himself landed on the telescope, and cocked his head to look at her. "Oh, Robin!" Marigold whispered gladly, so relieved that more tears pricked her eyes. The little bird chirruped sadly, then hopped onto her finger, as if trying to comfort her. She smiled bravely. "What are we going to do, Robin?"

Robin sighed, his head sinking dejectedly between his wings. Marigold felt at one with him. "How I *wish* you could talk," she murmured. "The ones we love are down there at Romans, and we have to find a way to rescue them. Or is it just me? Am *I* alone charged with the task?"

As Robin eyed her again, then gave another sad chirrup, she knew that the responsibility did indeed lie with her. "Very well, I accept that it's up to me, but I still don't know how to set about the task," she said, stretching out a finger of her other hand to touch the little bird's gleaming red breast.

He puffed his feathers, tilted his head to gaze at her with his bright brown eyes, and sang a few notes. Then he repeated the same notes more urgently. She felt helpless. "It's no good, Robin, I can't understand your language." He sighed again, and tilted his head the other way, to look down at Romans. Then he hopped down onto the grass, and huddled dejectedly next to some early harebells that were as blue as the heavens.

After a moment, Marigold resumed her surveillance through the telescope, and suddenly realized Sir Hindley Tern wasn't alone in the summerhouse, as without warning, Alauda stepped into view. Marigold's old foe looked ravishingly beautiful in a lime-green silk gown, and the ignominy of the pillowcase was clearly behind her, for she was all smiles as she held out her hand to the man she was with. It was Rowan, and Marigold's very soul was wrenched as he pulled his mistress sensuously close, then kissed her tenderly on the lips. His eyes were dark with seduction, and his pleasure could not be mistaken as Alauda pressed eagerly to him. His hands moved yearningly over the silk of her gown, and no one else seemed to exist for either of them as the kiss became more demanding and erotic. At last Alauda drew away, then took him by one hand to lead him toward the house. They went up the steps to the second floor, then turned toward the hunting tower and disappeared around the end of the balcony. It did not need to be spelled out that they were going to Alauda's bedroom to make love.

Distraught, Marigold tossed the telescope aside, and scrambled back from the edge of the slope. Far from being kept at Romans against his will, it was clearly very much to Rowan's *liking* to be reunited with the mistress he said he'd rejected! A discord of emotions pounded through her, and she was so upset she couldn't even cry. Robin fluttered anxiously beside her, but then there sounded some very cross-sounding quacks that heralded the approach of a certain mallard. The robin flew away as Sir Francis landed awkwardly a few feet away from Marigold, who sat up unhappily. "Oh, Sir Francis, what do *you* want?"

To say that he was angry about something would be to put it far too mildly, for he was positively incandescent with rage. He jumped up and down, quacking all the time, then waddled close enough to jab her painfully with his bill. "Whatever is the matter?" she gasped, recoiling in astonishment. His response was to resume his ranting. He was quite beside himself, gibbering and stamping as if she had caused mortal offense, but at last he calmed down a little, and confined himself to disapproving snorts.

Marigold stared. "Why are you like this?" she asked, as he clacked his bill, and muttered under his breath. She was indignant too; after all, Rowan's betrayal had been a terrible shock. "This is horridly unfair! If you knew how unutterably wretched I feel, you wouldn't—"

It was the wrong thing to say, for he erupted into another bombardment of cursing quacks, and rushed up to peck her again. After that he quivered from bill to webbed feet as he made himself tall and thin so he could be eye to eye with her. He oozed with outrage, and his ire was so intense that Marigold couldn't help but know he considered her to be gravely at fault. But what had she done? She hadn't even *seen* the drake since the breakfast when Perry, and Bysshe had been acquainted with details of recent events.

At last Sir Francis seemed to calm down a little. He waddled to the edge of the slope, looked over, and shook his head. Then he looked at her, snorted, and shook his head again. It was all too much for Marigold. She was devastated by seeing Rowan and Alauda together like that, and was in no state to cope with this as well. She simply wanted to run away from everything! Stifling another sob, she got up and hurried to her horse. Sir Francis gave a dismayed quack, and took to the air, diving so low over her head that she felt the draft of his passing. His clamor recommenced, and he harried her all the way back to Avenbury Park, so that by the time she dismounted again, her head was ringing with his endless quacking. She realized she'd left the telescope behind, but nothing would have induced her to return. She'd send one of the men. . . .

Sir Francis was just about to make another aerial attack, when he broke off midquack, and flew away very hastily. Marigold gazed after him with a mixture of relief and puzzlement. He'd seemed almost frightened. Why? The answer was immediately forthcoming, for Falk spoke a few feet behind her.

Chapter Thirty

Marigold whirled fearfully about, for no one had been in sight when she arrived. Falk was standing at the commencement of the garden path, and there was no sign of a horse or carriage. How had he arrived without her hearing? His wig was very golden as he came toward her. He wore a maroon coat and gray breeches, and a ruby pin sparkled in the folds of his muslin neckcloth. "I trust I find you well, Marigold?"

"I fear I cannot sincerely offer the same felicitations," she replied frankly.

"How charming," he murmured with a thin smile. Then his gaze moved beyond her as Perry and Bysshe came out of the house and ran to her side. She was later to discover they had returned from the search because Bysshe's horse had gone lame, but right now she was too intent upon Falk to give the boys' unexpected presence a second thought.

Perry placed himself between his mother and uncle. "Where is Lord Avenbury, Uncle Falk?" he demanded.

Falk's eyes flickered. "Right now he is with Alauda at Romans, as I think your mother will confirm," he said smoothly.

Perry turned inquiringly to her. "Mama?"

Marigold gave him a brave smile, then quickly addressed Falk again. "What makes you think I would know my husband is with your sister?" she asked.

"Because you watched them from the escarpment. Oh, by the way, you left this behind." He drew the telescope from his pocket.

Her hand shook a little as she took it. She no longer needed to ask him how he had arrived here without horse or carriage, nor did she wonder how he was in possession of something she had only just left at the earthworks, because she now knew the answer. Falk Arnold could not only turn his followers into birds, he could become one himself!

Falk gave one of his cold smiles. "Poor Marigold, how unfortunate you are when it comes to marriage. I trust you saw how overjoyed your new husband is to be with Alauda again?"

She strove to think clearly. So far in this conversation Falk had enjoyed all the advantages, and for Robin and Jenny's sake—if no longer for unfaithful, uncaring Rowan's—she had to redress the balance. How could she retain her power's credibility in Falk's eyes? She glanced at the topiary bush, and was startled to see Robin peeping out. Then from behind the bush there came a single belligerent quack that she knew was directed at Falk. It was somehow reassuring to know the mallard was close by as well, and it was certainly good to know that when it came to Falk Arnold, Sir Francis was her friend again. The two birds' support encouraged her, and she smiled coolly at Falk. "I trust Mr. Crowe is in a great deal of pain. He took such a fall last night, did he not? You know, I found him ridiculously easy to deal with." There, make what you will of *that,* she thought, determinedly ignoring Perry's incredulous stare.

A new wariness crept into Falk's cold amber eyes. "I'm not sure I understand you, my dear," he murmured. "A certain robin and wren were responsible, you had nothing to do with it."

"Please continue to think that way."

The reply irritated him. "I promise you will soon regret such flippancy."

"You are in error again, for I am in earnest. If I had been more vigilant last night, Lord Toby would not have caught poor Jenny. It was a lapse of concentration that will not be repeated." She slipped her hand pointedly into her riding habit pocket, and pretended to be toying with something about the size of a billiard ball. Let him wonder if she had an anguinum!

Falk's eyes became piercing. "Are you presuming to challenge me, Marigold?"

She managed a smile. "That is for you to find out, Falk," she replied, only too aware that Perry and Bysshe thought she'd taken leave of her senses. Perhaps they were right. Perhaps Bedlam was the best place for her.

"Look into my eyes and know you are playing with fire, for I am all-powerful," Falk said softly.

She could not help but be frightened, but wild horses could not have dragged the fact from her. "All-powerful? You ever were a braggart, Falk, and I have learned not to take anything you say at face value," she replied, and the moment the words were uttered, her sixth sense flashed with insight. Wasn't taking something at face value the very thing she'd done on seeing Rowan at Romans? He hadn't been lying to her about ending things with Alauda, and no matter how much to the contrary it might have seemed, he wasn't at Romans of his own volition, nor was he willingly with his former mistress. He was this man's prisoner! Suddenly she knew why Sir Francis had been so angry with her. Far from being the betrayed, she had, by her lack of faith, been the betrayer! The drake was supernatural, and was incensed by her reaction, because he knew Rowan was bewitched by druid magic and therefore not responsible for his actions. So the splendid but vociferous demon duck had come to the earthworks in very high dudgeon to put her right on the matter. She didn't know why Sir Francis should harbor such fierce feelings on Rowan's account, but he certainly did. Even now she could feel the sharp jab of the drake's bill.

"Perhaps you should believe me, my dear," Falk murmured, "for when I claim to have great power, I mean it, and I'm going to defeat your miserable challenge." Before Marigold knew what was happening, he raised his hand and pointed toward Perry, who to her horror changed into the peregrine falcon of his name. Panic-stricken, Perry gave a thin, piercing shriek, and flapped his wings.

Bysshe stumbled backward with a frightened gasp, but although Marigold was deeply shaken, her maternal instinct surged to the fore. Making soothing noises, she gathered her beloved son into her arms, and as he cowered against her, she could feel his sharp talons through the stuff of her riding habit. "Oh, Perry, my poor darling," she whispered, stroking his head, which together with his wings and upper body was dark gray, whereas his legs and lower body were more pale and banded. He was very beautiful, but completely terrified.

Falk began to laugh. "So much for your ability! There is nothing you can do for my unfortunate nephew, is there? You bluff well, my dear, but I have just proved you don't possess the anguinum. Perry is now mine. You should have remembered that he is of my blood, and therefore likely to be particularly susceptible to my will. It is because he is so close to me that I cannot kill him, but believe me, I am able to leave him as he now is for the rest of his life. He is my insurance against any reckless attempt to interfere. Do anything at all, Marigold, and he will never be other than you see him now."

She was choked with anger and distress. "No! Please, Falk, release him," she begged, her voice catching on a sob.

"At dawn on midsummer day, at the precise moment the sun's rays strike the mistletoe on the oak, I intend to again perform the ancient and solemn druidic rites of the wheel."

"What is the wheel?" she cried, still holding Perry close.

"It is what must be if I, Aquila Randol, am to have what has always been rightfully mine."

So Falk Arnold and Aquila Randol *were* one and the same, Marigold thought. Or was it just that Falk was convinced of the fact? Perhaps he was quite mad, and should be locked away!

Falk went on. "The wheel will only turn if all the elements are there, and when Alauda was last here at this house with Avenbury, she found the long-lost anguinum again. It was in the moat, where it had lain since 1534, and was only revealed when Avenbury himself had ordered that part of the henge to be dredged. Oh, foolish Avenbury, he was instrumental in my rise, and therefore his own fall. The moment the anguinum was placed in my hand again, I knew I could not fail in anything I attempted. Now nearly all the elements for the wheel are in my possession, from Jennifer to the thirteenth and last lord himself. Only Raddock remains, and he will fall into my hands yet."

Marigold glanced toward a nearby topiary bush again. Robin was still there, barely ten feet from Falk!

Falk drew a long, satisfied breath, then gave a cool, mirthless chuckle sound. "When the wheel turns, I will be assured of all this," he waved his arms to encompass Avenbury Park, "and Jennifer Avenbury will become my bride. Can you conceive what it is to desire someone across the centuries? Can you imagine the strength of a passion that has burned constantly in readiness for this one midsummer? The thirteenth and last lord has reached his time, and so have I. Jennifer is about to come to me, and when she does, my love will be complete."

"You aren't capable of love," Marigold whispered, wishing he could indeed be locked away.

Falk was amused. "Launder your best black, for you are about to be a widow again; but in the meantime, for Perry's sake, remember to bow to my will. You cannot save your husband, because his fate is preordained, nor can you do anything for Jennifer, who was always meant to be mine. As for that upstart Raddock, he will be alone for the rest of eternity, which is no more than his presumption deserves. And by the way, if you imagine you can muster help from the staff here or from the village, remember that they too are subject to the anguinum's power. I can ensure that everyone remains asleep, and that those who are awake become either what their name denotes, or anything else I choose."

Bysshe gasped with realization. "The tree by the orchard door. It was a rowan, wasn't it?"

"Of course. Avenbury very nearly escaped, but luck was on my side, not his." Falk's amber eyes swung coldly back to Marigold. "As for what will happen to you and this boy during the rites, let me say I intend to leave you as you are, for I want you to observe what happens. Just remember my abilities to change or transfix you if I so desire. Now then, do we understand each other, my lady?"

She cuddled her beloved son. "Yes," she whispered, for what else could she say?

Suddenly there was a whir of little wings as Robin darted from the topiary bush to attack Falk's toupee. It was David and Goliath again, just as it had been that day at Castell Arnold. Falk gave a howl of fury, and lashed out, but the resolute robin sank its claws into the false hair and began to tug. Then Sir Francis waddled purposefully from behind the bush, quacking and flapping as he deliberately got in the way of Falk's feet. With a yell, Falk fell heavily to the ground, and the loosened wig was jolted free. As he stretched out to retrieve it, Sir Francis dove on it first, and bore it aloft. The mallard flew strongly toward the lake, then disappeared down among the reeds. Marigold stared after him, and so did Perry, whose curved bill had opened in astonishment. Bysshe gaped as well, for the two birds had so clearly worked in concert that it was quite breathtaking.

Falk scrambled to his feet, looking a little ridiculous because two small sideburns of false hair had been left in place. He glowered at Marigold, Perry, and Bysshe as they drew uneasily together, trying to seem as if they hadn't really noticed anything. To their relief, he had other things on his mind, to wit the recovery of his precious wig. Before their eyes, he shifted shape to become a gyrfalcon, the largest of the falcons. More brown and speckled than Perry, he would have been very impressive indeed, were it not that the top of his head was totally devoid of feathers! He spread his enormous wings, and flew away toward the lake, his pate agleam in the sunshine. Marigold, Perry, and Bysshe watched as he made for the area of reeds where Sir Francis had disappeared with the wig, but just as he glided down toward the spot, there was sudden pandemonium as an immense flock of waterfowl took to the air. He had no time to get out of the way, and in a moment, he was hopelessly caught up in an endless stream of ducks, divers, grebes, swans, coots, and moorhens. At last they were all airborne, wheeling in a noisy cloud above the lake as Falk, shedding a bent feather or two, set off for Romans while the going was good. He didn't look at all the druidic magician turned gyrfalcon, but rather something that had only just escaped Mrs. Spindle's meat cleaver!

In spite of his dreadful predicament, Perry clearly delighted in the treatment Falk had received at the lake, for he swung his head from one side to the other, and gave several of his strange shrieks. Bysshe watched him, and then grinned, for if Perry wasn't laughing, he, Percy Bysshe Shelley, was a Chinaman. Tentatively he extended his grin to Marigold. "Perry approves of all that, don't you think, my lady?"

"It would seem so," she replied, stroking her son's beautiful feathers.

"Serves Falk right, eh?"

"Indeed so," she murmured.

Chapter Thirty-one

In the ensuing days, Perry was initially the most utterly forlorn bird of prey imaginable. He refused to come into the house, but perched instead on the balustrade of the dining room terrace, his head sunk low, and his feathers drooping. As he moped and shuffled, it was inevitable he would attract Mrs. Spindle's cat, but it wasn't until the tabby relieved him of several feathers that he elected to come inside and accord Bysshe the task of keeping the determined feline at bay.

Marigold and Bysshe decided it was best not to tell the servants that Perry and the peregrine were one and the same, for they were sure such a revelation would result in a hysterical mass exodus. So Perry's apparent disappearance was explained away by a sudden decision to return to Eton on the night stagecoach that passed through Avenbury village. No one could refute such a claim, especially as his things were carefully hidden to quell any whispers, and soon it was clear the staff accepted the tale, although they were puzzled that Bysshe should remain. Bysshe, meanwhile, told the servants he had captured a sick peregrine, and at first it had to be said that poor Perry did indeed look sick.

Perry struggled to settle into his new existence. He communicated with Marigold and Bysshe in his strange shrieking tone, and at nights perched on the top of Bysshe's wardrobe. During the day he was carried around on Bysshe's wrist, which was protected from his savage talons by a stout leather strap, but gradually Perry took to his wings more and more, and much to Marigold's dismay, began to do what falcons do. Once he had liked Mrs. Spindle's fine beefsteak pies, but now he preferred small rodents. Among these was a mouse he deliberately stole from the cat in an act of pure vengeance. He ate everything raw, and tried to join Marigold and Bysshe in the dining room, but his mother's idea of good table manners certainly did *not* run to such things. Perry therefore found himself and his rodents banished outside.

But Perry and his unlovable new eating habits did not detract from Marigold's other worries, chief and most harrowing of which was Rowan. The remaining days to midsummer were torture for her, especially as she was racked with guilt for ever having doubted Rowan. She spent many hours pacing the house and garden, endeavoring to think of a way out of the morass which Falk had conjured around them all, but her mind remained a blank, and all the while midsummer day continued to approach at an almost audible march. She had to force herself to remember that in her second vision by the standing stone, Robin and Jenny had told her the answer was in the portrait. This meant that Falk *could* be defeated, not that he just *might* be, yet when she studied the painting, there was nothing there, nothing at all.

Several times she returned to the escarpment, but she did so entirely alone. Bysshe offered to come too, bringing Perry on his wrist, but she hadn't wanted anyone with her. Robin didn't appear on any of these unhappy expeditions, nor was there any sign of Sir Francis, and never had she been more alone in her life than when she trained the telescope upon Romans, and again saw Rowan with Alauda, behaving for all the world as if he were the most happy man on earth. Poor Jenny was still trapped in her golden cage, hopping desperately from perch to perch, and calling out. Tic-tic-tic. *Help me, please help me . . .*

Marigold's solitary visits to the escarpment were observed with sadness by the servants and local residents. They were all much perplexed by Rowan's presence at Romans, which had soon became common knowledge, and their loyalties were torn. Until now he had always enjoyed their respect, but no one could approve of the seemingly callous treatment he'd dealt his bride, first disappearing, then coming to light again with his mistress. Marigold's distress when he first vanished had been too heartbreakingly genuine for people not to know how much she loved him; his conduct, on the other hand, seemed all that was cruel. Another aspect of local disapproval—resentment even—was the way he'd allowed everyone to search for him. They believed he'd deliberately led them all a merry dance, dodging from one part of Romans to another in order to pretend he wasn't there at all. In their eyes, Lord Avenbury had most certainly blotted his formerly spotless copybook. Marigold longed to tell them the truth, for she could not bear to know how low he'd sunk in everyone's esteem, but she knew it was best to say nothing. The Avenbury curse was known in fashionable London circles, but Rowan and his forebears had always striven to play it down locally, so to suddenly tell the truth now would be to reveal incredible occult goings-on that would surely be too much for simple country folk.

One day a letter arrived for Rowan from his lawyers, and because the seal had broken and she glimpsed Merlin's name, she couldn't help reading it. The contents left her not knowing whether to laugh or cry. Rowan was informed that his wife's first marriage had been genuine, although the investigator had at first thought it would be impossible to prove anything. This was because on arriving at the town of Kirkham in Lancashire, where the investigator believed the wedding had taken place, it was learned that recent clumsy attempts to smoke a large flock of starlings from the church roof, had resulted in the whole church burning to a cinder, registers included. On establishing this, the investigator had almost returned to London, but then the incumbent clergyman had mentioned there was also a *village* in Lancashire called Kirkham, and this was where the relevant record was at last discovered.

Marigold was so surprised to learn that proof existed after all, that she had to read the letter several times. She had no doubt the obliging starlings were Falk's doing, but he had made a singular error in thinking the town, not the village, of Kirkham was the site of the marriage. Without the benefit of the local clergyman's knowledge, the wrong church and its contents were burned down, and Falk was under the impression that his plot had succeeded. Anguinum or not, this was clearly one example of litigation that could be prevented from going Falk's way. Merlin's so-called new will could now be safely challenged, and Perry could be declared Merlin's legitimate heir.

Smiling a little wryly, Marigold refolded the letter, and placed it upon the hall table with the rest of the mail awaiting Rowan's attention. What a Pyrrhic victory this was, for when Falk discovered that proof of her marriage to Merlin had survived, it would be in his interest to make certain Perry remained in feathered bondage. That way Falk would *genuinely* become the true heir. Oh, the bitterness of this particular pill, for it would almost be better that the right church had burned after all, for at least then Perry would stand a chance of being changed back to his proper shape again.

It seemed midsummer eve was upon them all quite suddenly,

and Marigold was distraught. She knew Falk was preparing for the coming dawn, because Bysshe had gone to the earthworks to do a little spying. Rowan had been on the balcony with Alauda, watching the scene in the orchard, where the druids had commenced a vigil around a bonfire. Seated in a circle in their cowled white robes, they were passing Jenny's cage one to another, and chanting. *May the wheel turn, may the wheel turn.* As well as his robe, Falk wore the heavy golden torque around his throat, and a mistletoe crown graced his bald head, indicating that he hadn't retrieved his wig. Bysshe reported that Rowan did not seem to be concerned by the significance of it all, for he smiled and whispered to Alauda, sometimes kissing her, sometimes just holding her close. He showed no awareness at all that the coming dawn rites would entail his own demise.

Marigold went to bed that last night knowing that unless something were done, at dawn the husband she adored would die. In the seclusion of the bed in which she and Rowan had lain together, she sobbed inconsolably into her pillow. Her love for him was so overwhelming, and her desperation to save and protect him so ferocious, that gradually she became aware of the same awesome sensation she'd known when touching the standing stone. Energy began to surge through her, and she was carried away by a maelstrom of emotion. Something fearsome and primitive had been unleashed in her, a force so strong that she had no control. Vivid, sensuous colors shimmered through her, and she was engulfed by strange, unfathomable feelings as she was whirled helplessly around and round. Then, in the midst of it all there shone a bright alluring light, toward which she knew she must reach out. She heard Rowan calling, and she answered, begging him to pull her out of the vortex. Suddenly his hand, luminous and almost transparent, plunged down through the colors and light to rescue her. Although his fingers seemed to lack substance, they had a remembered warmth and strength as he pulled her to safety.

Then the maelstrom became calm, and they were lying together in the bed. He seemed ethereal, a shimmering apparition, yet he was very real. Her name was on his lips, her love reflected in his eyes. He was so precious, so adored and worshipped that she felt weak at his touch, and when his mouth met hers, it seemed her flesh would surely melt. She welcomed him into her arms, her lips bruising with the passion of the kiss, and as she waited for the longed-for penetration, never had anticipation been more sweet or erotic. He stroked her breasts, teasing her nipples between his fingers. Oh, how wonderful it felt, and how exciting was the new urgency in his kiss. She wanted to cry with love, for he was the air she breathed.

At last he took her, sinking deep into her warmth, and gasping with pleasure. She gazed up at him. How ghostly he was, a silvery phantasm she could actually see through, but there was nothing ghostly about his lovemaking. He was really here with her, he *was*! His eyes were closed in ecstasy as he thrust in and out of her, and exultation seized them both as the climax began to carry them away. They both became weightless with elation, but then the bright light shone blindingly through Marigold's consciousness, as if it had come to take Rowan from her again. So she held him more tightly than ever, for fear he would leave her again, but at last he drew away, and got up from the bed. She reached out, trying to make him stay, but already he was fading. He smiled lovingly down at her, and whispered her name, then he disappeared.

She lay there on the moonlit bed, staring at where he had been. He hadn't been a dream, or a hallucination, for her body was warm and slaked, as always it was when he made love to her. So what had happened? How had he been able to come to her? She tried to remember how it had begun, and realized her intense emotion had caused it. She had conjured Rowan's fetch, his doppelgänger! Marigold wriggled down in the bed, where the warmth of his body was still tangible. Was this another facet of her power? If so, it was one for which she was very thankful indeed. She had needed Rowan, and he had come to her. She only prayed he realized what had happened, and that while his essence and soul had come to his wife, only his shell lay in Alauda's arms at Romans.

She must have fallen asleep, because she was awoken by something tugging imperatively at the hem of her nightgown. Her eyes flew open to see Sir Francis on the bed, pulling almost willfully at the lace-trimmed lawn. The clock began to chime three; it was only an hour before dawn!

Chapter Thirty-two

Dismayed, Marigold got quickly out of the bed, and put on her wrap. Sir Francis chuntered beneath his breath, as if to chide her for taking so long to awaken, then he fluttered down to the floor, and began to waddle toward the door.

Marigold gazed anxiously after him as she dragged a brush through her hair. "What can we do? There's only another hour left. Oh, *why* did I fall asleep!"

"Quack! Quack!" The mallard turned to give her one of his superior looks, then continued out of the room.

Lighting a candle from the nightlight beside her bed, Marigold hurried after him. "Have you thought of a plan?" she asked rather pointlessly, for even if he had, he wasn't able to tell her. The drake thought it stupid as well, for he bestowed another withering look upon her.

In Bysshe's room nearby, Perry had been disturbed by Sir Francis's quacks, and gave a harsh call. Bysshe awoke, and came to the door just as Marigold hurried past in Sir Francis's wake.

"What's happening?" the boy asked sleepily, while from the top of the wardrobe, Perry made a noise that seemed to be the same question.

Hearing the falcon, Sir Francis squawked with alarm, and dove among the folds of Marigold's hem. Perry flapped down, and would have gone after the terrified drake, had not Bysshe caught him by the foot as he passed. "Oh, no, you don't! That's Sir Francis, not a likely meal!" Perry struggled, but Bysshe carried him into the room, fixed a chain around his leg, and then made him sit on the leather strap on his wrist. Perry wasn't at all pleased, but had to do as his friend wished.

Marigold lifted her hem, and looked down at the cowering mallard. "Come on, it's safe now." Eyeing the peregrine mistrustfully,

Sir Francis emerged from hiding, and shuffled quickly to the top of the staircase. Then he took to his wings to fly down to the hall.

As the others hurried downstairs as well, Bysshe looked inquiringly at Marigold. "What's going on?"

Marigold shielded the candle's guttering flame with her hand. "I don't really know. Sir Francis awoke me, and that's all I can say. Oh, Bysshe, I can't *believe* I actually went to sleep. On this of *all* nights! I'll never forgive myself if Falk wins because I was so weak!"

"You aren't weak, Lady Avenbury, you're the strongest, most determined lady I know. You went to sleep because you're exhausted, and no one can blame you for that," Bysshe said reassuringly, and Perry added a thin shriek, as if agreeing.

At the bottom of the stairs, they were surprised when Sir Francis waddled toward the kitchens, but they soon discovered what he wanted them to see. The kitchens themselves were deserted, but there was something very odd in the walled garden outside. The full moon was up, and another summer mist had arisen, threading softly between the branches of a small clump of trees—beech, spindle, whitebeam, and hazel—that hadn't been there before, and curled up asleep at the foot of these trees, were various maids and footmen whose names did not suggest anything into which they could be changed. It was clear to Marigold that Falk had somehow lured the servants outside in order to transfix them before the coming ceremony. Those who weren't here must have already gone to their beds, and were now deep in a very unnatural sleep indeed. Marigold gazed uneasily around. The mist swirled, and the light of the moon was quite bright enough for her to see the village through the wicket gate at the far end of the garden. There weren't any candlelit windows, and looming above some of the cottages she saw other strange new trees. The whole of Avenbury, except for Bysshe and herself, was now under Falk's spell.

Perry made an unhappy noise, and Bysshe drew a long, rather shaky breath. "There *is* a frightful fiend, is there not, my lady? He has two names, Falk Arnold and Aquila Randol, and I think he's very close behind us indeed."

Sir Francis gave another peremptory quack, and turned to waddle back into the house. They followed without a word as he led them across the hall to the dining room, where he fluttered up onto the table. Perry's fear in the kitchen garden was forgotten now as his falcon instincts swept to the fore. He had always been very partial to roast duck, and now didn't take his amber eyes off the plump drake, clearly assessing how best to pounce. As the mallard edged nervously away, Bysshe shook Perry. "Stop it, you're not *really* a peregrine, you know!"

Marigold placed the candle on the table. "So what now, Sir Francis?" she murmured resignedly, for it did not seem possible that anything could be done at this stage in the proceedings.

Muttering anew, the drake fluttered down from the far side of the table, waddled down the room a little way, then launched himself up at the portrait of the first Lady Avenbury and her small son. He rapped his bill against it, fluttered back to the floor again, then he repeated the exercise. After that he turned to stare at Marigold, as if to say "*Now* do you see?"

Mystified, Marigold and Bysshe went over to the painting. Bysshe shrugged. "Why on earth is he in such a state about *this* one? Surely it's the other that's important?"

Marigold gazed at the portrait, and then her lips parted. What had Jenny said? *The painting! The painting! Look at it, Marigold, look at it! The truth is there!* She gasped, and clutched Bysshe's arm. "We've been looking at the wrong picture! *This* is the one Jenny meant!" She could have wept with annoyance at herself. How stupid to assume Jenny was referring to her own portrait.

Forgetting Perry, Sir Francis hopped excitedly up and down, and treated them to a positive explosion of quacks. Had he tried, he couldn't have shown more delight.

Bysshe gasped at the painting. "But what on earth is there to see in this one? It's just a likeness of a sixteenth-century widow and her baby."

"I know, but there *has* to be something. Concentrate Bysshe. You too, Perry, and if you spot anything, just make a fuss like Sir Francis." Perry nodded, and made a grunting noise.

As Marigold racked her brains about what Rowan had told her about the first Lady Avenbury, his exact words suddenly came to her from the blue. *She, her husband, and the baby all succumbed to the plague. Lord Avenbury died first, and she was said to have been so griefstricken at his death that her baby son was born prematurely. They only survived him by one month, before they too fell victim to the pestilence.* The truth positively stared her in the face. "Oh, you foolish drake, why didn't you indicate this before?"

Sir Francis puffed his feathers indignantly, and gave her a look that suggested he'd done more than enough. Bysshe looked at him,

and then at Marigold. "What are you saying, my lady? Have you
seen something?"

"Yes, Bysshe, I have. Rowan isn't the thirteenth Lord Avenbury,
he's the fourteenth, as is shown quite clearly in this painting."

"Eh?" Bysshe's jaw dropped. Perry blinked, and gave a startled
squeak.

Marigold told them both what Rowan had said about this second
portrait, then she went on. "Don't you see? If the baby boy died
one month *after* his father, for that month he was the second Lord
Avenbury! The baby has been forgotten because according to all
the records, the first Lord Avenbury was succeeded by his younger
brother. It's like—well, it's like saying Edward IV was succeeded
by his brother, Richard III, when everyone knows one of the
princes in the Tower was actually Edward V for a while. Do you
see? It's so obvious. I can't understand how we didn't spot it before!"

Bysshe pursed his lips. "*We* wouldn't have spotted it at all. It
would never have occurred to me to think of the line of succession."

Marigold wanted to laugh aloud. "Oh, it's all so clear now.
Rowan's father was the thirteenth and supposedly last lord, yet
Rowan succeeded him to become the fourteenth. What price
Aquila Randol's famous malediction now?"

Bysshe's eyes began to brighten, but then he lowered them
again. "Even so, Falk still has the anguinum, and we *know* how
great his power is as a result," he reminded her.

"Falk believes the anguinum is infallible, but it isn't. Remember
how proof of my first marriage has survived after all?"

"Yes, that's true, but . . ."

"What if we were to interrupt the midsummer rites, as the first
Lord Avenbury did? What if Falk were to realize his precious anguinum isn't quite what it's supposed to be? What if Rowan were
told he is the fourteenth lord? Would Falk still be able to compel
him against his will? You heard what Falk said. Perry is particularly susceptible because of shared blood, and presumably the
other druids are receptive because they're devotees, but Rowan is
neither of those things. Falk has to control him in order to make his
horrid wheel turn, but if Rowan knows what we now know, he will
strike free!" As she spoke the clock began to strike. Dawn was now
only half an hour away.

Perry gave an unhappy squawk, and Bysshe exhaled heavily.

"All right, let's say we do it, but how can we even approach Lord Avenbury? Falk and his cronies will have left Romans by now, and the first we will even see of Lord Avenbury is when he is brought to the oak."

"If the confrontation has to be beneath the oak itself, then so be it," Marigold said quietly.

"But, my lady, Falk threatened to leave Perry like this forever if we tried anything."

"If sufficient disruption is caused, I doubt that Falk's first thought will be of Perry. At least, that is what I must hope." She reached out to stroke Perry's head. "Please understand, Perry. I can't let Falk win, I just can't."

As Perry nuzzled her hand and nodded, Sir Francis quacked approvingly.

Chapter Thirty-three

Marigold went to open the French window onto the terrace, and as she did so, Sir Francis suddenly flew past her and away into the half light of predawn. Bysshe went outside with her, and they gazed through the swirls of gossamer mist toward the common. The faint silver glow of approaching day had now begun to creep above the eastern horizon, and the uncanny new trees still adorned the village and kitchen garden. Magic and wickedness tingled in the air, and the sixteenth century suddenly seemed very close, as indeed did prehistory itself.

Marigold shook off her fears, and looked at Bysshe and Perry. "Come on, we must go to the oak. I want to be there when Falk and his cohorts arrive."

Bysshe was alarmed. "Actually at the tree?"

"As close as possible, yes."

"Don't you think that's a little too dangerous? I mean, maybe Falk's anguinum isn't infallible, but he still has some nasty abilities."

"What do you think we should do then?"

"You and Lord Avenbury hid in those brambles the night you scared the life out of Perry and me. I think we should hide there now, so we can gauge everything before acting."

She gave a wry little smile. "Before acting upon *what,* that's the question. I've been swept along with new hope because of what we now know from the painting, but I still haven't thought of exactly how I'm going to engineer anything." She lowered her eyes thoughtfully. What would cause uproar, and halt Falk in his tracks? He was now sure that her ability didn't stand a chance against his own, but what if he were tricked into thinking it did after all present a threat? He'd called her bluff when she pretended to have an anguinum in her pocket, but what if she actually appeared to possess one? Her eyes began to gleam a little. That day at Castell

Arnold she'd thought it was a red billiard ball that dropped to the floor. In the uncertain light of first dawn, might not such a billiard ball look convincing?" She turned briskly to Bysshe. "Give Perry to me, then run to the billiard room and bring a red ball."

"A red—? You surely don't mean to pretend that you have an anguinum as well!" Bysshe was appalled, and Perry gave a horrified shriek.

Marigold looked at them. "Have you a better plan? Think about it. Falk is bound to be cautious if he believes I can match him, amulet for amulet."

"And he may turn you into a marigold to be eaten in a salad!"

"Very well, I'll get the ball myself." Gathering her skirts, she ran along the terrace to the adjacent billiard room, selected the ball she wanted, then came out again.

Bysshe looked anxiously at her. "Please don't do this, Lady Avenbury, for heaven alone knows what Falk may be able to do to you."

"My mind is made up. True, I may fail and provoke Falk into something dreadful, but what is more dreadful than the present situation? Why should I believe that Falk will ever return Perry to his normal self? It simply isn't in his interest to have a rival heir around, so Perry will be left as he is. Rowan, whom I love more than life itself, is about to be a sacrifice, and what of poor Robin and Jenny? They sought my help, and are relying on me to do something. I am the only one with anything to lose, for I have decided that you and Perry are to stay here at the house."

"No!" cried Bysshe.

"Oh, yes, Master Shelley. If I allow you to assist me, Falk will have a grudge against you as well, and I cannot permit that."

Before Bysshe could reply, Robin suddenly flew onto Marigold's shoulder. He chirruped urgently, and she knew he was trying to tell her that Falk and his entourage were approaching. After giving Bysshe a look that brooked no disobedience, she hurried away, toward the path and ha-ha. Robin flew with her, chirruping constantly. She clutched the red billiard ball tightly, and her mind raced as she tried to decide how to set about the task in hand. The fates of her husband, son, and friends were in her keeping, and for them she was about to attempt the greatest and most dangerous of bluffs. Please don't let her fail. Falk mustn't be allowed to make the wheel turn, he *mustn't*!

On reaching the brambles, she paused to listen. Sounds carried through the dawn, horses being ridden slowly, and male voices chanting. Remembering how the druids' suspicions had been drawn to the brambles before, she glanced around for another hiding place. Suddenly she noticed an isolated standing stone she hadn't seen before. It was almost hidden in a knot of young sycamore trees about fifty yards to her right, and as she ran toward it, the hooves and chanting sounded ever more near. Once there, she pressed back a little breathlessly among the foliage, and Robin alighted on a branch next to her. Marigold was careful not to touch the stone, not yet anyway, for now that she was here, her sixth sense came to her aid again. She knew that when the right moment came, she would know what to do. Her hand tightened over the billiard ball.

The sky was changing color rapidly now as night gave way to day, and the brilliance illuminating the east heralded the imminence of sunrise. It should have been an ordinary midsummer morning, but there was nothing ordinary about what was happening here in the depths of Wiltshire. The faint blue lights of the will-o'-the-wisp hovered above the moat again, and in the distance she heard a vixen screaming. The sounds along the road from the village were quite loud now, and she watched through the sycamore leaves as an eerie cavalcade came into view. The white-clad druids were like phantoms as she counted them. There were fifteen altogether with Rowan and Alauda. How vulnerable and unaware he still seemed as he reached across to take the hand of the mistress who was luring him to his fate. Tears stung Marigold's eyes as the riders halted, and dismounted. One of them carried Jenny in her cage. Falk's cowl fell back, revealing the glint of golden torque at his throat, and the crown of mistletoe on his bald head. He held the sickle-headed staff, and went up to Alauda, who had diamonds in her raven hair, and wore a black silk cloak that hid her clothes. She took Rowan's hand and gave it solemnly to her brother. Rowan seemed a little puzzled, but he made no protest as Falk led him to the head of the column the others had now formed.

Alauda remained by the horses as the druids advanced in slow single file toward the oak. Their heads were bowed, and they were still chanting, for all the world like monks going to prayer. Each man's identity was concealed by his cowl, but Marigold knew Mr. Crowe by the broken black wing protruding from his sleeve, and she now guessed that it was Lord Toby who carried

Jenny's cage, for who else would carry the bride but the one who
had captured her? Robin fluttered down onto Marigold's shoulder, making sad little noises as he watched his beloved being
borne toward a destiny she dreaded. Marigold shared the bird's
unhappiness, for she too was watching her beloved. Rowan
walked as if in a dream, and on reaching the oak did not resist as
two of the druids tied him to its trunk, he even extended his
hands for his wrists to be bound. Marigold tasted the salt of her
tears. Oh, Rowan, Rowan . . .

A square of white cloth was laid on the grass at Rowan's feet,
and Lord Toby hung Jenny's cage from the lowest branch. Then
Falk stood facing Rowan, staff in one hand, anguinum in the other.
His followers formed a chanting circle around the oak, as he gazed
up at the mistletoe among the oak leaves, waiting for the sun. The
sky was brightening by the second now, and the mist swirled as if
alive, then at last the first rays broke over the horizon to fall directly upon the mistletoe. Falk reached up to strike a spray of the
magical mistletoe with the bronze sickle on his staff. The heavy
golden leaves tumbled onto the square of cloth, and Falk raised the
anguinum, which now glowed bright red in his hand. Strange
words fell from his lips, the ancient Celtic tongue of bygone
druids.

The air crackled with energy, and Rowan cried out as at last he
realized what was happening. Suddenly Jenny's golden cage shattered, and the faint image of a young woman in Tudor dress began
to appear next to Rowan. Robin made a soft whimpering noise as
Jennifer Avenbury returned to the human shape she had last known
in 1534. She was very beautiful indeed, but the sound of her weeping carried with painful clarity above the endless chanting.

Then something even more incredible happened. The circling
druids started to float around the oak as if weightless, and the
standing stones of Avenbury, small and large, hauled themselves
from the earth to dance! It was like something conjured by the
great wizard whose name her first husband had shared, but it was
happening here in the nineteenth century! Each stone was spinning
like a dervish, and the air seemed to roar with sound. This was the
turning of the wheel.

Marigold pressed back in fear as the stone by which she was
hiding uprooted itself as well. Then in a flash she knew the moment had come, and she reached out to touch it before it too joined
the dance of giants. A dazzling light blinded her for a second, and

an intense heat leapt through her fingers. She felt the billiard ball burning in her hand, and she looked to see that it was now scarlet glass that glowed like Falk's anguinum. It had become an anguinum! There was no need to bluff now, for she really could match Falk! Holding it high, she emerged from hiding.

Chapter Thirty-four

Rowan gazed helplessly at Marigold as she entered the terrible arena. He thought to protect her by remaining silent, but Alauda saw the red light in her hand, and screamed a warning to her brother. Falk made a swift movement with his anguinum, and Jenny seemed to freeze, then he turned sharply to face Marigold. His expression changed dramatically as he realized what she held up for him to see. Swiftly he used his own, and jagged shafts of lightning passed between the two. A wind rose from nowhere, billowing Marigold's clothes and making her red-gold hair stream across her face.

The wild dance continued, but everything now became silent, so that Marigold and Falk might have been entirely alone, and when he spoke, it was as if he were right next to her instead of many yards away. "Anguinum or not, you still cannot beat me, Marigold."

"You think not? Look, Falk, how many do you see?" She felt almost elated as she summoned not one, but three fetches of Rowan. Silver and radiant, they appeared outside the spinning circle of small blue stones, and Falk stepped back involuntarily.

Marigold was exultant. "I have already beaten you, Falk, for I know something that will shatter your dreams. You've miscalculated, Falk. Rowan is the fourteenth lord, not the thirteenth!"

He was very still. "You're lying!" he said then, but she was sure the supernatural dance began to slow a little.

Alauda called out urgently to him. "Don't pay her any heed, Falk! She's trying to trick you!"

Marigold smiled, and snapped her fingers to make Rowan's fetches disappear again. "It's quite a trick, Alauda, you should try it some time," she said, and was gratified by the hate-filled look Alauda directed at her.

Marigold gazed at Rowan. "Is it not a trick, my darling?" she said softly, and saw by his answering smile that he was aware of what had happened during the night. She felt stronger than ever as she returned her attention to Falk. "The truth is all there in history, Falk. A baby boy was lord for a month, which means Rowan's *father* was the thirteenth and supposedly last Lord Avenbury. You're a generation too late, and Jennifer Avenbury can never be yours now." She held her ground as more shafts of lightning flashed from his anguinum to hers, she even laughed with scorn. "Pretty lights are all you amount to now, for you've even failed to disprove my first marriage. You burned the wrong church!"

The dance became even slower, and one by one the revolving stones began to slip back into their places. The druids were gradually lowered to the grass once more, and their chanting ceased. The wind died away to nothing.

"You lie!" Falk's voice rose to a shriek as he saw his great plan coming to nothing before his eyes.

"Behold your famous wheel! It no longer turns for you!" she taunted.

"I warned that I would punish you for interfering, and so I will!" he cried, turning toward Rowan, but as he raised the sickle-topped staff, Perry suddenly swooped out of the brilliance of the rising sun to snatch Falk's anguinum with his vicious talons. Falk cried out with dismay, but there was nothing he could do except watch the peregrine fly away with the amulet.

Alauda ran forward, unable to believe that all the months of preparation were to prove of no avail. She caught her brother by the arm, and shook him bitterly. "Don't lose your nerve now! You are Aquila Randol, the greatest druid that ever lived!"

Marigold suddenly realized that Bysshe had also disobeyed her, for the moment Alauda had distracted Falk, the boy ran to the oak from his hiding place by the brambles. He seized the white cloth and mistletoe from the grass, and then tried to wrench the staff from Falk's hand, but he was grabbed by Alauda. With angry cries, the other druids closed in to deal with the brave but reckless boy.

Almost demented with disbelief that all this could be happening, Falk again raised the staff to strike Rowan with the sickle, but then a huge flock of waterfowl dove down from the sky, led by Sir Francis, whose furious quacking could be heard above all the others. The druids scattered as they tried to beat off the aerial army, and in the process they released Bysshe, who escaped with the cloth and mistletoe.

Alauda screamed hysterically as the two swans she'd driven from the Romans jetty alighted on the grass in front of her. They'd recognized her immediately, and were now intent upon revenge. They spread their enormous wings, then hissed menacingly as they pursued her toward the moat, where the eerie blue flames still hovered.

As soon as the other birds arrived, Robin darted upon Falk, treating his gleaming pate to such a barrage of pecks that Falk fought desperately to drive him away with one hand, the other being occupied with the staff. His mistletoe crown was dislodged, and fell forward over his nose, but still Robin kept up his attack, and eventually Falk had to drop the staff in an effort to defend himself with both hands. At this point Sir Francis joined in, clamping his bill onto Falk's nose, and holding on for all he was worth. What a splendid pair of candle snuffers was a mallard's bill, thought Marigold, as she ran to retrieve the staff. In a moment she'd hacked through the ropes holding Rowan, then she was in his arms, and his lips had found hers in a kiss more sweet and poignant than could ever have been imagined.

Falk now knew it was all up, and all he could do now was try to save himself, and his devotees. He managed to beat off Sir Francis, savagely dashing the mallard to the ground, then he raised both his hands and cried out in the same ancient tongue as before. Lightning flashed, and there was a roar of thunder from a sky that was empty of clouds, but although Falk did indeed still possess some powers, they were no longer quite what he or his followers would have wished. Somehow Taranis's original magic became confused, and instead of escaping by changing into the birds of their names, the druids became mere flightless chickens! Old English Whites, to be precise.

Falk was easy enough to pick out among them, for he still had the torque around his neck, and his head remained bald except for the remnants of the mistletoe crown. Mr. Crowe, clucking in dismay, hobbled hither and thither, causing more confusion than ever as he got in the others' way. A very wet and bedraggled Alauda scrambled up from the moat, and ran to join them all. She was draped with slimy green weed, and was in such a state of hysteria that her squawks were piercing. At first they were all so panic-stricken that they ran in all directions, but at last they had the wit to unite, then Falk marshaled them with a loud cry, and they all ran flapping toward the house. Sir Francis's aerial army pursued them relentlessly.

With the vanquishing of Falk's power, the servants had returned to their normal selves, but hardly had they time to glance at each other in amazement at what had happened to them, than the incredible chase hurtled through the garden toward them. Mrs. Spindle screamed with fright, and picked up her skirts to run into the kitchen. She was followed by the others, but as they started to close the door, the desperate chickens streamed noisily through the gap. Soon after that there were feathers everywhere as Mrs. Spindle recovered from her fright, and picked up her meat cleaver.

With the cook in hot pursuit, Falk and his companions fled through every floor of the house, but gradually the chickens seemed to disappear. At least, that was what Mrs. Spindle thought, but the truth was that they'd obeyed another of Falk's orders, and were now huddled in the darkest corner of the attic, wondering how everything could have gone so utterly wrong.

The waterfowl wheeled about and flew swiftly back to the common, where poor Sir Francis still lay where Falk had dashed him. The huge flock of birds glided to the grass, and moved concernedly near to see if Sir Francis was all right. Marigold knelt beside the fallen mallard, and gasped as he changed into a man of Henry VIII's time. Somehow he seemed familiar, although she did not know why. He was quietly handsome, with tawny hair and a pointed beard, and he wore a single pendant earring. There was a rich lace ruff around his throat, his doublet was turquoise slashed with gold, and his hose were gray. His eyes were closed.

Rowan leaned over to put a reassuring hand on her shoulder. "So, the name Sir Francis was appropriate after all. This is my ancestor, the first Lord Avenbury. I recognize him from his portrait in the great hall."

The man stirred, and opened his eyes. He gazed up at Rowan. "How now, Lord Avenbury," he said with a wry smile.

"How now indeed, Lord Avenbury," Rowan replied, smiling back and then holding out his hand.

The first Lord Avenbury struggled to his feet, then immediately turned toward his sister, who was still quite frozen. "Oh, Jennifer, Jennifer, you're safe from Randol at last," he said, going to embrace her. She remained stiff and unresponsive in his arms, but they knew that she heard and understood everything.

Marigold's immediate thought was to release Jenny from this

new imprisonment, but as she raised the anguinum, Lord Avenbury turned with a dismayed cry. "No!"

"But—"

"No one can ever be enchanted more than four times. Jenny was turned from woman to wren, then from wren to woman, then she was frozen. If you bring her to life as a woman, she will never be able to be a wren again, and that is what she really wants."

She was taken aback. "I don't understand. I thought she and Robin wanted to be together again as they once were."

"No, they want to remain birds. Marigold, of Jenny, Robin, myself, and your son, only Robin is in the form he desires." As he spoke, Robin fluttered to his shoulder and chirruped agreement. Lord Avenbury smiled at the little bird, then went on. "Your son wishes to be a boy again, and we wish to be birds, because we are content with our feathered eternity, indeed I am most happy indeed as a mallard, even a demon one." As he said this, he turned to smile at Bysshe, who had come to join them with Perry on his wrist. On seeing the falcon, the assembled waterfowl backed uneasily away, for no bird of prey was ever to be trusted.

Bysshe grinned sheepishly. "We really thought you *were* a demon, sir."

"After my initial disarray, it amused me to behave like one," Lord Avenbury admitted, then looked at Marigold again. "My life as a drake contains everything I could wish, for my wife and baby son are with me."

"Really?" Marigold was pleased. "But why have you never brought them to show us?"

"They're shy, but maybe now all this is done with, they will accompany me to see you. Provided, of course, you first return me to my desired form." He said this last in a tone of gentle persuasion.

Rowan put his arm around Marigold's waist. "If that is what they all want, my darling, then that is what you must do for them."

She glanced down at the scarlet ball in her hand. It was still glowing, and its energy still tingled through her. "But there are things I must ask." She looked at Lord Avenbury. "Why did you become a mallard? Did Aquila do it?"

"No. There was a very wise druid seer here at Avenbury, who fell foul of Randol and was banished. This seer had the power too, and when I lay dying, he was able to see that I became one of the eternal birds. As my life slipped away, I was to become the first bird that was heard. It happened to be a mallard from the lake here.

That's why my wife and child are also mallards, for I made absolutely certain that I was the first bird they'd hear!" He smiled.

She smiled too. "How very sensible of you, sir."

"I can be, even if as a drake I sometimes seem less sensible than irritating." He became more serious. "I owe you my life, for if you hadn't saved me from Mrs. Spindle . . ."

"You owe me nothing, sir, because I am now in your debt."

"Hardly."

"Then let us agree to hold each other in high esteem." She laughed a little. "Mind you, I didn't think you were all that estimable when I first saw—and heard!—you at Dr. Bethel's house."

"I was splendidly noisy, wasn't I?" he replied. "The reason was my annoyance that my delight at having used the boys' demonic circle to 'arrive' was ruined by the indignities heaped upon my person."

"You certainly registered your protests."

"Well, a drake has to speak up for himself," he said with a grin. "Anyway, I imposed upon Perry and Bysshe because I needed to be involved in what was to come, and I'd spied upon them enough to know they'd move heaven and earth to come here once they learned of your intention to take 'doomed' Lord Avenbury as your second husband." As Bysshe shuffled embarrassedly, and Perry gazed pointedly in another direction, Jenny's brother continued. "Before I made my presence known in Eton, I'd been in frequent contact with Jenny and Robin, for we were all three aware of what must happen this year. We knew about your as yet undiscovered power, and about Rowan being the fourteenth not thirteenth lord, but unless you discovered both things, Randol's scheme would have succeeded."

"It's of no consequence, I know, but I really would like to know why you left it to the eleventh hour to properly indicate which portrait I was supposed to look at. I know you went close to it before, but if you'd only told me sooner—"

He interrupted. "Time was ticking away, and I was afraid for poor Jenny." He looked lovingly at his beautiful sister again. "For her sake I decided to make certain you considered the correct portrait. Fortunately it did no harm, on the contrary it achieved what was necessary."

"But who decreed that I had to finally act alone? There isn't anything in the legend, is there?"

Instead of answering straightaway, he looked up at the mistletoe. Although the sun was almost up now, the rotation of the earth was beginning to cast the shadow of the escarpment over it. Several sprays were still bathed in dawn rays, however, and Marigold thought he seemed relieved that this was so. She glanced at the bright green-gold sunlit leaves amid the darker foliage of the oak. It was like the tree's heart, indeed, maybe that was exactly what it was. She cleared her throat a little. "My lord?" she prompted.

His attention swung back to her. "Forgive me, my dear, you asked a question, did you not? No, your crucial role isn't in the legend, but it *is* indicated in my sister's portrait, which happens to have been painted by the druid seer I mentioned earlier. He predicted that our salvation would come from the marigold, which is why he painted so many of your flowers into the portrait. He painted rowan leaves because he knew that tree would prove to be Aquila's stumbling block, and the wheel lies useless in the grass because he knew it could be prevented from turning. He also foresaw that the birds of the lake would help to finally prevent Aquila's victory. There are other things in the portrait as well, but right now I cannot remember them." He glanced up at the mistletoe again. "You must help us quickly now, my dear, for if the sun's rays leave the mistletoe, it will be too late."

At this, Perry shuffled alarmedly on Bysshe's wrist, and gave one of his thin shrieks. His fear of remaining as he was forever was almost palpable, so he directed the cry at Marigold. It was an imploring sound that cut through her like a knife, and she knew she dared not delay. Her gaze moved wistfully to Jenny, with whom she felt such affinity. It would have been so good to use the anguinum to bring her to life once more, and just talk to her, but there was no time; the anguinum had to be used to another end.

Clutching the amulet, Marigold closed her eyes, and concentrated. She felt energy flowing into her, and asked aloud for everyone present be granted their wish. But instead of English, she heard herself speaking in the same ancient tongue that Falk had used earlier. An absolute silence followed, and she was afraid to open her eyes because she thought she'd failed, but Rowan's arm tightened reassuringly around her. "You can look now, my lady," he said softly.

Then Perry cried out jubilantly. "Mama! Oh, Mama, you've done it!"

Her eyes flew open as he ran to hug her, and she could have wept for joy that he was as strong and handsome as before. She held him close, and then looked up to see her three bird friends, Jenny Wren, Robin Redbreast, and Sir Francis, flying happy and free in the morning sunshine. Suddenly the assembled army of waterfowl rose noisily from the grass, filling the early morning air with cries as they wheeled above the common. The unnatural new trees had disappeared from the village, which was now fully awake. People had emerged from their homes, and were going about their business as if nothing had happened, which indeed, as far as they were concerned, was the case. It was just an ordinary day, except that tonight there would be dancing and amusements on the common.

The great multitude of birds streamed noisily away toward the lake, led by Sir Francis, whose loud quacks could be heard above the general clamor. Robin and Jenny remained, and alighted on a branch of the oak. Jenny gazed brightly down at Marigold. "Thank you, Marigold, thank you so much," she said.

Tears filled Marigold's eyes. "You will come to me again, won't you? We've shared so much, and I feel so close to you both, yet we haven't had time to talk. I so long to know you better."

"We would like to know you too. We will come," the wren promised, then she and her robin lover flew away.

Marigold and Rowan lay naked in each other's arms. The bed was scented with lavender, and the early evening sunshine warm and hazy. They could hear music on the common, as the villagers celebrated midsummer day. Everything was quite perfect. Rowan leaned over her, cupping her breast with his hand. "I adore you with all my heart, Lady Avenbury," he whispered.

"And I adore you," she whispered back.

He hesitated. "Marigold, about what happened at Romans with Alauda—"

She put a finger briefly to his lips. "There is no need to say anything, for I know you were under Falk's control."

"But I was unfaithful, my darling," he whispered.

"I don't see it in that light."

"I was aware of what was happening, but I didn't seem to care. I even knew I was to be the sacrifice this morning, yet nothing seemed to matter. I was spellbound, I suppose." He took one of her heavy red-gold tresses in his hand, and parted the strands. "They spoke quite openly in front of me, you know. When Alauda sent that note trying to prevent me from leaving, she was going to deliver me into Falk's hands then. I'd ruined their original plan, you see. She'd wanted to spend time here with me, but my sudden marriage put a stop to that. If I'd been under their control here in this house, no one would have remarked anything untoward. As it was, they had to keep me at Romans, and you know what a stir *that* caused!"

"Your good name has suffered considerably," she admitted, thinking of the servants and villagers.

"I will do all I can to redeem myself."

"If that entails being very agreeable and attentive to your wronged wife, she will not complain," Marigold said softly, then she looked inquiringly at him. "Now that our little flock of chickens have been found in the attic, what do you intend to do with them?"

"I'm tempted to hand them over to Mrs. Spindle, but I can't quite bring myself to that point. Actually, I thought I'd send them to Salisbury Market. They should fetch a good price."

"Speaking of fetches . . ."

He smiled down into her green eyes. "You made very fast and loose with my person, madam."

"Did you like the experience?"

"Very much."

"I'm so glad you knew it was happening."

He laughed. "I knew, all right!"

"I wanted you so very much, and at first I didn't even know what I was bringing about. It was very agreeable, however," she added in a whisper.

"Just think, my darling, if ever we should be parted at night, you can summon me at will."

"Only at night?" she inquired, widening her eyes innocently. "What if the mood should take me in the morning, or afternoon?"

"Do with me as you please, my darling," he breathed.

"Make love to me again," she whispered, for they had done so more than once already, but still she wanted more of him.

"Madam, you are insatiable."

"I fear so. My lord, are you telling me you are too tired?"

He smiled. "What would you do if I said yes?"

She reached under the pillow, and drew out the anguinum. "You wouldn't stand a chance, I fear." she said teasingly.

"Have you no mercy?" He bent his head to kiss her nipple, drawing it slowly into his mouth.

She closed her eyes in delight. "No mercy at all." She sighed, her hands roaming over his back and then down to his taut buttocks as he moved on top of her.

"Then it is as well you have no need of an anguinum to arouse me," he replied, pushing deep into her. When he could push no more, he looked down into her eyes again. "What think you of your second marriage, my lady?"

"Oh, it compares very favorably indeed with my first."

"I'm relieved to hear it, because I intend this to be the last of Marigold's marriages."

"And I intend it to be the only one of Rowan's," she replied, closing her eyes with pleasure as he began to make slow, delicious love to her.

She was faintly aware of two tiny bills tapping at the window as Robin and Jenny peeped in and then flew off again. She was also aware of the distant quack of a very individual mallard, but the sounds drifted into oblivion as ecstasy melted her entire being.

Nadine Miller

☐The Duke's Dilemma

0-451-18675-3/$4.99

☐The Madcap Masquerade

0-451-19512-4/$4.99

☐The Misguided Matchmaker

0-451-19206-0/$5.50

☐The Unlikely Angel

0-451-19467-5/$4.99

Gayle Buck

DILEMMAS OF THE HEART

☐**THE SILENT SUITOR by Elisabeth Fairchild.** Miss Sarah Wilkes Lyndle was stunningly lovely. Nonetheless, she was startled to have two of the leading lords drawn to her on her very first visit to London. One was handsome, elegant, utterly charming Stewart Castleford, known in society as "Beauty," and the other was his cousin Lord Ashley Hawkes Castleford, nicknamed "Beast." Sarah found herself on the horns of a dilemma. (180704—$3.99)

☐**THE AWAKENING HEART by Dorothy Mack.** The lovely Dinah Elcott finds herself in quite a predicament when she agrees to pose as a marriageable miss in public to the elegant Charles Talbot. In return, he will let Dinah pursue her artistic ambitions in private, but can she resist her own untested and shockingly susceptible heart? (178254—$3.99)

☐**LORD ASHFORD'S WAGER by Marjorie Farrell.** Lady Joanna Barrand knows all there is to know about Lord Tony Ashford—his gambling habits, his wooing of a beautiful older widow to rescue him from ruin and, worst of all, his guilt in a crime that makes all his other sins seem innocent. What she doesn't know is how she has lost her heart to him. (180496—$3.99)

Prices slightly higher in Canada

Payable in U.S. funds only. No cash/COD accepted. Postage & handling: U.S./CAN. $2.75 for one book, $1.00 for each additional, not to exceed $6.75; Int'l $5.00 for one book, $1.00 each additional. We accept Visa, Amex, MC ($10.00 min.), checks ($15.00 fee for returned checks) and money orders. Call 800-788-6262 or 201-933-9292, fax 201-896-8569; refer to ad # SRR2

Penguin Putnam Inc.   Bill my: ☐Visa ☐MasterCard ☐Amex_____(expires)
P.O. Box 12289, Dept. B   Card#_____
Newark, NJ 07101-5289   Signature_____
Please allow 4-6 weeks for delivery.
Foreign and Canadian delivery 6-8 weeks.

Bill to:
Name_____
Address_____City_____
State/ZIP_____
Daytime Phone#_____

Ship to:
Name_____   Book Total $_____
Address_____   Applicable Sales Tax $_____
City_____   Postage & Handling $_____
State/ZIP_____   Total Amount Due $_____

This offer subject to change without notice.